Ellora's Cavemen

Jewels of the Nile
Volume III

Paperback Trade Inn
145 East Fourteen Mile Rd
Clawson, MI 48017
(248) 307-0226

Ellora's Cave
ROMANTICA PUBLISHING

ADRIFT
Elayne S. Venton

The fates are on Lorie Walker's side when she pulls long-term duty with the hunk of Space Station 5423, Dodd Henderson. Or maybe she's not so lucky. Their space capsule is drifting in a black hole and the gauges are nonfunctional. The odds of survival are slim whether they try to break free of the void or await help. Dare they take the time, perhaps the only chance they'll ever have, to explore the suppressed passion between them? Or will a diversion from their recovery efforts doom them?

PASSION'S SONG
Jory Strong

Aria's life on the mining world of Iyon is harsh. Her future made bleaker when her father gambles her away in a dice game. Refusing to accept a prostitute's fate, she flees into the night—and ends up in Raeder's and Haven's arms.

They're a fantasy made flesh—or a nightmare waiting to happen. After a night of unparalleled pleasure, she learns of their origins and runs from them, only to realize she's faced with a choice—listen to her heart, or to the rumors about the men who call the closed desert world of Adjara home.

PRIVATE LESSONS
Solange Ayre

Lonely widow Vanessa d'Aulaire reads Professor Robert Woodcock's marriage manual and marvels at its absurd, inaccurate statements. Determined to set the professor straight, she invites him for tea, only to learn she was his teacher ten years ago. Rob's schoolboy crush flares into a man's passion as Vanessa tutors him in pleasuring a woman.

Vanessa's stepfather is pressuring her to marry one of his friends. But how can she consider marriage to an elderly widower when her secret liaison with Rob fills her with sensual delight?

RETURN TO XANDER
Rowan West

Mia has ached for artist Xander since she broke up with him. She never expected to find him stripping at a club. Xander isn't pleased to see Mia but that doesn't stop him from having hot sex with her. When Mia shows up at Xander's studio, she agrees to a challenge—she will stay and pose for portraits. Xander plans to paint her, use her, then throw her out. But old emotions return. Mia needs to convince Xander she will do anything to be with him or they'll lose out on love.

SORCERER'S SONG
Cindy Spencer Pape

When Sorcerer Cian hears a siren's song on a cool Toronto night, he has no idea his life is about to change forever. Lyra's life has been a long cycle of loneliness and meaningless encounters with mortals. One night with Cian turns that life upside down. Can their night of passionate sex turn into a love that will last forever? Together they work to find a way, challenging even the gods themselves for their chance.

WHITE VALLEY
Lacey Thorn

Dakota was devastated when she caught her fiancé with another woman, so she heads to what she thinks is familiar ground for a little rest and relaxation.

Sebastian and Dimitri Cordova are surprised when they stumble upon an unknown woman bathing in the bridal pool in White Valley. The sacred waters are used only to help prepare a woman for joining with her new mates—werewolf mates. Determined not to leave her to suffer a sexual awakening on her own, the brothers do what any good werewolves would do. They claim her as their own.

An Ellora's Cave Romantica Publication

www.ellorascave.com

Ellora's Cavemen: Jewels of the Nile III

ISBN 9781419957932
ALL RIGHTS RESERVED.
Adrift Copyright © 2008 Elayne S. Venton
Passion's Song Copyright © 2008 Jory Strong
Private Lessons Copyright © 2008 Solange Ayre
Return to Xander Copyright © 2008 Rowan West
Sorcerer's Song Copyright © 2008 Cindy Spencer Pape
White Valley Copyright © 2008 Lacey Thorn
Editorial Team: Raelene Gorlinsky, Carole Genz, Sue-Ellen Gower, Helen Woodall, Denise Powers.
Cover design by Darrell King.

This book printed in the U.S.A. by Jasmine-Jade Enterprises, LLC.

Electronic book Publication September 2008
Trade paperback Publication September 2008

With the exception of quotes used in reviews, this book may not be reproduced or used in whole or in part by any means existing without written permission from the publisher, Ellora's Cave Publishing, Inc.® 1056 Home Avenue, Akron OH 44310-3502.

Warning: The unauthorized reproduction or distribution of this copyrighted work is illegal. Criminal copyright infringement, including infringement without monetary gain, is investigated by the FBI and is punishable by up to 5 years in federal prison and a fine of $250,000.
(http://www.fbi.gov/ipr/)

This book is a work of fiction and any resemblance to persons, living or dead, or places, events or locales is purely coincidental. The characters are productions of the author's imagination and used fictitiously.

ELLORA'S CAVEMEN: JEWELS OF THE NILE III

೫

ADRIFT
By Elayne S. Venton
~11~

PASSION'S SONG
By Jory Strong
~61~

PRIVATE LESSONS
By Solange Ayre
~105~

RETURN TO XANDER
By Rowan West
~155~

SORCERER'S SONG
By Cindy Spencer Pape
~201~

WHITE VALLEY
By Lacey Thorn
~249~

ADRIFT
By Elayne S. Venton

ଚ

Dedication

In memory of Rod Serling.

Acknowledgements

To my critique group, especially India Masters, fellow sci-fi fan.

Chapter One

✼

"Cryonic thaw is complete," a computerized voice droned into Lorie Walker's foggy brain.

The solid, curved front cover on her freezing chamber slid open with a soft hiss, allowing the warm air of the ship to wash over her cold body. She squinted against the light glowing from the emergency lamps inside the compact spacecraft. When her eyes adjusted, Lorie blinked at Communications Specialist Dodd Henderson's back as he floated just above the gravity-enhanced floor in front of the control panel, typing at lightning speed. Completely engrossed in his work, he didn't seem to hear her soft groans as she stretched her stiff arms and legs.

For a long, unfocused minute, she admired his wide shoulders, trim waist, contoured buttocks and long muscular legs showcased within his snug, shiny gray flightsuit. In the four years she'd worked on Space Station 5423, Dodd was the only man who'd made her pulse race. Luck had been on her side when the Interplanetary Defense Council reassigned them to Pluto IV together.

Or maybe not. Her gaze shifted to the black expanse outside the cockpit window. A shiver trickled across her shoulders. Where were the stars, the streaming comets and floating asteroids? She'd never seen space so dark, so empty. So lifeless.

This is what purgatory must look like.

She rubbed her cold arms in an attempt to chase away the bone-deep chill. After taking a deep, lung-filling breath, she stepped out of the cryotube on unsteady legs. The door hissed closed behind her. The unusually weak suction in the gravity-enhanced floor threw off her equilibrium. She slapped a palm on the hull wall for support.

Dodd spun around as if surprised to see her, and then relief eased the strained lines on his face. "Thank God I'm not in this nightmare alone." A muscle jumped in his tight jaw. "Simulation training didn't prepare me for this."

Lorie cleared her raw throat. "Where are we?"

"In a black hole."

"No." She took a step and her knees buckled.

Dodd lunged across the small space and clasped her arm in a firm grip. "Take it slowly, Walker." He clasped his other hand on her opposite arm to steady her, and looked deeply into her eyes. "You've been immobile for fifteen years."

"What?" She squeezed her eyes shut against the sudden pain in her head. "Fifteen years! What are you talking about?" She forced her gritty eyes open again and glanced up at her handsome crewmate. A wheat-colored five-o'clock shadow covered his jaw, as if he'd awoken from one long hard night rather than years in cryostasis. Concern darkened his dazzling eyes and furrowed a crease across his forehead. Still wobbly, and drawn by his heat, she leaned into his side, but only briefly, determined not to show her weakness. "The journey to Pluto IV was supposed to take no more than five years."

"Yeah." He looked beyond her at the closed cryotubes. "Something went wrong. The gauges are out of whack, which would explain why the cryotubes deactivated without the proper destination approach signal." Dodd flipped down a nearby jump seat and gently pressed down on her shoulders until she sat and the magnetic discs in the chair linked to the clips on her belt. The brittle material of her flightsuit tore at the knees, bearing evidence of long exposure to sub-freezing temperatures.

"Five years," she emphasized softly, as if repeating it might make it true. "Not fifteen." Her legs bounced up and down in a nervous tremble.

Dodd plucked the serum injector from the wall bracket. A piece of metal flashing caught the back of his hand and he absently rubbed the bleeding cut before he held the injector to her neck. "This will make you feel better."

The prick barely registered, but the medication rushing through her veins jolted her back to life. She sighed at the warmth. The tingle of instant thaw danced in her fingers and toes, and then spread inward to her belly and nipples.

When she glanced up at Dodd's probing gaze, a surge of lust shot through her system, making her clench her quivering thighs together. Certain her reaction was due to the therapeutic properties of the medicine, she disregarded the heat swirling low in her belly the best she could, and concentrated on the perilous situation.

During the short time they'd prepped for this flight, she and Dodd had become friends, not tell-me-all-your-secrets friends, but good buddies. She trusted him to give it to her straight. "What happened?"

"All I know is we're floating in a black hole and the date log tells me fifteen years have gone by. So far, I've had no luck hailing anybody. And there's no record of anyone trying to hail us." He hunkered down in front of her and smoothed his palms over her thighs, settling the quivering with his big warm hands.

Heat shot to her feminine core. She ducked her head, hiding any signs of yearning on her face. In the months she'd spent with a lover who'd claimed to both love her and hate her, she'd learned to hide her sexual desires. Too many harsh encounters had outweighed the enjoyable ones.

Since then, Dodd was the only male who made her smile, who made her feel sexy and alive. He was an outrageous flirt, winning the affections of more women than she could count. Whom he bedded, naturally, and usually not more than once. A real Casanova, he fed her private fantasies, and gave her hope she'd find someone as devilishly charming but with a darker side to suit her needs. He was very tempting. She kept her distance, though, knowing it was safer to simply imagine the wicked things she'd like to do with him.

A shudder rocked the ship.

Now is not the time to examine your sex life. Concentrate on the problem.

"Prognosis?" she asked, fearing the worst.

"You're the engineer. You tell me."

A quick glance at the flashing warning lights on the console tightened the knot in her stomach. "Do you believe in miracles?"

* * * * *

Dodd admired Lorie's lush backside as she leaned over the console doing exactly what he'd done when he'd first looked out the window into nothingness. She attempted to decipher the jumbled information stored in the database.

"That can't be right," she mumbled to herself.

That's what I thought too.

He still didn't quite believe they floated in a black hole. *Stars* vanished into the vast emptiness of black holes. How could a small craft like theirs remain intact? He must be dreaming while in stasis. After all, Lorie Walker filled his mind during waking hours. It made sense she'd sashay into his dreams during the long flight to Pluto IV.

Then again, he'd never heard of anyone dreaming during cryostasis. At least not that they remembered.

The cut on the back of his hand stung like hell. Did that prove anything? Lorie's solid yet feminine form felt amazingly real when he'd caught her before she fell. The citrus scent of her skin wasn't something he could easily imagine. He'd already tried pinching himself, and that accomplished nothing.

Real or not, he'd finally scored time alone with the elusive Lorie Walker. He had an opportunity to discover the real

Lorie, not the dull engineer who worked on Space Station 5423, but the vixen who played there. She hid her secrets well, but his job as a communications specialist taught him how to scrape away people's façades and find the truth beneath.

Okay, so he'd discovered her darker side by accident when he'd tapped into the com unit in her quarters and discovered she'd made appointments at the Sub Level within the Pleasure Club—under an alias. Miss Straight Arrow, it turned out, indulged in kinky fantasies right up his alley.

Casual interest in the redheaded engineer had exploded into rabid curiosity.

But she was a tough nut to crack, either ignoring or rebuffing any seductive comments he made. He'd never been able to pin her down alone, until now when fate intervened.

How they ended up in this limbo of time and space didn't matter. He intended to take advantage of every second.

In case he wasn't dreaming though, he'd better see what he could do to get them out of there. He didn't want to float in this abyss until life support depleted.

"Watch your feet," he said, patting her ass as he stepped past her. "I'm going to crawl under the console."

She shot him a guarded look and went back to work.

For a microsecond, he thought he saw a flash of interest in her eyes. After all, getting a spanking topped her list of naughty things to do in the Pleasure Club. Too bad anxiety clouded over the brief spark.

If she didn't act so damn unapproachable, he might take her into his arms and ease the fears that flickered in and out of her gaze. Any opening at all and he'd jump on it.

Before they crawled back into the cryostasis tubes in victory or defeat, he intended to break down her barrier and hold her close, preferably naked.

Determined to find a way out of this mess, Lorie fought the panic clawing up her throat. "The hull seems to be holding up against the outside pressure," she reported as calmly as possible. The ship's occasional shudders and creaking didn't encourage her, but she had confidence in the engineering and construction of their long-range transport. After all, she helped design it.

She turned her attention to pinpointing their current location on the star chart. The galaxy was vast, so much unexplored. In fifteen years, who knew how far they'd traveled from their original path before the black hole sucked them in?

"We veered off course long before we hit this black hole," she said, tracking their flight path on the navigation screen. "By the scratches on the nose cone, it looks like we ran into a meteor storm."

Dodd hummed an unintelligible response.

"My best calculated guess is that we're still…" A lump clogged her throat. She looked down at Dodd, stretched out beneath the com panel inspecting connections—quite an appealing position, she thought absently while she checked out the outline of his cock.

Jeez! Now was not the time to study Dodd's attributes.

"Twelve light-years from Pluto IV," she finished in dismay, dragging her gaze back to the viewing screen. "Running on impulse power, we might drift through this black hole forever, unless someone spots us. The automatic distress signal is on, but sonar pings probably fade away inside a void like this."

Lost in space was not how she envisioned her last days of life. She swallowed hard.

"Dodd?" *Give me a sign of reassurance. Tell me we're going to make it back to the stars.* "Any luck down there?"

He grunted in response, which she decided meant "No".

She took a deep breath and gathered her courage around her. If he could be composed about the situation, so could she. Still, her hand shook when she scrolled through the life-support readings for the third time.

"The oxygen meter indicates the pump isn't functioning, which is obviously wrong since we're breathing." She waited a full minute for Dodd to say something. "It's a good thing the oxygen wasn't supposed to initiate until the cryotubes opened or we would've depleted it a long time ago. The bad news is the oxygen tanks only hold a two-week supply of air." Still nothing from him. "Did you hear me?" She nudged his hip with her boot tip. "We have two weeks to live!"

"I heard you."

After waiting for something more and getting nothing, she nudged him again, this time closer to his ribs. "Hey! We're in deep shit here. I'm starting to freak out." She slapped her hands over her face. Why had she admitted that?

He grabbed her ankle, slid out from underneath the com station and jerked her off her feet.

She yelped as she fell, but the low gravity slowed her plummet, allowing her to land softly on her butt beside Dodd.

"Come here." He sat up, grabbed one of her legs and dragged her astride his lap.

Her mound brushed over the bulge in his pants before she sidled backward and slapped her palms onto his chest.

Undeterred, he wrapped his arms around her and pulled her close until his cock nestled against her pussy. He stared at her with a solemn expression.

"What are you doing?" she rasped.

"Making everything all right." He gave her a small smile and rubbed a soothing hand up and down her back. "We'll take things one step at a time. That's all we can do."

Relaxing into his embrace, she rested her forehead on his shoulder, thankful she didn't have to face the blackness alone.

He made her feel safe, which was ridiculous given their situation and the shifting bulge in his pants, but there it was. She slipped her arms around his waist and hugged him. "I can't think straight."

"Don't think, then." He tucked her head into the crook of his neck and kissed the top of her hair. "I'll take care of you."

Magic words. Seconds dragged by. Sitting in his lap comforted her as much as the gentle caress of his hands on her back. She turned her cheek and softly kissed his neck.

It didn't surprise her when he twisted sideways, lowered her shoulders onto the floor and rolled on top of her, belly to belly, thigh to thigh, his cock settled between her legs. Still, she felt safe—and excited.

He gripped her wrists and pressed the backs of her hands down next to her shoulders. "I've wanted to do this since before the trip began." His eyes darkened as he slowly dipped his head. A hairsbreadth from her lips, he stopped, watching her closely.

Anticipation fluttered in her belly.

How many times had she imagined falling under his spell like this, lost in those sky blue eyes, awaiting his kiss? Now, away from his admirers where she'd been one in a hundred, her turn had come. Despite her wariness, she needed his warmth, his strength, needed to push aside her fears, if only for the span of one kiss.

Little by little, he eased her arms upward and pinned her wrists to the cold floor above her head. Her breasts swelled. The skin around her nipples puckered. After an interminably long minute, he finally pressed his mouth to hers.

Her fingers slowly curled into loose fists. Her pulse thumped heavily beneath her jaw. As he glided his lips over hers in long, measured strokes, liquid fire pooled in her belly. Her pussy throbbed and desire dampened her panties.

It was only a kiss, for Pete's sake! It meant nothing. Dodd had a reputation for kissing every female on the space station.

She was simply another notch in his belt.

Did she care? Hell, no.

Weak and hungry, she parted her lips, easing the tip of her tongue past her teeth in a blatant invitation. Unexpectedly, he drew back and gazed into her eyes. Self-conscious, she covered her move by licking her dry lips.

"Lorie," he said, drawing out her name until it faded away in a whisper. "Lovely temptress."

Her pulse kicked up.

"No one makes my heart stutter like you do."

"I don't need your false flattery, Dodd. Just kiss me."

Rather than dispute his sincerity, which he looked like he wanted to do, he released one of her wrists and stroked her temple. The tension in her shoulders dropped away as he dragged his fingers through her hair until they snagged in the thick strands at the nape of her neck. The kiss roughened. His tongue slipped inside her mouth, probing, licking, sliding over hers in a sensual dance.

Longing surged through her. She kissed him back in equal measure, savoring the taste of lemon-ice, a remnant of the freezing solution, in his hot mouth.

A rumble of approval vibrated in his throat. He let go of her other wrist, swept his hand between their bodies and caressed her breast through her flightsuit.

A gasp rushed up her throat, but she didn't stop him.

Dodd's lips glided over to her earlobe where he licked and nipped on the tender flesh. His warm breath drifted into her ear, clouding her scattered thoughts.

"I want you," he whispered softly.

Was she ready for this? Now wasn't the right time. They were floundering in space, and if they didn't get back on track, they'd perish out here. In spite of that, she didn't want to let him go. Not yet.

He seemed able to read the acceptance in her eyes.

She flinched when he tugged open the side closure on her flightsuit, slipped his cool hand over her ribs and cupped the underside of her bare breast.

Oh, stars.

"I've thought about this moment so many times," he said, nibbling his way down her neck to her collarbone.

Have you? Really?

"All those times we'd run into each other on the space station and you never gave me a second glance." His tongue slid across her heated skin to the dip in her throat where he deposited feathery kisses that gave her chills. His hand gently caressed the swell of her breast. "I tested my charm on lots of women, and it seemed to be in working order, but when I aimed it at you, it seemed to fluster you. Turn you off, actually."

Dang if he didn't sound a little insecure.

"For a while, I thought you might be a lesbian," he said with a nervous chuckle. He kissed the underside of her jaw and then drew back until his whole face came into view. "You're not, are you?"

She caressed his rough jaw with her palm. "I've never tried it."

"Don't," he said adamantly.

She gasped as his fingers rolled her nipple into a hard bud.

"I want you all to myself."

His possessiveness made her a little nervous, and yet she liked masterful men.

Why did uncertainty haunt her? Deep down, she knew he wasn't anything like her brutal ex-lover. No woman had ever complained Dodd had been too rough, or too insensitive. Just noncommittal.

Of all the males she'd ever known, Dodd ranked first on the list of People to Be Stranded in Space With. She'd been attracted to Dodd from the first moment her friend pointed him out as the new member of the communications group. Looking at his handsome face made her sigh, inspecting his tight, hard body made her drool. Those intense blue eyes made her heart pound. But could he give her what she wanted? Would he be shocked by her desires?

"It's fate that the two of us are stuck in this black hole together, Lorie." He massaged her breast, at first gentle, then squeezing the plump globe, and then another gentle caress until she arched her back, silently begging for more.

Was it fate? Who knew? "Fate or not, I have no complaints about the company."

"So glad to hear it." He pushed her open flightsuit off her shoulders, trapping her upper arms close to her body and exposing her mounded breasts. When he looked down at her, longing and satisfaction clearly shone in his eyes, the gaze so gentle, it made her heart ache. He lowered his head toward one peaked nipple.

Oh God! Yes.

No.

No! What were they doing? One touch and she'd be lost. She'd want more and more until… Until they ran out of time.

"Stop." She grabbed his stubbled cheeks. "Are we crazy? We can't do this now." Her eyes pleaded with him. "Not now, Dodd. We have to find a way out of this mess."

With a dramatic groan, Dodd hung his head. Slowly, he lifted his chin, cocking his head to the side. "Be warned," he said quietly but firmly, "I won't be put off for long." His lips compressed into a straight line as he rolled off her and helped her to her feet. "Not this time."

Chapter Two

※

Lorie yanked her flightsuit closed over her chest, and the fragile material shredded in her hands. "Oh, damn." Her taut nipples peeked through two of the vertical tears streaking down the front as if the top had been designed to showcase them that way.

Opposite her, Dodd's eyebrows rose. Raw interest gleamed in his eyes.

"Stop staring at my breasts. We have work to do." Their transport rumbled as if to emphasize her point. She turned her back on him and glanced over the multitude of flashing lights on the control panel. As much as her body hummed for his touch, their bleak situation demanded her attention.

Big, warm hands slid around her hips, making her pulse leap.

"What can I help you with?" he asked, snuggling up to her back. Heat seeped into her spine. His hands skimmed up her ribs, his fingers wiggling into the open slits and tickling her skin.

Aching desire burned low in her belly. *Ohgodohgod.* She slapped at his arms. "Dodd—" As she spun away, he yanked his hands back. The rips lengthened, leaving open gaps all the way to her hips.

She looked down at her ruined flightsuit, and almost smiled at the way her skin peeked through the ragged tears. It reminded her of an outfit she'd seen another woman wearing at the Sub Level, except hers had been crotchless. And the woman had been bound spread-eagle to a wall. What would Dodd think if she told him things like that turned her on?

Laugh, probably. No one expected the quiet, serious engineer to have a naughty streak.

"You're so pretty when you blush," he said with a smile in his voice. "Not that you're not pretty anyway."

The heat in her face spread to her ears. "How many times have you used that line, Dodd?"

"Hmm. Well, in your case, it's true. I'm partial to redheads."

"I never noticed," she lied.

"None of them excited me like you do." He brushed the back of his fingers over her cheek. "Freckle Face."

"Oh? And why is that?"

A dark blond brow arched high. "Maybe because they were too easy to conquer." He swept his palm over the curve of her breast, pausing slightly at the nipple before she stepped back and he dropped his hand away. "Maybe because I couldn't find a smart, sensible female like you among them."

She looked away, feeling like a fraud. He didn't see the real Lorie Walker at all. No one did. In the early years, working undercover for the IDC had introduced her to dark desires she relished and hid from the world, for fear of being labeled or ostracized. Despite some encounters that made her question her choices, she couldn't stop yearning for passion's sharp edge. She couldn't stop hiding either.

Out of habit, she wrapped her cloak of respectability around her like a shield. "Yeah, I'm sure a smart, sensible girl was exactly what you were looking for in a bedmate."

His smile broadened. "Oh, did I forget to mention your body makes my cock rock-hard every time I look at you?"

"This body?" she asked, fanning her hands down her sides. "Covered in freckles? These wide hips and big thighs?"

In one quick step, he moved forward, grabbed her butt cheeks and pulled her against his firm, sexually lethal body. "Yes." He swept his head down and plundered her mouth.

Drowning in his sensual kiss, she gripped his flightsuit at the shoulders, unintentionally tearing the material from the hard muscles beneath. She fought the urge to rip open the rest of his flightsuit, run her hands over his chest, rub his nipples until they pebbled beneath her fingertips and caress his flat belly. She wanted to stroke his cock, guide him inside her, wrap her legs around his hips and ride him hard.

God, she was so weak!

She wanted him. This instant. While white-hot heat consumed her body and searing desire flooded her mind. The mind-boggling black hole could wait.

But the darkness surrounding their ship pressed in on her mind. The inexplicable situation distracted her. She wanted him, but on her timetable.

"Dodd," she muttered into his mouth as she pushed at his shoulders. She twisted her head to the side. "We won't have time to enjoy this if we're dead!"

His body stiffened.

She leaned back and searched his unreadable expression. He stared past her into the endless black sky. The color in his face drained to a pasty white. Finally! She'd gotten past his hormones to his common sense.

He glanced over at the cryotubes and back at her. "Maybe we should—"

"I'm not going back into stasis," she said, breaking body contact. "Not until we've tried everything we can to get out of here."

"What if it's impossible?"

"It's not," she said, tamping down the last burning embers of lust. Unable to stop herself, she skimmed her palm over his chest, careful not to tear his flightsuit any more. "Have some faith."

An odd look crossed his face. "You sound so positive."

She shrugged, not feeling confident at all. "Come on," she said, backing away. "Lend me a hand with the propulsion system."

He inhaled deeply and nodded. "Tell me what to do."

"Pull the crystal canister from the energy core while I take a look at the electronics."

Hours later, the hazard lights still flashed on the control panel.

"Damn it!" No matter what she did, it made no difference. "The only good news is we've managed to activate cruising power. The navigation history says we've been going in a circle since we entered the black hole. By switching the controls to manual mode, we can steer the craft."

Now which way should they go? No sense in wasting precious fuel on the wrong trajectory.

After hunching over in cramped spaces for so long, Dodd clasped his hands on top of his head and stretched, thrusting out his chest and flexing his biceps. Lorie tried not to stare at the masculine display. Still, heat flushed through her body at the sight.

With a grunt of relieved stiffness, he dropped his arms. "You'd think the massive gravitational pull of the black hole would've pulled us directly toward the middle."

She frowned. "Maybe we're spiraling toward the center?" Everything she'd ever read about black holes was pure scientific conjecture. Who knew how they really functioned? If the mass was so great, why wasn't their little space exploration capsule crushed? Was it possible they simply orbited the outer edges?

Little about the journey made sense. Logically, after fifteen years, they shouldn't have power to light the emergency lights in the floor let alone the flashing control panel. The liquid nitrogen feeding the cryotubes would've evaporated by now. They'd had enough for a ten-year round trip, that's all. She glanced at the two solid chambers that had kept them alive. Had the cryotubes opened due to a lack of nitrogen coolant? The level marker indicated they still had about five years' worth left, but then all the gauges were screwed up.

"Maybe we haven't been in cryostasis as long as you figured," she said hopefully. "Maybe the cryotubes opened on time, and we're closer to Pluto IV than we think."

"Look around you," he said quietly. "Does this look like everything is going according to plan?"

"Could it be we're on the dark side of the planet?"

"With no stars in our view? I doubt it." The sadness softening his gaze shot straight through her soul.

"Stop looking at me like that." She set her hands on her hips. "We *will* get out of here. You've beaten the odds before. I've heard a million stories about your early years in the tactical division."

His lips twitched with wry amusement. "A million?"

"Well…lots." More than he could imagine. No point in letting him know how many people she'd asked about him over the years. "I never pegged you for having a fatalistic viewpoint."

"I'm a realist. We're in a black hole with no apparent exit portal. We have limited life support, no communications and minimal guidance systems. Our chances of survival are slim to none."

Already aware of the dismal facts, she glared at him. "We have brains, and each other."

"Ah, yes. Each other." She watched in amazement as he chased the anxiety from his face and a lusty gleam lit his eyes. "Let's make the most of the time we have left," he said, waving her closer. "Come here."

A crooked smile pulled at her lips while she shook her head at him. "You have a one-track mind, Dodd Henderson."

He reached out, grabbed her arm and pulled her against his chest. "I can think better when my cock isn't aching for you. Put me out of my misery and I swear I'll give you a hundred and ten percent when we're through."

"Is this how you seduce all your women? 'Cause it lacks something for me."

His lips twitched at her mockery. "If you have your way," he said, sliding his hand between the slashed fabric at her hip and thrusting low, "we'll be too busy to explore anything but the stars." He cupped her damp panties, and slid his middle finger along the center crease. "Let's take a little time for ourselves and explore each other." He nipped her earlobe and then soothed the sting with a warm, sensual lick. "Who knows when—or if—we'll get another chance."

Her knees nearly buckled. *Wow, that worked much better.*

Although the lure of sex with Dodd tempted her beyond measure, staying here any longer than necessary made her nervous. Two weeks of oxygen was not a long time.

She looked forward to her new home. Unbeknown to the IDC, as soon as she'd received her transfer papers, she'd looked into a civilian position at the engineering school on Pluto IV. If all went well, she'd have an offer soon after she arrived. For the first time in a long time, she'd be in charge of her own life. No more impromptu undercover role-playing, at least not a role she hadn't selected herself, she thought with an inward smile.

She quirked an eyebrow at Dodd. Would he be interested in a game of master of the dungeon? She imagined him striding half-naked across a stone floor, a paddle in his hand, intent on driving her to orgasm. Her skin tingled thinking about it.

"As soon as we're on our way out of this black hole, I'll take care of your itch, Henderson." To back up her statement, she cupped his groin.

He grunted in surprise and froze, letting her stroke him from the base of his cock to the tip.

It was quite an inspiring little journey. He was long and thick, just as she imagined he'd be. She swore she could feel the blood pumping through the steely rod. Smiling into his eyes, she gave him a light squeeze for good measure. "I'll start with a blowjob you'll never forget."

Eyes narrowed, his quick fingers slid beneath her silky panties, easily tearing them away. Two fingers slid into her slick core, pressing deep, lifting her up onto her toes. "Let's start now, Freckle Face."

Heart in her throat, she raised her chin and grabbed his balls, gently rolling the palm of her hand around the big bundle in his pants. "When we set a course."

He eased his fingers in and out of her pussy, sliding through the wet heat with slow and deep strokes. "You want me as much as I want you."

"I'm not denying that," she said breathlessly, squeezing her thighs together and rocking against his hand. "But I've got priorities."

"So do I." He wrapped his free arm around her back, locking her into a tight embrace, and drove his tongue into her mouth at the same time he plunged his fingers deep into her cunt. His throat absorbed her cry.

Blazing pulsars.

She slid one knee up the outside of his thigh, clinging to him like a drowning victim. While she held on to the outline of his big cock, she rode his fingers, too involved now to stop. It had been so long since she'd been more than a convenient sex partner, since she'd felt desired. Orgasm was going to hit her fast. She could feel it coming…tightening into a whirlwind of ache and pleasure.

His breath hitched as she leaned into his heat, clamping down as he pushed inward. Lust, hot and greedy, slammed into her. The need to have him deep inside her flushed her skin with heat. She'd willingly take his fist inside her if he'd make her come. Right. Now.

His fingers plunged through her creamy juices with a loud slurp, bringing her closer. Higher...

She thrust back her head, breaking the incredible kiss, and gasped for air. "Dodd! Oh God!" Her hips shook.

He drove his fingers in and out faster. Deeper. "Beg me, baby!"

"Don't stop," she huffed. "Please. Oooh."

Fire licked at her core.

The heel of his hand slapped her pussy with each thrust. He captured the back of her head with his free hand and sucked the stretched column of her neck.

Goose bumps rose across her shoulders and down her thighs. Pussy muscles clamped down on the delicious agony licking at her clit. "Oh...oh...yeeesss!"

The tight coil inside her snapped. It unfurled with lightning speed, shooting sparks all the way to her taut nipples. "Ooooooh!"

As Dodd slowed his deep strokes inside her, she squeezed every last tremor from her body.

Trembling thigh muscles forced her to lower the leg clasped to his hip. "Wow," she said with shaky breath. She forced a deep breath through her nose to slow her speeding heart rate. Then another.

The loss of his warm, thick fingers inside her slick pussy left her feeling bereft, and yet his closeness and his other hand absently gliding through her hair kept her warm and made her feel cosseted. She closed her eyes and squeezed her inner muscles one last time.

A soft kiss on her temple loosened the tension in her shoulders.

Belatedly, she realized she held his cock in a vise grip and he hadn't complained at all. She eased her fingers loose. "Sorry," she mumbled.

"You didn't hurt me," he said with a crooked smile. "Much."

"I suppose you want me to kiss it better now."

His smile grew. "If you insist."

She pursed her lips at him, close to giving in. He deserved a good blowjob for the knee-weakening finger fuck he'd just given her, but she couldn't. Primarily because she had to catch her breath. "As soon as we're under way to...somewhere. I promise."

He clutched the back of her neck. "Damn, you're a stubborn woman." He dropped his hand to his side. His nostrils flared as he drew in a deep breath. "Fine." He crossed his arms across his wide chest and stared out into the infinite night. "Here's my theory. Since no light escapes a black hole, we need to travel faster than the speed of light to escape gravitational pull. If we concentrate the crystal fuel into one power boost, we may be able to break free." His expression deadly serious, he tilted his head and looked her straight in the eye. "Are you willing to risk *everything* for that one chance?"

Chapter Three

Lorie pressed her fist over the knot in her stomach. "I've never heard of a spacecraft this size exceeding the speed of light."

"Me either." The desolate look in Dodd's eyes said they didn't have a chance in hell of escaping the black hole. Ever. Yet he didn't stomp on her hope. "The question is, do you want to try? We could become famous as the first explorers to see the inside of a black hole and come out to tell about it, or we could be missing in action for a long, long time."

A chill skipped across her shoulders. One chance for freedom. Dare she take the risk? If they failed…

They mustn't fail.

"The likelihood of getting rescued from inside a black hole is extremely small." She shoved her fear aside. "So what do we have to lose? I think the chance of getting out is better than staying," she said softly.

"Right." He didn't sound convinced.

For the first time since she'd met him, he looked disappointed. He took her hand in his and stared at her.

"What?"

He gave his head a small shake and squeezed her fingers. "Damn, if you're not the first woman who's twisted my guts in a knot since Hannah Mitchell stole first place from me in the sixth-grade science fair. And I'm going to lose you."

Her heart jumped into her throat. "What are you saying?"

"If we make it back, there's going to be a media frenzy, scientific inquiries, psych tests and more. Then we both have to focus on new IDC positions. No time for *us*."

"You want there to be an us?" she asked with surprise.

"It would've been nice." He gave her a wobbly smile. "But then you would've discovered all my faults, like how arrogant I am and quick to judge. I'm not always honest either," he said with chagrin. "Sometimes my charm is more sarcasm than flattery."

She raised her brow at his admissions.

"There are things from my past that haunt me," he said solemnly. "You don't seem to have that problem. I'm flawed. You're not."

She dropped her head to hide the incredulous expression on her face and raised an eyebrow in disbelief. He had a dark past? It couldn't be half as bad as hers. "I have plenty of flaws."

"Not in my eyes."

A blush of delight warmed her cheeks. "Is this where your sarcasm comes into play?"

"Not at all. I've never met a more selfless, honest, hard-working and caring person. Everyone in Engineering speaks highly of you. Yogaslav told me you covered double shifts for four weeks when he had a family emergency on Earth. Goodson still talks about the time you shoved him away from an electrical panel right before it flared and fried everything within three feet."

She shrugged. "They would've done the same for me."

Warmth glowed in Dodd's eyes. He cupped her cheek and gave her a sad smile. "You're everything I wish I could be."

"I've heard similar stories about you."

"Ha. I've never saved anyone."

"No? What about that misunderstanding by the Hubbard visitors who thought our signal lights were weapons? Your calm intercession avoided disaster that day."

"They weren't a big threat. If they had been, I would've recommended the station commander vaporize them. Not very diplomatic of me." He gave her a roguish smile. "I especially wouldn't want anything to happen to you." Before she could say a word about defending herself, he swept her mouth with a light, sweet kiss.

"You know, Henderson, this tender side is why the whole space station population is in love with you."

He tilted his head. "Including you?"

The question took her off guard. "I...uh, sure. I'm your biggest fan."

His smile stretched into a cocky grin. "Is that so?"

She looked away, afraid she'd revealed too much. With a negligent shrug, she said, "Yeah. You're all right."

He reached out and grasped her chin, forcing her to face him. "I think you're all right too."

Time stood still for a moment as she stared into his beautiful blue eyes. Was it possible the catch of the galaxy truly cared for her? It was unfathomable, and yet, the way he looked at her seemed...special.

"I have one request," he said softly, dropping his hand from her chin.

"What's that?" she asked, totally under his spell.

"You give me that blowjob you promised *before* we're blasting through space faster than the speed of light. It might be difficult if you try it during super-G mode."

His dancing eyes and smug tone raised her hackles, but she couldn't call him on it. First of all, she saw it as a defense to cover his moment of tenderness, and second, she *had* made the offer. Besides, she was eager to see the hard planes of his body and his legendary big cock.

The timing sucked, but would there be a better time than right now? Her gaze dropped to the long ridge at his crotch, clearly outlined by his tight flightsuit. Great Jupiter, she'd like to hold him in her hand, stroke his silky length and make him beg like she begged for release. If she relieved him of his sexual frustration, maybe he'd focus on the crisis at hand.

Ten minutes of play wouldn't alter their situation for better or worse, would it? "Since it's going to take all our concentration to work out—aah!"

A triumphant gleam lit his baby blues as he wrapped both arms around her and jerked her against his body. Heat leapt from his gaze. Each heartbeat thumped against his chest and pounded against her skin. "I need you, Lorie," he said seriously yet savagely. He tilted his head and crushed his moist lips to hers, stealing her breath away.

Heaven knew she needed him, too. Fear and desperate yearning had her clinging to his solid strength and his warmth, unable to let go.

The neck of his flightsuit ripped like tissue paper beneath her sharp nails. It was too tempting not to take advantage, so she stripped it away from his muscular shoulders. "Mmm," she moaned with delight into his mouth and then broke the kiss so she could ease back and drag the ripped fabric down the rigid contours of his torso. His chest flexed as she ran her fingertips over the hard planes. Eagerly, she smoothed her palms down his flat stomach, tearing the thin material along the way until she bumped the tip of his erect cock. "No skivvies, Henderson?"

"Pointless," he mumbled as he nuzzled her neck.

"Oh," she gasped softly, lifting her shoulder against his tickling kisses.

She grabbed his burgeoning shaft, learning its size and shape using long, firm strokes. "I approve."

A chuckle shook his chest. "Of going commando or the size of my cock?"

"Both."

While he licked circles on her neck, she kissed the space

between his collarbones, and then dragged her wet lips down between his pectoral muscles. The hand not wrapped around his silky-steel rod slid around his back and squeezed one firm ass cheek.

With a muted grunt, he set his hands upon her shoulders, gently pushing her lower. As she dipped down, following the thin line of hair between his ribs, his fingers tightened. When she stopped and slipped her tongue into his bellybutton, he sucked in his breath, drawing in his stomach. The stiff shaft encased in her hand twitched.

"Suck me, baby."

With a mischievous grin, she raked her teeth over the skin below his navel and sucked a bit of his flesh into her mouth.

"Oh. Mmm." He laced his fingers into her hair. "That's not what I meant and you know it."

She licked the rosy mark she'd left on his skin. "Oh. You mean this?" she asked while she stroked him.

"Yesss." He sounded breathless as he guided her mouth to the tip of his cock. "Right there."

"Here?" Her tongue skimmed over the slit in the tip, lapping at a pearl of pre-cum.

"That's...a good start," he said brokenly.

It was fun teasing him. She smiled inwardly at the power she held over him, amazed he didn't push her faster than she wanted to go. Oh, he wanted her to hurry up, she knew, but he held back. Good thing. Nothing killed the mood faster than forceful, rushed foreplay. She slipped her mouth over the big knob and gave it a little suck.

He rocked up and down on his toes.

Taking pity on him, Lorie settled into a more comfortable position on her knees and took his cock deep into her mouth. This beat worrying about their immediate future.

Above her head, a rush of breath swooshed from his lungs. "Oh fuck. Yeah." His breathing skipped as she slid her mouth up and down a little faster. "Oh my God, that's good, Lorie." Beneath the fingertips of her left hand, his buttocks clenched.

Long moments of silence passed, broken only by the slurp of her wet mouth and Dodd's sporadic low groans. His fingers tightened on her scalp whenever she took him deep and stroked her tongue up and down his thick shaft. He especially liked it when she sucked and lapped at the bulbous head while stroking his shaft. His breathing grew more erratic with each sensuous slide.

"I'm close!" he shouted as he pushed her away.

For a second, she was confused by his action, but then he slipped his hands beneath her arms and lifted her up off her knees. In one long fluid stride, he backed her up to the control panel and set her down on the rounded edge.

"Whoa! What am I sitting on?"

"It's all useless communication equipment," he said, plucking her breasts through the torn slits of her flightsuit. "You should tear all your clothes like this, Lorie." He grasped both mounds within his broad palms and caressed them roughly. Heat flashed in his eyes as he pressed the bountiful flesh together, creating a deep cleavage. "Oh, baby." He swooped down, dragging his tongue over one nipple and then the other.

He blew on the glistening tips. With a little hum, he homed in on the left one, wrapped his lips around the bud and sucked.

On a gasp, she gripped the sides of his head, wanting to stop the sudden ache that shot down to her cunt and then, never wanting the ache to stop. He licked and sucked and nipped until her breasts swelled with passion. She wrapped her legs around his thighs, hungry for him.

He released her tender nipple and turned to the other one already taut with wanting. A few sensual licks later, he plunged a hand between her legs and ripped open the center seam. He shoved aside her torn panties and stroked her center, searching for entry.

Her breath seized in her lungs when two thick fingers plunged into her moist channel.

"This is just a preview of what's coming, Lorie," he said with a sensual growl. "Wait until I sink my cock into this juicy pussy of yours."

Hot arousal tugged low in her belly.

"But…" They'd both received a clean bill of health before the flight, but how had the cryonics affected her STD-birth control inoculation? She stared helplessly at him, wanting him inside her more than anything, but smart enough to act wisely. She expected to escape this black hole and she didn't want any surprises down the road. "Protection?"

He brushed his lips across her cheek. "Don't worry. That shot I gave you earlier contained plenty of protection."

Relief rushed through her veins. "All right then." She spread her legs wider for him and smiled shyly, unable to say anything more as she watched his fingers glide past the torn fabric into her flushed, swollen sex.

"You're super wet. Ready for me."

It wasn't a question, but she nodded anyway.

After a few more deep slides, he withdrew his slick fingers. Grabbing her behind the knees, he pushed her legs up, forcing her back onto the flat panel, and ripped the inner seam wider until a huge gap appeared. "Hold your legs up and open, sweetheart. I want to look at you."

Hot and eager, she obliged him.

An instant later, he knelt before her. "A natural redhead, I see," he said, running his damp fingers through her bush. Her pulse skittered as he flicked a fingertip at her clit and then slid his fingers between her lips, collecting her cream. "And a pretty rosebud, too," he said as he smeared her cunt juices around her puckered hole. "Do you like anal play?"

"Sometimes," she admitted warily, squirming beneath his light touch. "I, uh…"

She lost her train of thought as a single finger found her anus and pressed into her to the first knuckle. Reflexively, she squeezed the digit and moaned quietly.

"Easy, honey." Holding his finger in place, he spread her labia with his thumbs and licked the lush interior.

"Do you like that?" he asked huskily, glancing up at her with dark fire in his gaze.

"Yes." Heart in her throat, she shimmied closer to his steamy breath. Shards of icy-hot pleasure broke low in her belly when he lapped her cunt a few more times. "Definitely."

"Just say 'fire' if I do something you don't like."

The ease in which he'd given her a safe word stunned her. Had it slipped out unbidden? She hadn't heard that his exploits leaned toward sexual play that required a safe word. Maybe they were more alike than she thought.

"Okay," she said, sucking in a deep breath as he wiggled the finger into her ass until it slid to the second knuckle.

His mouth descended on her pussy, kissing and licking and sucking. She bit her lip at the incredible yearning that shot through her. Her body bowed in pleasure. *Oh, Dodd. You live up to your reputation.*

"Relax."

She tried, especially when he wiggled his tongue over her clit like that, but every touch made her bear down and rock against him.

He withdrew his finger and primed her ass with more of her cream. "I'd love to fuck your ass," he said as he dipped his finger in and out in a steady rhythm. "But I want to feel your cunt wrapped around my cock first. I want to see your face flush with desire as I plunge into you over and over again." He gave her clit a quick hard suck. "I want to hear you scream my name."

"Oh God." Her inner muscles clenched with need. She clutched the edge of the control panel until the muscles in her forearms burned. Between his tongue laving her pussy and his finger teasing her anus, she rocketed toward orgasm. "Fuck me, Dodd."

Dodd stood and looked down at her with a hint of victory twisting his lips. The hands that had held her, excited her, now gripped her hips. She missed the intimate touch in her ass and his hot breath on her pussy. Craved it. But the promise of his long rigid cock plunging in and out of her sopping cunt made up for the loss. She stared hungrily at the masterpiece at his groin, thrust outward from the dark nest of curls at a perfect forty-five-degree angle, probably something only a sexually ravenous female engineer like her would notice, she thought with an inward grimace. She inhaled deeply. "Take me any way you want. I am *so* ready."

"I've waited a long time for you to say that," he said with a sincerity that surprised her. Eyes sizzling with heat, he braced one arm on the panel, took his erection in the other hand and guided it to her cunt. With a steady glide, he pushed deep.

She arched up as he slowly withdrew. The pressure of his cock set a flash fire burning beneath her skin.

"I've wanted to fuck you for so long," he said as his slick shaft slid along sensitive inner muscles, filling her and retreating, driving her mad.

"All you had to do was ask," she panted.

"Are you kidding? That's not…" He shook his head. "You're so damn snug." He closed his eyes for a few long, deep strokes. His lips parted as he rocked between her legs.

Pressure on the ship's hull shook the panel beneath her ass, the vibration darting straight through her cunt. As good as it felt, the shock wave worried her. *Please, no catastrophes now*, she silently pleaded to whatever deity held their fate in its hands.

Dodd pushed deep and stilled until the tremor faded away. "Wow," he exclaimed in a rush of breath.

When he looked at her again, the dazed look in his eyes cleared, burnt away by the searing heat of passion. "I want to know the real you, Lorie." He leaned forward, scooped his arms beneath her shoulders and drew her up against his damp chest, driving deeper into her center.

Held tightly in his embrace, her heart swelled with warmth and happiness. She wrapped her legs around his hips and threw her arms around his neck.

"Especially the naughty vixen you hide from the world," he added with a look of reproof.

A guilty flush burned her cheeks. How did he know? She kept her erotic toys in a biometrically sealed container. Intimate play had been limited to private appointments at the Pleasure Club. Even her best friend thought she was sexually challenged. Did he sense the white-hot flame in her no one else did?

"I don't know what you're talking about." With a playful grin, she rubbed her breasts over his solid chest. The friction shot a warm tingle from her nipples to her belly.

Dodd must've liked it too because a moan rumbled in the back of his throat. One hand slid down her back and gripped her ass, his fingers digging into one fleshy cheek. He tucked his chin into her neck and pumped faster, harder.

Heat rushed up her neck into her face. Low in her belly, the spiral of an orgasm spun tighter and tighter. "Dodd," she murmured softly, desperately, clinging to him. In her mind, she formed the words to tell him how good he felt inside her, how she'd dreamed of this and never wanted this moment to end, but he distracted her by slipping his hand lower on her butt, into the gap of her torn uniform, and working two fingers past her tight ring into her ass. A gasp tumbled out along with a sob of joy.

"Yes!" She wriggled closer, riding him hard, wanting to

take as much as he could give. "Fuck me. Fuck me!"

He plunged in and out of her sopping pussy, grunting with each thrust, while he pressed his thick fingers inside her ass. Perspiration gleamed on his forehead. The strain of his exertion creased his brow.

She loved watching him drive into her body with the tenacity of a conqueror. Her gaze riveted on him, she imagined her face was just as flushed, her eyes as bright, shining with the willingness to give him everything he desired.

Boiling passion raged through her like a flash flood. She squeezed her eyes shut and tossed her head back, drowning in burning, tumultuous sensation. The climax hovered just out of reach. "Dodd!"

He buried his cock as far as it would go. He pushed his fingers deep within her anus.

Oh. Oh. Oooh! A hot spasm rippled through her cunt, and then another. A lengthy groan reverberated inside the small transport, and yet her pleasure-racked brain barely registered the erotic sound as her own. Every neuron focused on the heat wave rolling through her, making her squeeze Dodd with all her might while her taut body shook.

Before the last contraction shuddered and faded away, he came, filling her with his fluid warmth.

Through lips parted by ragged breath, she whispered his name again. This time in awe. Unwilling to let go of his neck, she rested her cheek against his stubbled jaw.

Silence reigned as their heartbeats slowed together.

No wonder the whole female space station crew mooned over him. Making love to him was like being catapulted around the sun where the dazzling sun flares reached out and seared you.

Just how many other women had he made feel this way?

"You're as sexy as hell," he said, easing his fingers from her ass and discreetly wiping them on the uniform hanging in shreds from his hips. Using his other hand he pushed back a strand of hair stuck to her hot forehead.

All her insecurities rushed back. How many times had he told a woman she was sexy after they'd made love? Yes, he'd said he admired her, and he seemed to like her, but men would say anything to get what they wanted, especially a womanizer like Dodd.

He was still buried inside her, physically linked to her, but emotionally, they'd disconnected.

She mentally slapped herself. He hadn't pulled away from her. She was the one who'd thrown up the emotional barrier, afraid of believing what might be a lie. Equally afraid she'd found someone who related well to her, and it was too late.

She dropped her feet to the floor. It had been wonderful, and she'd always treasure her brief liaison with the stud of Space Station 5423, but in the scheme of things, it meant little. If they survived the exodus from the black hole, who knew what awaited them? If they didn't make it out of the black hole, they'd be dead and nothing would matter at all.

"What's the matter, Lorie?" Dodd's grip around her back tensed.

She pulled her arms from around his neck and gently pushed down on the arms encircling her. "Time to get back to reality."

Chapter Four

For a long moment, Dodd didn't move. *Was that another brush-off?* Lorie's abrupt shift from passionate woman to detached engineer hit him low in the belly. No female had ever cut him off so casually after sex, and he desired Lorie more than any other. Damn it, he wanted to howl like a banshee.

His cock still pulsed inside her, warm and sated. She had him so fired up, in another few minutes, he'd be ready to go again. Now that he'd tasted her sweet nectar and soothed his longtime ache within her pliant body, he wasn't going to put up with her hot and cold attitude anymore.

Based on her fetish choices at the Pleasure Club, he knew exactly what she wanted, and he was more than happy to oblige her. In fact, his boss at the Interplanetary Defense Council insisted he do whatever it took to keep her safe and content en route to Pluto IV. She'd pissed off some dangerous fugitives lately, and she'd been making noises about quitting the IDC. Since the council considered her a key asset, they wanted to make sure she arrived at her destination alive and happy. Her sexual pleasure fit that goal, didn't it?

"I'm not done with you yet."

"But-but," she sputtered. "You came."

"Yeah." He pulled out his spent cock. The smell of their mingling juices kept him semi-hard. "So did you. But only once." He gave her a quick kiss. "And I'm thinking you're a multi-orgasm kind of girl."

Her mouth popped open in surprise.

A grin tugged at the corner of his mouth. When he'd first met Lorie, her reserved personality clashed with the passionate vixen he'd imagined. She'd perplexed him, constantly sending mixed signals that drove him crazy.

Now he knew his instincts had been right. She had scorching fires burning in her soul.

As he skimmed his hands over her shoulders and down her arms, she watched him with hot anticipation burning in her eyes. Gently grasping her wrists, he pulled her arms behind her back. "You'd like to come again, wouldn't you, Lorie?" His gaze briefly dropped to her taut, extended nipples. Too bad he'd shipped his sex supplies ahead to Pluto IV. He had some jeweled nipple rings that would look gorgeous on her.

Her eyelids fluttered closed over passion-glazed eyes and opened again. In the few seconds she hesitated to answer, he imagined her screaming a resounding "Yes!" but that's not what she said.

"We've got to try to get out of here, Dodd," she said quietly, pushing him away. "Life support may have been compromised when we entered this black hole."

"This transport contains space survival suits certified for five days. That should give us enough time to break free of the black hole's hold and find a space station, colony or nearby cruiser. Indulge me just a little longer, baby."

He looked down at her tattered flightsuit, annoyed by its hindrance. "I want to see all of you, Lorie." Without waiting for her permission, he tore the fragile fabric from her shoulders. "You brought a regulation spare outfit, right?" he asked as he ripped the rest of the suit from her limbs. *I doubt anyone will ever see you in it, but I'm not going to prick your optimism.*

She stood still and proud as he admired her. Not an anatomically perfect body, but all woman. He gave her a smile full of male appreciation, and she smiled back.

"Fair is fair," she said, tearing into his suit with equal fervor.

"Do you know how sexy your freckles are? Especially that one, right there," he said, lightly touching one close to her nipple, and then drawing an invisible circle around her rosy areola.

She slapped his hand away and resumed tugging his pants off his hips.

When they were both naked except for their ankle boots, he spun her in his arms until her bare back pressed against his chest, delighting in her feminine shriek of surprise. He loved the way her breasts overflowed his palms, and the breathy sounds she made whenever he dug his fingers into the fullness. He really liked how his cock nestled into the crack of her ass.

Her musky scent wrapped around him, firing his blood. For a long moment, simply holding her satisfied him. He savored the fit of her curves along the length of his overheated body, content in listening to her soft moans as he teased her nipples. Before long, he craved more.

He gripped her wrists and drew her hands up to her breasts. "Play with your nipples."

Without a flicker of hesitation, she latched her thumb and fingers on to her taut peaks and rolled them back and forth. She dropped her head back until it rested on his chest, perfectly at ease.

Ah, he thought with a smile, she's done this before.

"That's it," he whispered encouragingly while he slid his palms down her belly to her damp curls. Without an order from him, she spread her legs, giving him easy access to her cum-slick inner thighs.

With the ease of an eel gliding through water, he slipped two clean fingers into her cunt, and used his thumb to play with her clit. He drew her ass back firmly against his cock until his hard shaft was cradled within the plump cheeks.

"Pinch those breasts," he said as he drove his fingers in and out of her drenched pussy.

If she had any misgivings about not proceeding with an escape plan, she didn't show them now. Lips parted, panting lightly, she pinched and pulled on her taut nipples while her cunt contracted around his sliding fingers.

Oh, yeah. She was perfect.

Sexy, levelheaded, open-minded, full of determination, and yet willing to yield to him. What more could he ask for?

He loved the feel of her silky skin as she rubbed against his chest, groin and thighs. He licked the delicate skin beneath her earlobe, sucked gently, then harder. Her pulse tripped beneath his lips. *That's my babe.* The backward grind of her hips stimulated his cock into a rigid pole.

Cream drenched his fingers, making it easy to add another to her soaked pussy. She bent her knees and slid her damp back up and down his chest as she rode the three fingers stuffed inside her.

"Are you ready for that ass fucking now, Lorie?"

Her movements stiffened. "It's been a long time…" Despite her balking, the muscles in her ass clenched, briefly tightening around his cock.

To entice her further, he rubbed his thumb relentlessly over her clit. "You'd like to be stuffed full, wouldn't you?" He pulled one slick finger free and eased it into her ass.

She gasped and jerked but never let go of her reddened nipples. In fact, she pinched them harder.

Dodd grinned. After letting her get used to his firm hold on her, he tapped his middle finger against the thin wall separating her pussy from her ass.

A pink stain crept up her neck into her face and deepened to a rosy hue. Without a word, she spread her legs wider and rolled her hips.

A surge of lust shot through him. "You remember our safe word?"

"Fire," she breathed huskily.

"That's right." A chill of anticipation danced down his spine. "Lean down," he whispered against her hair. "And brace yourself." As she stretched toward the floor, he slipped his fingers free and stroked his cock down her crack. Using the slick juices from her cunt to coat his shaft and her anus, he pushed the broad pink head past her tight anal ring.

"Oh!" Her butt cheeks clenched and released.

Dodd gritted his teeth at the tight pressure. "You're so beautiful, Lorie," he said as he slid deeper into her warmth. "So fucking beautiful," he whispered roughly, searching between the sodden folds of her dripping pussy until he found her engorged clit. Grasping the nub firmly between his thumb and forefinger, he gave it a little tug.

"Mmm!" She arched her back and clutched the edge of the com station.

"Are you all right, babe?"

"Yes," she said shakily. "Don't stop."

With his heart thumping hard against his ribs, he stroked her clit while he gradually pulled out until the bulbous head of his cock rested just inside her. A satisfied grin spread over his face at her low moan of ecstasy. A few more short, leisurely slides in and out to make her ready, then he gripped her hips and pumped slow and deep.

Goose bumps popped out on her shoulders. "Dodd—" Her delighted gasp ricocheted around the inside of the space capsule.

"More, sweetheart?"

"Harder," she rasped, watching his reflection in the dark cockpit window. "Make me scream."

He shot her a predatory smile, grasped a handful of her flaming red hair and slowly pulled her head back until her neck arched into a beautiful elongated curve. "With pleasure." He bucked into her.

"Ooooh." She held still, one fist pressed against her chest, while he drove in and out. "Yes."

He watched her in the window as she'd watched him. Although a line creased between her brows and her expression looked strained, keen desire burned in her eyes.

"If I had a free hand, I'd swat that pretty pale ass of yours until it glowed a rosy pink."

Her lips parted in a silent O and then a smile slowly transformed her face. With a mischievous twinkle in her eyes, she wiggled her hips. "Spank me."

Hot lust whipped through his body. Taking his fingers out of her sopping cunt, he brushed his hand over the cool smooth skin of her ass. As he slid his cock into her warmth, he smacked the fullness of her right cheek, making it jiggle.

Instantly, she tightened around him. In the window reflection, he saw her pressing her lips together. He spanked her again and she briefly clenched her muscles again.

He hissed through his teeth at the slice of ecstasy that hit him low in the belly. "Oh, babe." He pumped in and out in a slow sensuous glide and then slapped her butt for another jolt of white-hot pleasure.

"Yes," she cried. "Make me burn."

The heavy pulse in his neck jumped. He'd never met a woman who showed such pleasure in anal sex. Swept up with her sizzling passion, he buried his throbbing cock as far as it would go into her anus and thrust in and out. He watched her neck flush to a deep pink which matched the radiance of her right ass cheek.

Her fingertips pressed into the silver console top until they turned white, but she didn't complain. She let him lean over her back and fuck her hard.

His fingers slipped through her juices as he rubbed and plucked her swollen clit. For a brief time, he let go of her hair and smacked her left butt cheek until it matched the right.

Groans of approval rumbled from deep in her throat.

His balls pulled up tight, pulsing with the desire to release his hot cum, but he wasn't ready to let go yet. She felt too damn good.

"Put your fingers in me, Dodd. Please," she begged between short deep breaths.

With a content smile, he slid two fingers into her clenching pussy. "You like double penetration, don't you, babe?"

She turned her head to look back at him, bit her lip and nodded. Her eyelids drooped, covering her glazed, lost look.

Pleased beyond words, he nipped her shoulder and then tenderly kissed the spot. If they made it to Pluto IV, he'd put a vibrator in her ass while he plunged his cock into her wet pussy. He'd bet she'd like that. He knew he'd like it. For now, though, he was happy pleasuring her this way. Very happy.

"I've been looking for a woman like you for a long time," he said in a hoarse, uneven whisper. "Don't plan on ditching me when we get to Pluto IV."

"Not…a chance," she huffed in between his brisk lunges.

The low moans she emitted each time he plunged in and out of her ass drove him on. Soon he was grunting more than Lorie, which was saying a lot. He didn't want to stop, but his balls ached for release.

"Got to come," he ground out between clenched teeth. Frantically, he slid his fingers between the swollen lips of her pussy, loving how they glided through her fresh cream. "Come with me, babe."

She clenched her butt muscles and rocked fast, oohing and aahing with enthusiasm.

Hoarse grunts erupted from his throat as she shoved her ass backward against his thighs. Through his sensual haze, he reached around her hips with his other hand and tapped her inflamed clit. "Scream," he rasped loudly, picking up her fast rhythm and pounding into her. He grabbed the tight bud at the center of her desire and squeezed.

She slapped her hand blindly at the control panel. "Dodd! Oh God. Oh God." Her whole body trembled.

He wouldn't be able to hold back much longer. He shoved three fingers deep inside her constricting pussy and held her tightly, his rigid leg muscles quivering. The hold on her clit tightened to a hard pinch.

She screamed, long and loud. With a wild throw of her head, her body jerked.

Her orgasm catapulted him over the edge. Blood rushed up his neck. His face burned hot as his semen shot into her.

"Oh!" they shouted together.

With a breathy sigh, she reached back and grabbed his thighs as another orgasm made her legs shake.

More cum spilled from his cock. A shudder racked his body. He'd never felt so drained.

Drawn by her jiggling breasts, he palmed the globes and drew her upright. The slick heat of her back meshed against his chest. God, he wished he could pick her up, throw her on his bed and make love to her over and over. Of course, the transport had no sleeping compartment, except the cryotubes and he was in no hurry to get back into one of those.

So he simply held her, dotting kisses on her temple as her heartbeat slowed to normal.

Yes, she was perfect for him. He anticipated a long, fulfilling relationship.

If they survived this totally screwed trip to Pluto IV.

* * * * *

Now that Dodd held her in his arms, Lorie's body glowed with contentment, and yet it wasn't enough. She wanted him all to herself, forever.

Off shift on the space station, Lorie had filled her free time with fantasies of the two of them, most of which she'd acted out solo using her private stash of sex toys. Once, she'd rented a metallic sexbot, downloaded a 3D image of Dodd's face into the customized features software and programmed it to chase her around her quarters. Eventually, she'd let it catch her, and then it took her up against the wall with its double-dildo cock. It had been fun but not nearly as exciting as expected.

She should've known only the real thing would satisfy her.

Would he really want her—only her—if, no, *when* they escaped this vacant hell?

"Are you ready to try to bust out of here now?" he asked softly.

She gently squeezed the arm wrapped around her waist and nodded.

A few minutes later, dressed in the more stylish flightsuit appropriate for meeting dignitaries on Pluto IV, she tinkered with the propulsion system, modifying it for maximum speed.

Dodd stood by, watching solemnly. "No matter what happens, I want you to know you're not just another fling. We have more in common than you know. I don't want to lose you, Lorie."

The glow inside her chest spread through her body in a flushed heat. A joyful smile stretched across her face. His speech lifted her spirits beyond the darkness surrounding them, giving her motivation to work harder and faster. "Glad to hear it. I don't bend over for every good-looking, smooth-talking space traveler, you know." She shot him a teasing glance.

"As soon as this last adjustment is finished, I'm going to..." His hot gaze swept down her body.

"Hand me the amp meter, Henderson," she said with a grin.

He slapped the tool into her outstretched hand, closed his hand around hers and swept her into his embrace. Their lips met in an open kiss full of heat and promise.

Lorie had to push him away, or she'd never finish the job. "Keep it in your pants. I'm almost done."

He stepped back with a growl. "Hurry up."

She chuckled at his impatience.

One last check, a prayer to whatever gods might exist, and she stepped back from the glowing energy crystal. The ship shuddered with renewed power.

"As much as I'd love to get naked with you again, it's now or never, Henderson."

His expression serious, he nodded with understanding and drew her into a tight embrace. "Let's strap in and give it a go."

They shared one last lingering kiss, perhaps the last one they'd ever share, and reluctantly broke apart.

The spacecraft rumbled and shook as Lorie coerced it toward light speed. With no celestial markers to judge their speed against, she had to trust the digital readout on the pilot console. Still, she squinted into the blackness.

Her heart hammered in her chest when she spied a fleck of light. "Look!" She glanced over at Dodd to watch his reaction. "Do you see the strip of light?"

His brows lifted in surprise. "I see it."

Shaking violently in her seat, she adjusted their trajectory and aimed for freedom, praying the ship would hold together long enough to break free.

After a few interminable minutes, she frowned. "We're not getting closer." She glanced down at the instrument panel. Their momentum wouldn't last much longer. "Damn it, we're not going to make it!"

Dodd cursed beneath his breath.

She looked over at him with fierce determination. He looked back at her, sorrow softening his eyes, along with the impression that it had been hopeless from the start.

"I'm not giving up!" she shouted at him. "I'm going to give it everything we've got." Her fingers gripped the thruster.

"Don't." His palm slapped on top of her hand. "You'll break the ship apart."

Anger flared. "What difference does it make now?" she yelled.

The engines choked.

"No!" Tears welled in her eyes. She shoved the thrust lever forward, giving the engines all the power the ship had left.

The ship sputtered into a stall.

She sat back in her chair, stunned. The light disappeared.

They were going to die, gasping their last breath in a tiny metal shell no one would ever find.

She couldn't move, couldn't think. She stared into the blackness, seeing nothing but the reflection of her distraught face and the ship's interior behind her.

Her gaze locked on the cryotubes.

"There's still hope," she said lifelessly, unstrapping the restraints and leaving her seat. "Somebody, someday, is going to solve the mystery of black holes. Who knows what they'll discover when they find a way inside." She strode toward the cryotubes, glancing back at Dodd's bleak expression as she pressed the chamber release button. "I'm not giving up on us, Dodd."

He nodded and rose from his seat.

The curved panel on her cryotube slid open.

A shocked scream tore from her throat. She jumped backward and bumped into Dodd's solid chest.

Strong hands latched on to her shaking arms. "What the—"

"Ohmigod, ohmigod." She couldn't stop staring at the preserved body inside the chamber. *Her* body.

Her heart pounded in her chest. "Am... Am I dead?"

With profound dread, she swung her gaze to the life-support gauges, all nonfunctional because they didn't friggin' need them!

She broke free of Dodd's hold and spun on him. "Are you—" She hit the release button on his chamber before he could stop her.

She couldn't breathe. He looked so peaceful. So still.

"Holy fuck," he said softly.

Lorie stared at Dodd in disbelief, the Dodd she thought was alive, but couldn't be. Which meant she wasn't living either, at least not in a physical sense. She pressed shaking fingertips against her temple. "What happened to us?"

Dodd didn't reply. He pulled her close and banded his arms around her. "Do you feel my heat? Can you hear my heart beat? We're not dead, Lorie. I don't know what we are, but it's not that."

A chill raced over her skin. "Could this—us—be a dream?" *Another one of my wild fantasies about you, Dodd.*

"Yours or mine?" Dodd asked with skepticism. "'Cause the last two hours seemed pretty damn real to me." He raised his hand to her shoulder and glanced at the raw cut on the back of his hand.

"Me, too." She sighed, wrapping her arms around his waist and pressing her cheek to his chest, listening to his rapid heartbeat, at a loss to make sense of it all. "Purgatory," she whispered with dread. "My father warned me working undercover with bad guys would—" Her fingernails dug into his warm, solid back.

"There's no point in making yourself sick with wild conjectures. Whatever the situation, it looks like we're still in stasis, safe and unharmed, with enough liquid nitrogen for another five years." Keeping one hand wrapped securely around her, he leaned forward and closed the cryotube doors. "Our subconscious is free. Is that so bad?"

Better than their minds imprisoned, she supposed. She looked up into his resolute face. "What do we do now?"

A devilish grin slowly lit his face. "We seem to have a lot of time on our hands, Freckle Face. I plan on making the most of it." One of his hands slid down her back and pressed her pelvis against the bulge in his pants. "I have a lot of ideas for filling the hours."

She melted into his embrace. "Do you think we'll remember any of this when we're roused from our frozen sleep?"

"Mmm. I hope so," he said, dragging a moist kiss from her temple to her cheek. "If not, I'll seduce you again. I've had you in my sights for a while and I'm not backing off."

"Are you planning to break your one-night stand trend?" She said it lightly, but she needed to know.

His brows dipped together. "Why would I go back to that when I have you?"

A slow smile broke the tension in her face. "Sounds good to me."

Epilogue

"What is the status of the transport crew who sent the distress call?" the commander of the IDC ship, *Unity*, asked the medical cyborg.

"Cryonic thaw is complete," he replied in his computerized voice.

"Good."

"Their bodies are healthy, but they remain unconscious. I have tried every method to revive their mental state, sir."

He made a small incision on the back of the male's hand and watched it clot. "All body functions operate normally. It appears the IDC placed a telepathic block in their minds in case of mission interference. Fairly standard procedure five years ago, sir."

Vaguely familiar with the IDC's controversial safety measures, the commander nodded. "The ship's log indicates they were headed for Pluto IV. Something—or someone—knocked them way off course into uncharted territory. They're lucky our new long-range sensors picked them up. Who knows how long they'd be drifting out here, otherwise." He studied the duo's bio readings scrolling across the headboard of each cot, not that he really understood much. "What can you tell me about this mind game the IDC has instigated?"

"The block is deep and strong. Based on their similar brain wave patterns, I believe it has connected them together in some way. A key phrase is probably required to rouse them."

"You haven't found a computer file or anyone at IDC who knows the pass phrase?"

"No luck yet, sir." The medic adjusted the brain scan band on the male's head. "Inquiries are difficult because I cannot locate identity records for either individual. It's as if their transport never existed."

"Or the IDC has reasons for not sharing," the commander muttered. He took a hard look at the pair lying on the med cots. Speculation about the unidentified crew ran rampant through his brain. They could've been mercenaries, political refugees, prisoners, undercover operatives or in the witness protection program. The IDC had more secrets than all the other galactic agencies put together.

The cyborg's electronic eye rotated from his patients to the commander. "Instructions?"

The commander hesitated. It seemed unlikely that the crewmates would wake on their own, but if they did, he couldn't afford any more distractions. The ship required his full attention. "Put them back into suspension and store them in the hold." He clasped his hands behind his back, comfortable with his decision. "We'll hand them over to the IDC at Space Station 5423 and let them figure out who they are. We refuel there in three months."

He turned on his heel and strode toward the door. "Possibly sooner if we can't fix the engine shudder problem."

PASSION'S SONG
By Jory Strong
ജ

Chapter One

Restlessness rode Raeder du'Faerin. It howled along his nerve endings with the same force as the sandstorm battering and rubbing against the outer walls of the tribe's tent city.

He wasn't the only one on edge.

Men he claimed as friends looked up, their expressions ranging from guarded to hopeful as he passed where they gathered in small groups, waiting—as he waited—for the council to finish its contemplations and send word to those who'd be lucky enough to claim a female, a third joined to a pairing that had already proven itself stable and useful to the tribe.

Among the Faerin, there was no petitioning for a joining as there was among some of the other tribes on Adjara. The Faerin elders met in council, listened to reports from the scouts—men who traveled to other planets in order to locate and identify the females who should be brought into the tribe—then decided which bonded pair of males would take her as their third.

The council's decisions were final. Its word, law. And the matching of a given female to a pairing wasn't subject to negotiation, only to acceptance or rejection.

Raeder had never heard of anyone turning down the chance to add a third, though occasionally a pair returned to their home world without the female they'd gone to claim. It was not an outcome he understood or found acceptable. It didn't matter whether the females were initially willing to be brought to Adjara or not—in the end they all made a place for themselves in the tribe and most found great happiness.

As he drew near the tent that was home, Raeder's hand went to the erection hidden beneath the loose folds of the robe he wore during those months when the tribe lived in the desert. Anticipation turned his thoughts away from the council elders and their deliberations.

Raeder knew even as he reached for the tent flap that he'd find Haven inside—waiting not on the council's decision, but for him to return home so they could spend the time when the sandstorm raged making love.

He tightened his grip on his penis, steeled himself against revealing any weakness. It was a game they played, a test of dominance and masculinity, each trying to make the other beg first. And though he was most often the victor, he made sure Haven had no cause to complain.

They'd been together for years, knew every inch of skin, every sound of pleasure—and yet still Raeder's cock throbbed when he stepped through the tent opening and saw Haven sitting on their sleeping pallet.

Dark eyelashes framed gray eyes guaranteed to inspire fantasies of fucking. And unlike most of the Faerin men who wore their hair short, Haven's was a black mass of waves flowing down his back to stop at his hips.

Raeder had wanted Haven from the moment he first saw him at the spring gathering. He'd known the attraction was more than physical even then.

"Come here," he said, his voice harsh with command as he unbelted the robe and it slid to the floor, leaving him standing in only a loin covering.

Haven smiled at having correctly guessed the mood Raeder would return home in. He flopped backward in a lazy sprawl so his loosely fitted trousers settled against his hardened cock, revealing its state and tormenting Raeder with it.

"You know I don't obey those kinds of orders," he said, sliding his hand beneath the waistband of his pants and wrapping his fingers around his penis. Reveling in the tightening of Raeder's face and the pant that escaped before Raeder clenched his jaw against another one.

Haven slowly pumped his hand up and down his shaft, shivered as exquisite sensation shot through him. The only thing better would be Raeder's mouth, and if this played out the way he'd planned, that's what he would get. He lifted his hips on a moan, letting Raeder see and hear how needy he already was, knowing that only rough, dominating sex would take the edge off Raeder as they waited for the elders to finish their contemplations.

Lust pooled in Haven's belly, fueled by fantasies of sharing a woman with Raeder, of making love to her together and separately. He imagined her soft and submissive, delicately featured and wonderfully curved as she knelt in front of him and took him in her mouth as Raeder watched, as Raeder mounted her.

Arousal leaked from the slit in his cock head. Haven used his free hand to push the light trousers down, watched Raeder's hand tighten on his cloth-covered penis before taking a step, and then another—silently conceding a measure of defeat as he closed the distance between them.

Haven's nipples were pebbled points, a weakness Raeder wasted no time in taking advantage of. Masculine fingers captured one nipple. A mouth covered the other, sending icy-hot bolts of lust straight to Haven's cock.

Raeder straddled him, bringing potent heat and a masculine scent. Haven's hips lifted off the mattress in a silent plea, with the urgent desire to touch his cock to Raeder's and rub against it until they were both panting.

Haven freed his own penis in favor of stripping away Raeder's loin covering and cupping the heavy testicles in one hand, circling the thick, hard length of Raeder's shaft with the other. Teeth clamped down in reaction, fingers became punishing on nipples that had been trained so pain and pleasure blurred into a perfect merging.

The silken crest of Haven's cock grew wetter. He moaned, bucked when Raeder increased the torment to his nipples in a silent command that forced Haven's hands back to his own penis and tight ball sac.

Haven's buttocks clenched as he fucked through the fist of his hand in quick frantic jerks. It'd be so easy to give in, to utter the single word necessary to signal his capitulation, his acceptance of the submissive role.

Haven fought against saying please. His buttocks clenched and his fist tightened mercilessly around his cock. He refused to come so quickly, to spill his seed across his chest and abdomen like a man with his first lover.

He wanted to draw their play out, to make Raeder fight for his victory. Then it'd be so much sweeter for both of them.

Mindless lust and the bestial urge to dominate and fuck roared through Raeder. He knew he was being managed, that Haven was giving him an outlet for the frustration he felt at having no control over the council's decision and whether they'd gain a third, but Raeder didn't care.

He gave Haven's nipple another rough tweak, another stinging bite and felt savage pleasure in the way Haven jerked, moaned, fought not to beg just as hard as he fought to keep from gaining release from the use of his hand.

Raeder was torn between twin desires, to kiss upward and ravage Haven's mouth, or to kiss downward and take Haven's cock. Raw hunger twisted and clawed in his chest and belly, poured into his testicles and made his foreskin retract in anticipation of possessing Haven in a way as carnal as it was intimate.

He moved downward, knowing if his lips pressed to Haven's, if his tongue slid against Haven's in a mimicry of fucking, then he wouldn't be able to stop himself from settling his weight on Haven, from rubbing his cock against Haven's until all it would take was canted hips and spread thighs, the promise of ecstasy and it would be all over.

Beneath him Haven started panting, moaning as Raeder used his teeth, his lips, the wet lash of his tongue to build the passion. The veins on the underside of Haven's shaft stood out, dark purple against dusky brown skin as the tip glistened with arousal.

Haven's hands speared through Raeder's hair as if afraid Raeder would stray from his course and fail to take him in his mouth. Another time, Raeder might have drawn the torment out longer, but at the moment he was a prisoner to his own frantic need to hear Haven's shout of release, to experience his own.

With a groan, Raeder curled his fingers around Haven's penis, felt it pulse in greeting as an answering throb of pleasure had his own cock bobbing, licking his abdomen in a sensual caress. They knew each other so well, were rarely separated from one another for more than a few hours on any given day, loved with the depth of a pair committed to each other for the duration of their lives, bound by law as well as in body and soul.

Raeder tightened his grip on Haven's cock, stroked from base to tip as his other hand found the soft globes of Haven's testicles. The dual assault made Haven arch and cry out, tighten his grip in Raeder's hair and say the words guaranteed to free Raeder from the tight leash of control.

"Please. Please suck me."

White heat scorched Raeder. But he didn't give in immediately.

He punished Haven with his tongue, rasping and rubbing it over Haven's engorged penis until Haven was shuddering, held on the razor's edge of release. And then he took Haven's cock into his mouth and started sucking, controlling the depth as Haven thrust upward in a violent frenzy that soon ended in a cry of total surrender.

Raeder retrieved a tube of lubricant from underneath the edge of the sleeping pallet. His cock stood full and proud, pressing and throbbing against his abdomen in eagerness. He squeezed lubricant onto it, coated it until it was slick — ready — and then he kneed Haven's thighs apart, forced a pillow under Haven's buttocks before coming down on top him.

They both groaned at the contact, at the exquisite feel of cock against cock, chest against chest. Raeder claimed Haven's lips. He thrust his tongue into Haven's mouth, shared the taste of sex and submission as he lifted, guided his cock to the tight pucker of Haven's anus and forged inside.

Raeder's heart thrilled to the sounds of Haven's pleasure, the moans that were close to being whimpers. His thrusts were shallow but they conveyed the rawness of his emotion, the possessiveness and love that overwhelmed him any time he was intimate with Haven. And Haven responded by raking his fingernails down Raeder's back in a signal that he wanted harder, deeper, faster — the blend of pain and pleasure only Raeder could give him.

There was no fighting the primitive response that rose with Haven's urging. Raeder fucked in and out of Haven, loving the feel of Haven's cock trapped between them, hard again from the exquisite agony and unbearable pleasure of their desire.

Raeder's breath grew ragged, tortured. His testicles pulled tight against his body, but he hung on to his control, didn't give in to his own release until Haven arched, cried out as ropy jets of semen escaped to coat chests and abdomens in a celebration of passion.

* * * * *

Aria Cajelais braced herself when her father entered the ramshackle cabin. Her fingers tightened on the small paring knife as waves of his emotion reached her along with the smell of liquor and sweat and mine dust.

She erected what mental blocks she could, but in close confines it was harder to escape the empathic gift she kept secret for fear of the consequences in revealing it. When he crossed his arms over his chest, making the muscles on his arms stand out in brutal relief, Aria tensed out of habit even though her father radiated nervous excitement and giddy expectancy instead of anger.

"We've got company coming," he said.

The four words were enough to make bile rise in her throat and fear settle in her belly. Her heart rate sped up and she wanted to escape the tiny shack, to run and keep running until she found a safe place. But there was no safe place for a lone female, not on the mining world of Iyon. The only roles allowed a grown woman not living in the home of a male family member were that of wife or prostitute.

She dropped the shields protecting her from the full impact of her father's emotions so she could measure what he was feeling against the other times he'd announced a visitor. Her heart stuttered when she was buffeted by waves of greed along with the stirrings of sexual anticipation.

Aria slammed the mental barrier back in place, a cold clamminess settling over her skin. "Who's coming?" she asked, the words faint, pathetically weak to her own ears.

"Lodur Marr."

The whore-master.

This time Aria couldn't suppress a shudder. Had her father decided to sell her into prostitution? Or did he plan to trade her for one of the women no longer generating enough money to satisfy Lodur?

Aria's chest tightened, trapping her breath and squeezing her heart in a painful fist. In her mind's eye she saw the brothel at the edge of the mining town, its windows barred to prevent the females trapped there from leaving.

The women who entered it were rarely seen again outside the brothel. It was rumored that some of the prostitutes died at the hands of the men who visited the house, and those who were used up, broken by the life they'd been forced into, were sold to men living in remote locations or to the savages who populated the desert planet of Adjara.

Another shudder passed through Aria. For the last month her father had brought more and more men home. He'd paraded her before them and at first she'd thought he was looking to collect a bride-price for her. But instead he'd plied his guests with cheap corn liquor then coaxed them into rolling the dice and spending the night gambling.

They'd all been rough, brutish men and the thought of becoming their property, of yielding her body to them whenever they desired her was terrifying. Aria knew she'd die under the onslaught of their violent emotions, if not from their fists. Each of them was so far removed from the man she fantasized about, the husband who would love and protect her, that she'd been forced to use her body, flashing skin and cleavage so they became distracted, foolish in their betting.

Her father's sly grins sickened her, revealed his game. But what choice did she have except to play the part he'd assigned her when time after time it was her he bet when a losing streak wiped out his coins?

Aria swallowed, forced herself to say, "Why is he coming here?"

Lodur had a brothel full of women to service him. He had a houseful of servants to see to his comfort.

Her father's gloating laugh was enough to make nausea pass through her in waves. He said, "Lodur thought he was being clever, coming to the mine and just happening to stop near the scales where my haul for the day was being weighed. He started talking to the foremen about some girl he heard singing in the capital city, and how he had a hankering to experience it again.

"Well, the foreman points to me and says, 'Don't know about singing, but he's got a daughter whose flute playing is beautiful enough to make a groan man cry.' So Lodur turns and I can see it in his eyes, he's already heard about you, only it ain't your flute-playing he's after. He wants to see what you look like.

"Well, girl, he's going to see all right, and lose some coin for the privilege. He thinks he's smarter than me. He thinks he can come into my home and cheat me rather than offering a fair price to turn my daughter into one of his fancy whores."

Aria's father rubbed his hands together. "When he leaves here tonight, he's going to be in my debt. Now hurry up and finish getting dinner ready, then put your entertaining clothes on."

Chapter Two

Raeder idly raked his fingers through Haven's long hair, the strokes gliding over a smoothly muscled back and lean buttocks, then up an arm covered with the exotic tattoos proclaiming Haven's lineage and personal feats.

"Do you think they'll reward us with a third?" Raeder asked, the restlessness no longer riding him though the ache for a female to complete their union and give them children did.

Haven leaned back far enough so his eyes could meet Raeder's. Tenderness filled him at the vulnerability he read in Raeder's face, the hope and longing he heard in Raeder's voice. Raeder liked to think it was his superiority on the game field during the tribe gathering and his prowess in bed that led to their bonding, but it was the softness and uncertainty well hidden beneath a shell of fierce dominance and masculine confidence that had completely ensnared Haven.

"We'll gain a third when the time is right," Haven said, tracing the tattoos along Raeder's shoulder with his finger before sliding down a muscled chest and finding a tiny nipple.

He brushed the pad of his thumb over it gently, slowly, loving the way Raeder's eyes closed and his cock hardened again. Raeder's desire for a female was no greater than his, but it had to be the right one.

"If we're not named this time then it means the woman who's a perfect fit for us has yet to be found," Haven said. "Wouldn't you rather wait?"

Raeder's eyes opened. They were as black as his hair, but they held the truth of his heart. "No more pleasure workers.

I'd rather never experience a woman's cunt again than see you taking a stranger neither of us cares about."

Haven nodded. He found only emptiness in the memory of the paid-for sex and practiced, professional responses of the females who made their fortunes on the pleasure planet of Z'nyia. "I feel the same. The scouts will eventually find a female for us. Until then, we have each other."

He rubbed Raeder's nipple with his thumb then took it between his fingers, squeezed until Raeder's buttocks clenched and his cock was fully engorged, eager.

"When she's given to us to claim," Raeder said, "we won't return to Adjara without her."

"She won't stand a chance against the two of us."

Haven smiled as he remembered being on the receiving end of Raeder's single-minded pursuit and steely determination. He knew the length of his hair and his quieter demeanor led those who didn't know him to think he was submissive to Raeder, a wife in everything but gender.

Nothing could be further from the truth. Raeder might ultimately be more dominant, but the balance of power could shift in a heartbeat or with a touch.

Haven let his hand trail downward to grasp their cocks in a fisted sheath. He reveled in the way Raeder's face flushed with hunger and heat.

Need rose. Sharp and painful.

He leaned in and claimed Raeder's lips. Lured Raeder's tongue into his mouth and sucked in the same ruthless rhythm as his hand worked their cocks.

Lust built and skin slickened. Hips jerked, faster and faster, until with shouts of pleasure they came, their semen mixing on chests and bellies as the scent of sex covered them like a blanket.

For long moments they lay together on the sleeping mat, both of them breathing hard. But finally they rose, shared the tiny rock-floored shower stall and the small amount of sun-warmed water that could be spared for bathing, then dressed.

They both froze when a knock sounded on the other side of the entrance flap. Gray eyes met pitch-black ones, mirrored the same emotion. Hope.

"Enter," Raeder said.

One of the youngsters who served the council as a messenger stepped inside with a rolled parchment in his hand. He handed it to Haven, who was closest, then left.

With slightly shaking hands, Haven unrolled it. "Aria Cajelais," he said, his voice little more than a whisper, his heart filling with joy as her name settled into his soul. "Her gift is music. She plays the flute."

"Where is she?"

"Iyon."

"Let's go claim her."

* * * * *

Aria fought the fear making her thoughts race like a rabbit being pursued by hounds. Sweat darkened the underarms of her father's shirt in wide patterns. His face was ruddy, his nose swollen from drink, and his eyes held the desperate edge of a man down to his last few coins as he chased Lady Luck.

"Shall we play again?" Lodur Marr asked, indicating the dice on the table between the two men.

Fat, be-ringed fingers reached over and caressed the bone-white cubes. His gaze flicked to where Aria stood wearing a skimpy dress no woman would be seen out in public in. His attention lingered on her chest, as if he imagined the snake-eyed pair of dice he fondled represented nipple-peaked breasts.

I can't let him take me, she thought, knowing in another roll her father's coin would be spent and he would bet her future, her life, in an attempt to recover his losses and make a killing.

"Shall we play again?" Lodur repeated, a snail-slick tongue sliding from the cavern of his mouth to lick plump, repulsive lips.

Aria couldn't suppress a shiver of pure revulsion. His greedy lust had battered at her mental shields since the moment he arrived.

Nausea rose, clearing her head of panic and giving her an excuse to leave the shack. "I need to step out back," she murmured, the polite way of indicating she intended to go to the privy.

Her father's head jerked up, a vicious scowl on his face, but Aria turned away quickly. A lump formed in her throat at the sight of her flute on the kitchen counter where she'd set it down when her father brought out his dice and ordered her to stop playing and to serve their guest the corn liquor.

The flute was the only thing of value she owned. She ached to retrieve it from the counter, to feel the comfort of wood made smooth by the caress of her fingers but gathering it would alert her father and Lodur to her intention to flee the fate waiting for her with the roll of a dice.

The immodest nature of the dress she'd been forced to wear and the chill outside gave her an excuse to slip on her heaviest cloak, a patchwork of dark fabric salvaged from discarded clothing and what she'd been able to acquire from the rag seller. Her heartbeat sounded like thunder in her ears as she opened the door and stepped outside.

She hesitated, allowing her eyes to adjust to a night revealed in the light of coldly glittering stars and by the muted blue of the pleasure planet, Z'nyia, and its orange-yellow moon-planet, Adjara.

Aria shivered at the sight of Adjara. But the nightmare tales of the savages calling it home and leaving only to acquire women for breeding were less terrifying than the future waiting for her if she didn't escape.

Icy fear slid down her spine when her gaze settled for a moment on Lodur's ox-driven carriage, its windows barred just as his brothel was. Her only chance was to get to the stream. The bloodhounds he was sure to use would find her if she tried to hide in one of the abandoned mine shafts or in someone's outbuilding.

Aria stepped away from the door. Despair filled her when two figures immediately emerged from behind the carriage, the silver glint of their whip handles and truncheons proclaiming they were Lodur's guards. She ducked her head and headed for the outhouse, hoping they'd assume no woman would be so foolish as to stray far from her home at night, and would stay with the carriage long enough for her to get a head start.

She lowered her mental shields and concentrated, felt traces of the guards' emotions along with their eyes on her back. The distance spared her from the worst of their predatory anticipation, but she felt their intention to enjoy Lodur's newest prostitute.

No! She refused to accept that as her fate. As soon as she passed from their sight, she began running.

A shout sounded almost immediately, spurring her on. Heavy footsteps raced after her.

She stumbled on rock and loose dirt, hindered by the thin-soled shoes and long cape. But she kept running, thought only of escape despite the hopelessness of it.

Aria felt her pursuers' emotions before she felt their hands, the steely fingers grabbing her hair and arms, sending pain wrenching through her as they ended her flight to freedom. The cape fell away as they dragged her back to the cabin. And though she knew it was useless, she fought, hating the feel of their hands on her skin.

The sounds coming from her mouth were primitive, feral, and grew more so when Lodur and her father emerged from the cabin. She knew by their expressions and the emotions swamping her that the dice game was concluded—and she was the loser.

Lodur pulled a syringe from the pocket of his elaborately stitched overcoat. "A pity I have to do his. In the old days the sight of a female struggling as she was taken into the brothel was good for business. But now with some of the town leaders taking up the new religion and turning into rabid dogs over the evils of prostitution, I don't need the trouble."

His lips curved into a spit-slick smile. "You'll learn soon enough that plenty of men prefer their women unwilling."

He jabbed the syringe into Aria's shoulder. "Put her in the carriage," he said, before great waves of darkness pulled her under.

The muscles on Raeder's arms bunched and rippled underneath Haven's staying hand. "Just a few minutes more," Haven said, his own fury pushing at his control, urging him to take his hand from Raeder's arm so they could attack the men who were unaware of being watched.

Raeder's hand balled into a fist. His slight nod indicated his agreement to waiting until Aria was clear of the impending fight.

A shudder passed through Haven at how close they'd come to beginning their life with Aria in a nightmare. They'd arrived just in time to hear the whore-master's words, but if they'd delayed leaving Adjara for even a few minutes, they would have been too late to save their third from being taken to the brothel and raped.

He was grateful the remoteness of the mining community with its scarcity of good building spots meant shacks were far apart. There was little chance of being seen or identified as Adjaran when they attacked and took Aria away with them—

to Z'nyia, where they'd spend time getting acquainted before returning to Adjara and presenting her to the tribe as their third.

"They've earned their deaths tonight," Raeder said, his voice a savage growl.

"But not by our hands if it can be avoided. Justice and retribution aren't why we're here. There will be trouble for our joining if we kill them unnecessarily."

Raeder's fist clenched and unclenched. He pulled away from Haven's restraining hand and took his weapon from its holster.

Haven breathed a sigh of relief when Raeder didn't adjust the setting from stun to kill. He slid his own gun out as one of the guards opened the carriage door. The other scooped Aria into his arms then climbed inside with her.

"Let's go," Raeder whispered, the tilt of his head and their years of working together all that was needed to indicate what would come next.

They moved through darkness, remaining concealed with the ease of hunters who'd learned the art of it on a desert planet where stealth and quickness of action meant the difference between eating and not eating.

The guard emerged from the carriage just as Haven was within firing range. He pulled the trigger, the primitive weapons at the waists of the two guards no match for the stunners, though neither guard, nor the two men who stood discussing the play of dice, knew what struck them as they tumbled into unconsciousness.

Chapter Three

೩⊃

Possessiveness. Lust. Tender concern. The emotions pressed in on Aria and swamped her in their intensity. Sensation bombarded her—the pleasant sting of freshly washed skin, the scent of flowers, the feel of bedding so soft she wanted to luxuriate in it, the hot touch of masculine hands and silky hair.

Her body tightened with need, feeding on the desire so easily breaching her mental barriers to find an answering swell of hunger at her core. Fingers traced her eyebrows, her nose and lips, stroked over her forehead in a gentle caress that made her whimper as she struggled to shed the cloying confusion and darkness that held her in its grip.

There were two voices above her, holding worry as well as anticipation. They called to her, their presence urging her to return from the fathomless place she'd been just as their touches stirred her longing and touched her dreams, her hopes.

She trembled when a masculine hand smoothed over her belly, burned through the material separating it from her skin. Its nearness to her cunt made her folds flush and part, grow slick. She wanted the hand to move downward, to cup her bare mound as she sometimes did in the night, to pierce her with stiffened fingers and find the spot that would send pleasure cascading through her.

Her nipples became hard points and the lust deepened. It was so pervasive she couldn't tell where their desire ended and hers began. Fantasies surfaced, dark, dark fantasies she'd allowed herself only when the flute's song no longer had the power to keep her spirits from sinking into despair. In those forbidden dreams she was protected and loved, watched over by two men who shared her bed and her heart, who ensured she never had to fear the roll of the dice.

Memories returned, broken, jagged things that made her heart race and her muscles tense. But before panic overtook her, a man said, "You're safe now." And despite the potential for violence, the savage desire for vengeance she heard in his voice, she felt the absolute truth in his words.

Slowly she became aware of the rigid cocks pressed against her. She started to struggle but was stilled by gentle hands, by a voice holding only the desire to care and protect her. "Easy," he said. "We thought you'd feel better if you woke clean and comfortable." And again she felt the truth, her empathy a gift instead of a curse.

Aria forced heavy-lidded eyes open. Her breath seized in her chest at the images captured in moon-glow. The men might have stepped right out of her fantasy. They lay on top of the bed clothing, dressed only in thin trousers, beautiful and utterly masculine—alike and yet different—exotic and enthralling with their hungry eyes and intricately tattooed arms.

She licked her lips and felt their lust spike through her nipples and turn them into aching centers of need. "Where am I?" she managed, rising to her elbows and looking around, taking in the glassed room, the starlit night visible through each of its eight walls, a gasp escaping when she saw the Adjaran moon so close.

"You're on Z'nyia," the first of them said, his fingers stroking her cheek, his black hair hanging down in waves, his gray eyes with their thick lashes filling her heart with song and making her want to reach for her flute. "And I'm Haven."

"I'm Raeder," the other said, hand splaying possessively on her belly and sending pulsing waves of molten lust to her clit and parted cunt lips.

"Z'nyia," she whispered, hardly daring to believe she was on the pleasure planet, a place where all were said to be free.

Her heart skipped a beat then raced. Her breathing became fast as she remembered Lodur jabbing the needle into her arm. What if the stories about Z'nyia were a lie? What if Lodur had sold her to Raeder and Haven? "How did I get here?"

Raeder's raw fury had Aria's eyes flashing to his in sudden alarm. She tensed out of habit at the anger she saw on his face and her reaction made Raeder's features grow taut and the desire for violence burn brighter in dark, dark eyes.

"Easy," Haven murmured, to her, to Raeder.

"We witnessed what happened on Iyon," Raeder said, his hand growing heavier on her belly, more possessive. "Was that your father who thought to turn you over to the whore-master?"

"Yes." A shudder passed through her.

Haven leaned down and pressed a kiss to her forehead. "Don't fear. Only Raeder and I know you're on Z'nyia. And though neither the whore-master nor your father nor the guards deserved mercy, we did nothing more than stun them so we could get you to safety."

He brushed his lips over her forehead again and her heart rate slowed. It was impossible to be frightened, not when their emotions were laid bare, when they enclosed her in a cocoon of warmth and safety, of possessive carnal need as well as tender desire.

"Are you pleasure workers? Is that why you brought me here?" she asked, the flash of amusement she felt in them giving her an answer before they did.

"No," Raeder said. "On Z'nyia we deal in gems."

Again she felt truth, just as she felt truth—and so much more—when Haven's lips gently touched hers and he whispered, "We brought you here because we wanted to get better acquainted. From the first moment we learned of you, we knew…we hoped…we believed you'd be the perfect woman for us. We want to give you a chance to know us better."

She shivered—not in fear, but with the need to let thought and questions yield to lust, to make love to these men who'd saved her from Lodur Marr and whose emotions buffeted her like a hot, erotic storm.

There'd been so many nights when loneliness and fear had eaten at her soul, when she'd touched herself in the darkness and dreamed of men like Haven and Raeder, of lovers who made her feel safe and desired, who surrounded her with their masculine strength and fierce caring. And here she was on Z'nyia, a place of pleasure but also of freedom, given a chance to turn fantasy into reality.

Aria tangled her fingers in Haven's black wavy locks. She felt the wild rush of joy her action sent crashing through him, the smoldering intensity of his desire and the answering surge of feverish lust that pulsed through Raeder and had him ripping the concealing sheet downward.

Raeder watched as Haven's mouth settled on Aria's. He was mesmerized by the sight of Haven kissing her, by the low moans and sensual whimpers after Haven stripped out of the thin trousers and his hand caressed her breast, tormented a dusky nipple.

He knew all too well what Haven was capable of with his lips and tongue, with his talented hands, but Raeder felt no jealousy as he watched them together. He felt only escalating desire, a fierce possessiveness of both lovers.

The scent of their arousal was an erotic mix of masculine and feminine. Their moans a siren song drawing Raeder's gaze downward to Haven's wet-tipped cock and then to Aria's parted thighs and flushed, swollen folds, the bare soft skin that had very nearly made him come when they'd undressed her in order to bathe her.

He stripped out of his own trousers and took himself in hand. His cock throbbed against his palm, grew slicker as his lust increased, as the need to claim her became a ravaging hunger. A pant escaped, then another, leaving him no longer content to play the voyeur and let Haven be the one to bring her to ecstasy.

Raeder slid downward, kissing her belly as he did so. He positioned himself between her splayed thighs, used his forearms to pin her to the mattress, his face only inches away from her erect clit and slick channel.

Intoxicating. Enthralling. For long moments he could only breathe her in, memorize the sight of her. But then he dipped his head and trailed his tongue through the silky moisture of her slit, knew the joy of hearing her whimper as she thrashed and lifted, tried to coax him into piercing her.

Haven's cock bobbed and rubbed against Raeder's arm, dislodged from its place against Aria's thigh by Raeder's assault on her drenched folds. Raeder lifted his face. He compared Aria's tiny stiffened clit with its delicate head to Haven's blood-filled penis, the tip glossy and purpled. The differences excited him, made him want to fuck them both, dominate them both.

Raeder pressed a kiss to Haven's engorged flesh. He licked and sucked, sent heated breath over Haven's testicles until Haven trembled, rubbed desperately against the forearm holding Aria's thigh open.

Then Raeder turned his attention back to the female they would share, the woman who would be their third. He circled and teased the small swollen knob. Rasped his tongue back and forth over the unprotected head before forcing it between rigid lips, sucking until she strained upward.

Raw hunger twisted in Raeder's gut. He wanted to put her on her hands and knees, to order her to take Haven's cock into her mouth as she took his into her sheath. And then he wanted to do the same to Haven, force him onto his hands and knees, mount him as Haven's mouth covered Aria's bare mound and Haven's tongue fucked her.

Soul-swallowing lust gripped Raeder. The muted sounds of Aria's submission and the sight of Haven's straining cock tested the limits of his control.

A growl of denial escaped as Raeder's testicles pulled tight and fire streaked up his penis in impending orgasm. He became aware of his own movements, the way he was rubbing, humping against the sheets like a boy not yet old enough for a lover.

He intensified his erotic assault, sucked more aggressively on Aria's clit, driving her upward until she reached the violent peak of ecstasy then went completely limp, her first cry of release captured by Haven's lips.

Raeder rolled away, gripping his cock to keep from coating his belly and chest with semen. Pain lashed through him, fiery lust clashing with steely control and leaving him panting, barely hanging on as he struggled to allow Haven to give Aria her next orgasm.

Haven's heart raced in his chest. He wanted to kiss downward, to suckle at dusky nipples. He wanted to bury his face between Aria's thighs and know the sweet taste of her arousal, to explore the silken folds and smooth mound with his tongue. To worship her as she deserved to be worshipped and convey with his caress how much they treasured her, how he and Raeder had dreamed of this moment when they'd add a third. But he didn't dare.

Raeder's need for release was too great, his dominant nature too close to the surface—as was his own. They'd been riding the edge of emotion even before learning of the council's decision, and then to find Aria in the hands of the brothel owner...to rescue her and endure the erotic torture of bathing her...

With a moan, Haven covered Aria's body. The heat of her bare cunt against his cock made him shudder. His hips jerked, his thighs widened hers, instinctively positioning her so he could find her opening and forge into it.

Haven lifted his face, the muscles along his arms and shoulders straining as he fought to give her gentleness and choice even though his back stung from where she'd raked her fingernails over his skin when Raeder made her climax.

He wanted her fierceness again as desperately as he wanted to possess her. She was beautiful to him, feminine and delicate, soft where both he and Raeder were hard, curved and smooth in the places where their sexes differed.

"Aria, do you want this?" Haven asked, his question whispering across her lips as his cock bathed in honeyed arousal, pulsed with the need to slide through wet folds and know the tight fist of her sheath.

She answered him by tightening her grip on his hair, by whimpering softly as she closed the distance, touching her mouth to his.

Haven moaned. His tongue sought hers, rubbed and tangled as his cock head found her opening. His buttocks clenched and unclenched with the effort to go slowly, to savor each moment as inch by inch he slid into her.

Her mews of pleasure nearly undid him, as did the ferocious intensity of Raeder's gaze as he witnessed Haven's claiming of their third and waited for his own chance to mount her. Haven shuddered when Aria's legs wrapped around his waist, trapping him in sultry heat and ecstasy.

For a single heartbeat he remained still, held in the perfect balance of exquisite agony and unbearable pleasure. But then her sheath fisted and unfisted on his cock, and her lips separated from his long enough to say, "Please."

The word had the same effect on Haven as it did when he was able to wrest it from Raeder. Lust roared through him, the urge to dominate.

He settled more of his weight on Aria, took her lips in a kiss meant to convey ownership, possessiveness. His cock grew harder, thicker and he forged into her, relentless in his determination to fill her with his seed and hear her cry of surrendered release.

Emotion rode him, primal in its fierceness, a wild erotic dance that spiraled out of control and left him thrusting feverishly. He ate hungrily at Aria's mouth, as if only the sounds of her joy and ecstasy had the power to sustain him.

Skin grew slick. The scent of sex was an intoxicating musk. The feel of her wet core a paradise he knew he'd never tire of.

Haven cried out when she scratched her fingers down his back. He thrust harder, deeper, instinctively trying to reach her womb as he panted and fought off the first wave of orgasm until she climaxed beneath him with the searing squeeze of her sheath.

Shudder after shudder took him, each marking the milking of his semen, the ecstasy of yielding everything to the female who belonged to them as much as they belonged to her. It left him lightheaded, boneless, his only reality her hot core and silky wet mouth.

He kissed her repeatedly, wanted to stay melded to her, trapped in feminine heat and sensual pleasure. But a low growl ordering him to move served as a warning that if his cock continued to claim Aria's channel, then Raeder would take him where he lay on top of her and she would be one step closer to the truth of who they were.

With a final kiss Haven lifted himself off Aria. His heart swelled with happiness as his eyes met hers and he read complete satisfaction there. Words tumbled over themselves in his mind, tender declarations and passionate promises left unspoken when Raeder crowded in aggressively and roughly positioned Aria onto her hands and knees.

Haven opened his mouth to protest, but before he could do it she lowered herself onto her elbows and widened her thighs to provocatively display her swollen cunt lips and open slit, driving Raeder into a frenzy with the evidence of another man's seed filling her channel and coating her labia.

White heat filled Raeder's mind and burned away all thought. He mounted her, shoving every inch of his cock into her in one hard thrust and reveling in the way she rocked backward, her channel tightening on him like a hungry mouth.

His hands caressed her buttocks before going to her hips, holding her in position as he began pistoning in and out of her. Her whimpers of pleasure filled the room along with the sound of his testicles slapping her swollen flesh and rigid clit.

There was no gentleness in him, but she didn't demand it. She softened, pleaded with him, as if she understood the rawness of his hunger, the savage need he had to dominate and have her beg for release.

Raeder glanced away from her only long enough to meet Haven's gaze, to share a look of triumph and joy at having found and claimed their third. And then he hunched over Aria, pressed his chest to her back in a desperate craving for the feel of skin against skin as his fingers found her clit and she came, taking him with her into white-hot bliss.

Chapter Four

Sensual lethargy left Aria feeling boneless and sated, unable to even contemplate moving, though the idea of bathing in the sunken tub a few feet away from a glass wall held great appeal. Haven's and Raeder's emotions pressed against her as intimately as their bodies did, their joy and satisfaction keeping her in place with a realness equal to the tangled limbs penning her between them.

Haven's exotically tattooed arm curled around her waist, holding her back to his chest as he pressed tender kisses to her neck and nuzzled her ear. Liquid heat pooled and wet her labia when his tongue traced the shell of her ear before darting into the sensitive canal.

Gentleness and utter contentment flowed from him, making inroads into her heart and leaving her with no desire to think about the future—not so soon after escaping the reality of her life on Iyon. For the first time she was free of fear and worry, free to explore the passion whose only voice, before Raeder and Haven, was the flute's song.

Sadness filled her as she thought of the wooden flute she'd been forced to abandon when she made her bid for freedom. It was poor in quality, crude in workmanship, its very worthlessness to others what had kept her father from gambling it away or selling it. But it had been priceless to her.

A feathered kiss brushed her forehead. Haven's concern curled around her like a warm blanket and brought tears to her eyes. Since her mother's death from the fever, tenderness and gentleness had ceased to exist in her life.

"What's wrong?" he asked, a tendril of fear ebbing into the emotions she seemed powerless to erect a mental shield against. "Were we too rough?"

"No," she said, renewed heat filling her, her body tightening in remembered pleasure. "I was thinking about my flute. By now my father will have destroyed it in a rage."

A shiver of fear slid through her along with images of her father's beefy hands curled into fists, his face reddening with anger instead of drink. Haven's and Raeder's feelings of protectiveness surged to the forefront, identical in fierceness, turning her thoughts away from memories of violence.

"We won't let anything happen to you," Haven said.

Raeder's hand cupped her breast, his thumb brushing over her nipple and sending renewed spikes of need to her clit. "You belong to us now."

Feelings of possessiveness accompanied the words, primal, raw emotions that touched her core and made her want to rise to her hands and knees and offer herself to him again. She pressed her breast into his hand, moaned when his fingers tightened on the nipple already hardened and aching from his thumb's teasing.

Behind her Haven moved, shifting their positions so she was once again on her back. The hand on her belly stroked downward, found her clit as he leaned over and captured her nipple between his lips.

Fire streaked through Aria, going from her breasts to her cunt and intensifying when Raeder mimicked Haven's actions, began suckling as his fingers found her wet folds and slipped inside. Even without their emotions pressing in on her, fueling the lust their touch inspired, Aria knew how much pleasure they found in her response to them, in the way she submitted.

She gripped the bedding as her hips jerked, arousal and spent seed escaping from her slit each time Haven stroked her clit and her inner muscles spasmed to clamp down on Raeder's fingers. Need burned in her womb, made her press into their mouths, beg them to suck harder, to bite.

They turned her into a creature of pure sensation, a song of passion reaching toward a crescendo. Her heart raced. Her body strained. And their touch became even more demanding, even more possessive, until finally she screamed in a shattering agony of release.

Aria made a small sound of appreciation when Haven picked her up and padded across the room to slip into the heated waters of the sunken tub. She didn't protest when he put her on his lap, her back against his chest, her legs straddling his.

The water soothed her, might have lulled her into sleep except for the hard presence of Haven's penis behind her and the sight of Raeder following them to the tub. His muscled, well-toned body made her think of the dangerous mountain cats that sometimes grew hungry enough to hunt in the mines.

His cock was still hard, thick and proud, glistening where it pressed against his abdomen. The heavy testicles swinging freely between his thighs were a primitive display of potent masculinity. And the sight of them made the muscles of her sheath clench and unclench as if hungry to milk him of more of his seed.

Raeder slid into the water as Haven lathered his hands with soap gathered from an artfully concealed dispenser built into the design of the tub, then used it on himself and her.

Aria moaned at the feel of Haven's slick hands, at the sight of Raeder lathering his own before gliding them over his skin in a slow, sensual invitation.

Raeder's dark eyes were impenetrable as his hands slipped beneath the water to his hardened cock and full testicles. She felt his lust intensify as his gaze traveled over both her and Haven, knew in that instant his carnal desire wasn't limited to her.

Shock made her stiffen in Haven's arms. Fear followed, but lasted only until she remembered she was no longer on Iyon, where men who lay together were stoned to death. This was Z'nyia, a world dedicated to the pleasure of the senses.

Dark, forbidden curiosity made heat coil her belly. Her labia filled with blood again, parted. "You're lovers," she said, her voice unable to hide what the thought of watching them couple did to her.

Erotic fear skittered along her nerve endings at the predatory expression her words brought to Raeder's face. He leaned in, placing his hands on the edge of the sunken tub, trapping her in heated masculinity. "It excites you to think of Haven and me together."

"Yes," Aria whispered and felt the effect her admission had on them.

Behind her Haven's breath became ragged. His cock pulsed against the curve of her buttocks and tension filled him, anticipation. In front of her, Raeder's lips firmed, dominance radiating from him in waves that had her shivering.

Perfect, Haven thought. *She's perfect for us.*

He'd dreaded the moment she discovered he and Raeder were intimate, had known if she couldn't accept their love for one another—emotional and physical—then he would insist they return to Adjara without her. Doing so would have left a gaping hole in his heart, a terrible wound to his soul, but he couldn't deny the part of himself that craved and was satisfied only by his relationship with Raeder.

There were men on Adjara who partnered with cousins or brothers and found release only with their own hand until they gained their female. He didn't condemn them for their choice. For some, the thought of coupling with another male went against the fabric of their being. But he wasn't like them, and neither was Raeder.

Raeder's hand left the edge of the tub to trace over the tattoos on Haven's arm. The touch made him harden further.

There'd be no foreplay to determine which one of them submitted, no sensual battle until someone moaned the word please. Determination was etched on Raeder's face. The first time Aria saw them together, he wouldn't be the submissive partner.

Raeder pulled Aria from Haven's arms and lap. He placed her on the plush material that surrounded the sunken tub, commanded her to lie back on her elbows.

Pleasure coursed through Haven at the way Aria obeyed, at the way she so readily submitted. He took himself in hand when Raeder pushed her thighs apart to display her flushed, rosy slit. He shuddered as Raeder's fingers toyed with her clit and she lifted her hips, wanting to be touched and petted.

Haven didn't resist when Raeder's hand circled his arm and guided him so he knelt on the ledge beneath the water. Without urging, Haven leaned forward to press his lips to Aria's wet folds. He moaned with the first taste of her. Lost himself to the silky smooth feel of heated skin and the intoxicating scent of the woman who belonged to them.

It was an intimacy he'd never desired with a paid pleasure worker, one he'd never experienced with a woman. But as he pressed his lips to Aria and ran his tongue through honeyed arousal, Haven knew he'd forever crave her. He'd be her willing slave if it meant he could bury his face between her thighs.

Haven sucked on her heated woman's flesh and the tiny, erect clitoris. He made her thrash and moan, surge upward to fuck the tiny organ through his lips.

It was unbearable pleasure, an intimacy that had him air-humping, moaning even before Raeder parted his buttocks and coated the rosette of his anus with lubricant.

Haven pushed backward, impaled himself on Raeder's fingers. Wanted Raeder's cock.

And then it was there. Breaching him. Filling him one slow inch at a time.

Haven felt Aria shudder. He lifted his face to find her watching, her eyes dark and carnal, her nipples tight with need.

Hot lust washed over him. He thrust his tongue into her sheath aggressively. And when she clamped down on him hungrily, canting her hips off the plush floor covering, he used his forearms to pin her down, to hold her open and helpless.

The steel band of Raeder's fingers encircled Haven's cock in a tight, commanding grip, ensuring there'd be no release until he allowed it. The lack of control intensified Haven's focus on Aria, translated into a need to dominate even as he was being dominated.

Haven conquered her with his lips and heated breath, with his tongue. He fucked her to the same rhythm as Raeder's cock took him, denied her the sweet bliss of orgasm until Raeder's hand went from torturous vise to stroking ecstasy, making Haven cry out as semen escaped in lava-hot jets and Aria's sheath clamped down on him in convulsive pleasure.

Haven slid back into the water, taking Aria with him — at least until Raeder claimed her, pulling her onto his lap then lathering his hands, making her moan as he bathed her. Contentment flashed hot in Haven's chest and his cock stirred despite how many times he'd come. He found it erotic watching Raeder bathe Aria, seeing the hands capable of meting out death or wielding a heavy pick caress feminine skin so gently, so reverently.

Love and need settled in Haven's belly at the tender expression on Raeder's face, the softening of hard muscle and the protective curl of his body around Aria's as he saw to her comfort, took care of her in a way that wasn't acceptable between males — even between males with a bond like the one he and Raeder shared. Having a third was everything Haven had dreamed it would be.

Haven followed when Raeder rose from the sunken tub and stepped under the heated air of the drying wand. He was fully aroused by the time they returned to the bed. Only instead of lying down with Aria between them, Haven positioned himself next to Raeder, took advantage of a mellowness usually encountered only after a successful desert hunt.

As soon as Aria was settled comfortably, Haven rolled on top of Raeder and knew the icy-hot pleasure of cock against cock, the satisfaction of having Raeder cant his hips, offer what usually could only be claimed after an erotic struggle.

He glanced at Aria and found her watching with her hand between her thighs. The thought of those delicate fingers fucking in and out of her sheath as she witnessed him fucking Raeder was intoxicating.

It took only a second to find the concealed dispenser, to coat his penis with lubricant and do the same to Raeder's opening. And then it was Haven who controlled, who orchestrated the dance of passion and demonstrated with thrust after thrust that he and Raeder were equals in bringing each other pleasure—and that their pleasure was Aria's as well.

Masculine grunts and moans joined with softer, feminine whimpers and sighs. The sounds of pleasure becoming a symphony that raced toward a shouted conclusion and was followed by the silence of completion and satisfaction.

Haven rolled off Raeder. He smiled when he saw Aria's face relaxed in sleep, her hand still between her thighs, the fingers wet from the sweet honey of her release.

"Tomorrow we take her home," Raeder said.

"Tomorrow we take her to the market and replace the flute she lost on Iyon," Haven countered.

Chapter Five

ജ

Everything about Z'nyia is meant to please the senses, Aria thought as she stepped through the doorway of the bungalow and entered a world of brightly colored flowers and exotic birds, sweet scent and beautiful song. A blush rose to her cheeks as a warm breeze slipped underneath Haven's borrowed shirt, traveling the short distance up her thighs to caress her bare mound in a sensual reminder of her nakedness beneath the thin material.

Nervousness made her take a step backward. On Iyon, a woman dressed as she was and out in public invited abduction and rape.

"It's okay," Haven murmured, his hand on her back halting her retreat. "In the marketplace you'll see women wearing far less and leaving little to the imagination." He leaned in and traced her ear with his tongue, sucked the lobe into his mouth and sent a shiver of ecstasy to her cunt along with the comfort of his steadying emotions.

A moan escaped when Raeder's hand followed the path the breeze had taken, slid up her thigh before cupping her heated woman's flesh and stroking wet, parted folds. "No one will bother you," he said, his voice as possessive and sure as the feelings radiating from him.

In the open air it was easier for her to shield herself from the emotions of others. But Aria found she didn't want to separate herself from Raeder and Haven, either physically or mentally.

A shiver of a pleasure went through her as she remembered Haven's earlier words, his hesitant admission.

From the first moment we learned of you, we knew...we hoped...we believed you'd be the perfect woman for us.

She didn't resist when they each claimed one of her hands and led her to the marketplace. Anticipation crowded in on her as open-air stalls gave way to glass-walled shops. She glanced at Haven's and Raeder's faces, wondered what it was they were excited about showing her.

A burst of warmth exploded in her chest, a sheer joy to be with them. Reluctantly she blocked her mind to their feelings, wanting to give them the gift of her surprise. There'd never been a time in her life, even in those short fuzzy years when her mother lived, that she'd ever felt as cared for and cherished.

They halted a little while later. "Close your eyes," Haven said and Aria obeyed though her hands tightened on theirs when they began walking.

When they stopped again, a door opened, the muted tinkle of a bell announcing their presence. They guided her into a shop and to a distant wall.

Footsteps approached, muffled by carpet. The air smelled of wealth, of wood and metal, paper and resin.

Haven pressed a kiss to her cheek. "Raeder and I want you to choose the gift that will please you best. You can open your eyes now."

Aria did and emotion clogged her throat. Tears formed at the corners of her eyes and slid down her cheeks at what they offered her.

In front of her was a display of flutes.

"Choose," Raeder said, his voice gruff.

Aria allowed the mental barrier to fall away and felt Raeder's panic at her tears along with Haven's understanding of them.

Haven brushed her wet cheeks with the gentle swipe of his thumb. "Take your time. Choose any one of the flutes and it's yours."

She took a shaky breath, expelled it, thought only fleetingly of refusing their offer. The hollow place left in her soul by the loss of her music wouldn't let her turn away from the counter and the small man hovering behind it, anxious to assist and excited by the prospect of a big sale.

Aria looked at the flutes. The selection was overwhelming at first. The sparkle of gold and silver competed against glittering inlaid gems and elaborately engraved patterns.

The designs became simpler as she moved along the counter. The small man grew resigned to making only a tiny profit, finally giving a disappointed sigh when her gaze settled on a wooden flute.

In shape and design, it looked much like the one lost to her, though the wood was different and the quality of craftsmanship higher. Perhaps it was its familiarity that spoke to her heart, but Aria knew the instrument in front of her was the right one for her.

"I'd like this one," she said, glancing up quickly when she felt Raeder's consternation and Haven's conflicted concern.

Raeder pulled a gem pouch from the pocket of his trousers and dropped it onto the counter. Its heavy thud was a testament to the wealth it contained. "You won't beggar us with a different choice, Aria. Haven and I can afford this gift."

Bristly masculine pride accompanied the words, making Aria think of the porcupines she'd occasionally encountered on Iyon when she went to the stream to haul water. But before she could attempt to soothe Raeder, the music seller said, "Try as many of the flutes out as you wish."

A small smile played over Aria's lips with thoughts on how best to convince Raeder of the rightness of her choice. "I'd like to try this one," she said, indicating the wooden flute.

The excitement generated by the sight of the gem pouch diminished in the music seller as he retrieved the instrument and handed it to Aria. With the first touch, she knew her heart had spoken truly.

Aria closed her eyes and lifted the flute to her mouth. The emotions so hard to block in the enclosing walls of the shop became notes in a larger song, a wellspring of feelings with infinite depth. She gave herself over to the music that flowed into her and became a part of her, found its voice through her.

Time and place had no relevance. There was only haunting melody and sacred truths, the feeding of the soul through song.

Only when the last note faded away did Aria open her eyes and become aware of her surroundings and those with her. In front of her the music seller wept unashamedly. Next to her Haven and Raeder were spellbound, their gazes fixed on her in wonder, their feelings a tangle though she sensed their pride.

"This is the flute I want," she said, breaking the spell, pleased when no one suggested she try another instrument.

Raeder picked up the gem pouch and opened it, shook out a small part of its contents onto his palm. He studied the colorful jewels for a moment before selecting a dark blue stone to offer as payment for the flute.

The music seller wiped at damp eyes before accepting it. He turned to Aria. "You have only to name your price for the privilege of hearing you play. Please come back if you seek employment. I'll introduce you to those in a position to make you wealthy beyond imagination."

Aria felt the absolute truth in his words and nodded, but her heart raced with the sudden tension radiating from both Haven and Raeder. And as they led her from the shop, their emotions buffeted her and made her uneasy though she found it impossible to fear them, just as she found it equally impossible to question them and erase the joy of their gift so quickly.

"Let's get something to eat before returning to the bungalow," Haven said, his fingers circling her arm with a sure, confident grip while Raeder's hand was a possessive shackle.

They were such a contrast, and yet at the core they were very much alike. She couldn't prevent herself from responding to their touch, the dominance that was so much a part of them.

Lust made her cunt lips swell and part. Liquid arousal escaped to slide down her inner thighs. Small tremors went through her, worry about the future intermingling with the desperate need to cling to the feeling of being safe and cared for.

They returned to the section of market containing open-air stalls. The smell of roasting meat and baking bread made Aria's stomach growl and her mouth water.

But when they turned down an aisle-way full of food venders, it was the planet's moon, Adjara, that drew her attention. Its face seemed near enough to touch and she wondered how those who lived on the pleasure planet could be at ease in such close proximity to a place populated by men whose way of life was so harsh that those who no longer served a purpose—including the women brought there to become broodmares—were put out in the desert to die.

Aria's grip tightened on the flute. Images rose up, of the shack she'd shared with her father, the hardscrabble existence and the constant fear she'd be gambled away. Her stomach clenched, not in hunger but in remembered fear of the slug-tongued whore-master and his carriage with its windows barred. She shivered at how close she'd been to ending up in the brothel Lodur owned, a place where the women who entered were rarely seen again. If Haven and Raeder—

"Aria?" Haven asked.

Her attention was drawn to the food sellers who were calling out, trying to entice them to colorfully decorated stalls. "I'm hungry enough to eat anything. You and Raeder can choose."

They chose tender meat and fried vegetables wrapped in thin layers of bread. And afterward, a pudding-like dessert served in browned, melted sugar.

Despite being in the midst of a marketplace bustling with activities and filled with stalls she'd yet to explore, after the last of the food disappeared Aria felt as if she could curl up for a nap. She excused herself to visit one of the washrooms set aside for women, felt how loath Raeder was to let her out of his sight, and how calming a touch and word from Haven were to him.

Their closeness deepened her desire for them. Out in the open air, she could tell Haven and Raeder shared more than sexual attraction. They were bonded in a way she'd only encountered between a few married couples on Iyon.

Her clit hardened in reaction. She very nearly abandoned her trip to the woman's lounge in favor of going back to them and suggesting they return to the bungalow so she could be a part of what they shared.

But just as her footsteps faltered, shimmers of titillated excitement slid through her, followed by a whispered female voice saying, "See those men, the ones with the tattoos on their arms? They're Adjaran."

Aria needed only to feel alarm flash though Haven and Raeder to know they'd also heard the words. Panic seized her, the same heart-thundering panic that had sent her into the Iyon night.

Adjara! Where women served only as broodmares and were killed as soon as they'd given birth.

Her hands tightened on the flute. Her breathing was fast even before she turned the corner of the aisle leading to the washroom and began running.

Fear gripped Raeder and he had no outlet for it, no refuge except in anger and determination. His fingers curled into fists as he looked beyond the empty woman's lounge.

Pain slid through his chest like the sharp edge of a knife's blade. She'd betrayed their trust, given her body and seemingly accepted them, then run. "When we catch her, we take her to Adjara."

"No," Haven said.

The single word made Raeder's emotions flash to fury. Primitive emotions assaulted him. Words of blame filled him in a red, blinding haze.

It was Haven who wanted to bring her to Z'nyia, Haven who wanted to take her shopping. It was Haven who allowed her to leave their sides.

The muscles rippled along Raeder's arms. If Haven refused to—

Nausea and heart-thundering pain abruptly replaced anger and blame as Raeder realized the direction of his thoughts.

He'd looked down on those who returned without their third, seen them as less and pitied them. On Adjara he'd vowed such a thing would never happen when he and Haven were given a female to claim. But as Raeder considered the dark thoughts of blame that had lodged in his heart, the physical violence he'd been close to, and saw his pain reflected in Haven's eyes—deepened by what had almost happened between them—he realized Aria must join with them willingly or the agony of this moment would pale in comparison to what was to come.

"We wait for her in the bungalow?" Raeder asked, his hand curling around Haven's arm, needing touch. Seeking comfort and forgiveness and getting it when Haven leaned forward, pressed his lips to Raeder's.

"We wait. We give her time. And if she doesn't come back, we find her and ask for a chance to allay her fears. And then we allow her the choice as to whether she'll return as our third."

Within minutes Aria stopped running. Thought and shame stopped her, along with the realization that she'd been a fool to let old fears and rumors, mindless panic control her actions.

A lump formed in her throat and her heart slowed to a painful throb. She closed her eyes and relived what she'd experienced with them, what she knew of their true feelings. She shouldn't have run away without giving voice to her fears and questions. They'd saved her from the horror of Lodur's brothel, had done nothing to deserve her fear. And she'd repaid them with distrust, by viewing them in the same way as she did the whore-master and her father.

Already she cared for them, felt the first stirrings of love. How could she not? They were a fantasy of body, an irresistible combination in personality. Haven with his tender steadiness, Raeder with his fierce dominance.

In the past her music had always filled the hollow places in her heart and soul. She could make a life for herself on Z'nyia, but having been with Haven and Raeder so intimately, she knew the flute's song would no longer be enough.

Aria opened her eyes and turned back in the direction she'd come from, her feet and heart racing—not with fear, but with hope.

* * * * *

Raeder was pacing when she stepped through the doorway of the bungalow. Haven was sitting on the bed, hands clasped between his knees. Both came to her immediately, enfolded her in their arms and swamped her with their relief and happiness.

"You're Adjaran. I—"

Haven stopped her with the touch of his fingers to her lips. "Those outside Adjara don't know the truth of how we live. There are almost no female children born to us. Being allowed to claim a woman and bring her home as our third, our equal, is an honor. It's a privilege males in every tribe pray they'll be deemed worthy of as soon as they grow old enough to dream of taking a lover. When Raeder and I were given your name..."

His emotions bombarded her, so intense that tears welled up in her eyes. She turned her head, kissed his cheeks, his mouth, tried to tell him with her actions what it meant to her to be cared about and wanted so desperately.

"You'll return to Adjara with us?" Raeder said and she felt the effort it took to turn a command into a question.

"Yes."

They pressed against her more tightly, their feelings escalating and translating into a need for physical intimacy. But despite their happiness over her return and her agreement to go to Adjara, she felt the pain of her betrayal still lingering—sharp in Raeder, less so in Haven. Later she'd tell them about her empathic ability, just as later she'd ask them more about life on Adjara, but for now she wanted only to chase their pain away with pleasure.

"I'm sorry I hurt you," she said, instinct urging her to her knees. "Let me show you how much I want to be with you, how much I want to please you."

She rubbed her cheek over Raeder's cloth-covered erection then did the same to Haven's, loved the way their hips jerked and their breathing quickened.

Aria freed their cocks one at a time. Pressed her lips to satin-smooth skin and measured their lengths with her tongue.

Their thighs bunched. They trembled with her attention.

The pain of her desertion disappeared under the lash of her tongue, as she took them in her mouth and sucked, separately and together, her torment driving Haven and Raeder into each other's arms for a carnal kiss.

Their desire fed her own. Her pulse throbbed between her thighs, filling her labia with blood. Arousal slid from her channel to coat her skin and scent the air.

With a shuddering groans Raeder and Haven ended their kiss and pulled her to her feet. Clothing gave way. Heated skin touched heated skin, making all three of them ache for deeper contact.

Aria went willingly to the bed. She didn't resist when Haven pulled her on top of him and filled her with his cock.

Her breath caught and her sheath clenched on Haven's penis when he spread her buttocks and Raeder stroked his fingers over the tight rosette of her back entrance, prepared her with lubricant. She shivered, moaned, wanted them both at the same time and felt how much they also wanted it.

"Yes," she said. "Oh, yes. Please."

No words had ever sounded so good to Raeder. Just as nothing could rival the feel of working his way into Aria's tight entrance and rubbing against Haven's cock in the heated warmth of the woman who was their third, who would always share their bed and would one day bear their children.

It was everything he had dreamed it would be. And he knew it would become even more as they lived together, as they loved together.

Raeder met Haven's gaze and saw his own emotions reflected there, felt a happiness and contentment that was soul deep. He pressed a kiss to Aria's shoulder, a gentle tribute to how important she was to them. And then he began thrusting, each stroke bringing ecstasy, each stroke sounding the notes of pleasure, forming the melody that was passion's song.

PRIVATE LESSONS
By Solange Ayre

ಏ

Dedication

To my dear friend Laurel F., with whom I learned to write historicals.

Chapter One

The innocent must seek out the innocent. To this end, young men must strive to come to the marriage bed untainted. They should engage in healthy sports and pleasant, energetic pastimes to sate their animal natures. They must avoid spirituous liquor, billiard halls and, most importantly, Scarlet Women.

Professor Woodcock's Guide to Success and Happiness in Marital Relations (1st edition, 1893)

"Pour out the tea when I ring the bell, Annie—not before," Vanessa d'Aulaire said, stepping into the kitchen. "I detest lukewarm tea. Once you've brought in the cucumber sandwiches and macaroons, you may take the rest of the afternoon off."

"Yes, ma'am." The cook wiped her hands on her apron and turned back to the stove, muttering something under her breath about "improper clothing" and "looks like an evening gown with that low neckline".

"It's an afternoon dress, not the least unsuitable," Vanessa said. "Royal purple is quite acceptable for second mourning."

Annie's arms went to her hips and her lower lip pushed out truculently. "That color is red, Miss Vanessa. Scarlet-red. Your mother would be rare mortified to see you wearing such."

"But she isn't here, nor will she and my stepfather return for three days," Vanessa answered, maintaining a pleasant tone.

"'Taint proper to entertain a man without your parents here," the cook continued with the freedom of a longtime servant.

"I'm a widow, not an innocent girl." Her voice turning stern, Vanessa added, "I am expecting the professor at two o'clock. Please show him into the parlor upon his arrival." Wishing to hear no more chastisement from Annie, she left the room with a swish of her velvet skirt.

Entering the parlor, she seated herself on the blue settee, arranging her skirt becomingly. She glanced around the room, observing the garish hangings and ornaments with distaste. She and her mother had never seen eye to eye, either in home decoration or in her mother's choice of second husbands.

She plumped the pillow beside her. "Jesus Loves You," the cross-stitched wording on it read. He was the only one who did, in this house.

Sighing, she reflected on how much happier she had been in her own home.

She stroked the mourning brooch on her bosom, the onyx stone surrounded by hair from her deceased husband. "Bertrand, you left me too soon," Vanessa murmured. The thought of the handsome older man, with his loving words and kind eyes, made her blink back tears. Eighteen months had passed since his death. Although she missed him, she longed to rejoin life again.

She remembered a day when Bertrand had said, "Life is short, ma belle," then kissed her ear in a way that made her tremble. "We must pursue pleasure while we live, for surely it is God's gift to us."

Professor Woodcock did not share her deceased husband's admirable philosophy. Vanessa picked up the professor's book from the marble-topped table. *The poor man*, she thought as she skimmed through the pages, pursing her lips at several of the professor's more absurd statements.

Men! Too many of them thought they knew everything in life, from her tyrannical stepfather to Professor Woodcock, with his many erroneous ideas about women.

Would the professor be a rawboned string bean of a man with a vulgar, ranting voice, like the revival preacher who had pitched a tent at the fairgrounds last summer? Or a portly older gentleman with a rotund belly, peering at her over his spectacles?

Well, if the man would only listen to her, she would soon sort him out.

Annie threw open the parlor doors. "Professor Robert Woodcock, ma'am."

Vanessa stood to receive her guest.

I have sorrowed to hear young men boast of "stealing kisses" from attractive maidens. Little do they know what harm they do, both to themselves and to those they debauch. Such activities excite the senses and tempt even those who have vowed to retain their precious chastity. An honorable man never dishonors the lips of his beloved until they are betrothed.

Professor Woodcock's Guide to Success and Happiness in Marital Relations (1st edition, 1893)

Robert Woodcock stood rooted, gazing at the beautiful woman who had haunted his dreams since his sixteenth year. Her rippling waves of ebony hair were dressed in a more elaborate fashion than he remembered, while her stylish gown and jewelry proclaimed her matronly status. But she had the same doelike brown eyes and tender mouth he recalled from the days when she had been his teacher.

"Good afternoon, Mrs. d'Aulaire. Thank you for your kind invitation." He bowed to her. "But surely you are Miss Hartley who taught at Bram's Crossing school?" Quickly stripping off his leather driving gloves, he stepped forward and took the hand she offered in his. The gentle touch of her long fingers made him tremble.

"How delightful of you to remember." Her smile was like a caress. "And I recall you as well. Robert Shelby—do I have that right? What made you change your name to Woodcock?"

"I needed a pseudonym when I wrote my book. I chose Woodcock because that is my favorite of all birds."

"Truly? I thought perhaps you had another reason for your choice."

He shook his head, unsure of her meaning. "No, indeed. When I informed my parents of my plans to publish such a work, they begged me to take a false name. Respecting their wishes, I did so."

He realized he was still holding her hand. Hastily, he let go.

"I hope you'll take tea with me this afternoon," she said. Stepping to the corner, she pulled the cord. "Cook will bring it shortly." She led him to a small table set with teacups and plates.

He hurried to pull out her chair for her, taking the opportunity to inhale her lovely fragrance. She smelled of violets still, an aroma that transported him back to his schooldays. He remembered how she would seat herself beside him and show him how to work his mathematics problems. Although only four years older than him, her brilliant intellect had made it easy for her to demonstrate the equations that puzzled him.

Ten years had passed since those long-ago schooldays, yet her proximity was having the same embarrassing effect. His unruly member had awakened. Quickly he sat and spread his napkin over his lap.

"So your family does not approve of your book?" she asked.

"My mother was shocked by its intimate nature."

"I never thought you would become a writer." Her movements were as graceful as a ballet dancer's when she unfolded her napkin and laid it over her knees. "You always said you wished to farm with your father."

"He promised me two hundred acres of my own after I graduated," Robert answered, suppressing a sigh. "I had so many ideas—new techniques, new crops—but alas, the bank that held my father's money failed in the Panic of 1893. He lost the farm."

A singular look crossed her face, as though she recalled an unpleasant memory. But all she said was, "Writing a book is a far cry from agriculture." She tilted her head questioningly. "What made you wish to write about the marital bond?"

He leaned forward across the table, hoping she would understand. "As a devout follower of science, I feel that no subject is immune from the gaze of rationality. At the university, I was shocked by the ignorance I encountered regarding the secrets of marriage. How can young men be expected to guide their wives properly if they know nothing themselves?"

"How indeed?" she murmured with a tiny smile.

"So I wrote my book, had it printed and took to the road. I lecture in the larger towns—unless the good citizens object. And I sell the book at my lectures. You would be surprised, perhaps, at how many ladies purchase it."

Mrs. d'Aulaire turned her head as the cook entered the room with a silver tray. Rob looked eagerly at the teapot and plate of sandwiches. Life on the road was uncertain and meals were not always as regular as one would wish.

"I'll be going then, ma'am," the cook said. She turned a look on Rob that made him wonder what he'd done to offend her. Had she possibly read his book?

"Certainly, Annie," Mrs. d'Aulaire answered. "Have a pleasant evening."

"The sandwiches look delicious," Rob said, smiling at the cook. "Did you make them?"

"Who else?" the cook answered pertly.

"Annie!" Mrs. d'Aulaire gave her a reproving look, but the servant left the room so quickly it was doubtful that she saw it.

As soon as the servant left the room, Rob said, "Your Annie seems to disapprove of me."

Mrs. d'Aulaire poured the tea. "She thinks it improper for me to entertain you while my parents are out of town. However, I feel sure you will control your animal urges and not ravish me."

Across the table, her dark eyes met his. Rob wondered if he was blushing. Her words had conjured up the most extraordinary picture in his mind. He saw her lying back on the settee, her nakedness exposed as he pushed up her skirt and petticoat. Her quivering sex was revealed to his gaze. He unbuttoned his trousers and his stiff member sprang forth, eager to plunge into her...

"Mrs. d'Aulaire!" he exclaimed. "Of course, I-I mean, of course *not*. Surely two old friends can meet without anyone finding it improper."

She laughed, a sound that made him think of fairy bells. "'Evil to him who evil thinks,'" she quoted. "Although it can't be denied that you felt a great affection for me ten years ago. Did you not?"

He had always wondered if she'd been aware of his adoration. Recalling how often he'd stayed late to fill the schoolhouse's woodbox or draw water to clean the floors, he realized his youthful passion must have been obvious.

"How could I help it?" he answered. "You were the most lovely and intelligent woman I'd ever met. I must tell you, Mrs. d'Au—"

"Vanessa," she interrupted. "I make you free of my Christian name. And I shall call you Rob, as I always did."

"Thank you," he said. The liberty she was allowing warmed him. "Vanessa, even when I attended Ohio State

University, you remained the pattern card for my ideal woman. Your image has never left my mind in the intervening years."

"Ten years." Her expression clouded with melancholy. "How much has changed since then!"

"Yes, much has changed," he agreed. "Your beauty has increased tenfold."

Her liquid gaze captured and held his. "It's kind of you to say so. But seeing how you have altered brings the years home to me. I remember a gawky farm boy with hands and feet too big for his frame, coming to school with straw in his hair. Now I see a tall, handsome man with broad shoulders, clad in an elegant suit. How time flies!"

She finds me handsome? Her praise had him lifting his shoulders and chin with pride.

And yet he couldn't bear the low note of sadness in her voice. In the past, her cheerfulness had brought joy to those privileged to be near her. Her students had loved her for her smiles, her gaiety.

What a shame that one so fair had been visited by sorrow. How could he offer commiseration?

She rose and went to stand by the window, her bountiful curves framed by the gold curtains so that she seemed like some artist's conception of beauty.

Rising, he joined her. "Please do not distress yourself," he said, putting a comforting hand on her arm. "I know how hard it must have been for you to lose Mr. d'Aulaire."

"Yes, he was a fine husband," she murmured. "A wealthy man who gave me everything I wanted. But you too have known sorrow, Rob. In your book, you tell about how your beloved fiancée was lost at sea."

"Well— Yes. Poor Emily," he said, unwilling to admit that "broken engagement" was a rather more accurate description of their parting. "But surely it is worse to lose a spouse."

"The loneliness is hard to bear." She gazed up at him, her red lips parted and quivering.

Before he considered his actions, his hands were on her smooth white shoulders and his mouth claimed hers.

Good heavens, her lips were so enticing as they moved softly under his. He half expected her to back away, but instead her warm mouth urged his on.

Her lips *opened* under his. Was it possible she wanted him to kiss her in the French style? Hardly daring to believe it, he entered her mouth with his tongue.

Her tongue welcomed him, gliding against his in a silken caress that inflamed him instantly. And he realized as he drank in the wonderful taste of her, sweet milky tea, that she was what he'd desired his whole life.

She was the reason he'd accepted his dismissal without argument, when Emily broke their engagement. *She* was the reason he'd ignored the flirtatious glances and smiles of the women he'd met on his travels.

Soft and yielding in his arms, her violet scent filled his world. He drew her closer, shaken by the way her full breasts pressed against him.

Although the bosoms of the Gentle Sex are of great interest to the masculine gender, husbands must practice reverence when approaching the fair white breasts of their wives. Even the great Solomon forgets this when he says, "Thy two breasts are like two young roes that are twins," praising appearance at the expense of utility. The breasts are not *for providing selfish pleasure to men, but to nurture the next generation.*

Professor Woodcock's Guide to Success and Happiness in Marital Relations (1st edition, 1893)

Drawing back, Vanessa looked up into Rob's face with astonishment. Yes, she had flirted with him. Yes, she had let him kiss her, amused by the way his schoolboy infatuation for her still lived on.

But that passionate kiss he'd given her left no doubt in her mind. This was no boy holding her in his arms, but a man. An ardent man who desired her. His warm lips had sparked an answering heat in her body.

The four-year age difference that had loomed so large ten years ago had faded away like early-morning fog.

He stared back at her, his blue eyes troubled. "Pardon me," he said. "I shouldn't have taken such a liberty. I let my feelings run away with me."

She stroked his cheek. How wonderful it felt to touch a man's skin, after so many months lacking that pleasure. "Lesson number one, Rob. Never apologize for a kiss when the lady has participated willingly."

He put his hand over hers. "Do you know how often I've wanted to kiss you? When I was in your classroom, I'd daydream that I was Robin Hood, rescuing you from the evil Sheriff of Nottingham. My reward was always…your kiss."

"Do I still remind you of Maid Marian?"

Lifting her hand to his mouth, he laid his lips against her palm. The caress sent a fluttering of desire through her body, pooling in her womanly core.

"You remind me of all the beautiful women of literature. Juliet. Ophelia. Cleopatra."

"All women of tragedy," she reminded him.

"Yes. Perhaps because I see the sadness in your eyes."

"But just now, your kiss made me happy."

His eyes darkening, he said, "I hope that means a second one would not be amiss."

"Didn't I always encourage my pupils to experiment?" she asked.

Mercy, she loved his mouth. So fresh and eager. This time she tunneled her hand through his hair, holding him close as his tongue explored her mouth. Her body ached for his touch. Would he know how to caress all her secret places until she was alive with desire, ready to be filled by his cock?

She sucked on his tongue, delighting in the arousal flowing through her body. A whimper of pleasure broke from her throat. Dear Rob! She'd always been fond of him, the awkward but intelligent country boy. It would be easy to grow even fonder of the man he'd become.

Yet there was something tentative about him, something still a bit awkward. Had he ever seduced a woman into bed before?

Perhaps she would have to take the lead, just as she had when she'd been his teacher. Once shown the way, no doubt he'd learn quickly. In the past, he'd always responded eagerly to her teachings.

Perhaps he would enjoy the new lessons she had in mind even more than geometry.

Breaking the kiss, she took a step back, looking up at him. How tall he'd become!

She took a deep breath, inhaling the pleasant way he smelled—the starch of his clean white shirt and another spicy aroma, perhaps the lingering scent of his shaving soap.

"Do you know why I invited you here—Professor Woodcock?" she asked, putting a playful emphasis on his pseudonym.

He lowered his eyes. "I thought perhaps…well, many ladies have asked me to autograph a copy of my book for them."

"I'm afraid not," she said, suppressing a smile. "When I read your book, I noticed some errors. Or perhaps I shouldn't say errors," she added quickly when his brows drew together. "Generalizations about ladies—about men and women—that are not always true, in my experience. I thought we might discuss them."

"I would be glad to, Vanessa," he said, but his voice was stiff. "Of course I strive for accuracy in my work."

She wound her arms around his neck. "Do not be offended. I think unraveling these errors might prove amusing for you. Now that our connection has been reestablished, I believe that an actual *demonstration* might prove superior to mere discussion."

"Ah, indeed." The glint in his eyes showed that he suspected what she had in mind. "I believe strongly in the value of demonstration."

She released him. Assuming a serious tone, she said, "Consider that silver teapot." She waved her hand at the table.

"The *teapot*?" His voice expressed disappointment.

She smiled. *Be patient, dear Rob. The lesson will proceed at the pace I choose.*

"Yes, the teapot. What is its primary function?"

"To serve tea," he said with ill-concealed impatience.

"Of course. However, I might also hide money in the teapot and bury it. If I were a miser, that might be its most important function in my estimation. Thus an item may have multiple uses." She picked up his book from the table, opening it to one of the sections she had marked. "And yet, you speak of breasts as though they have only one function, 'to nurture the next generation'."

He stroked his chin thoughtfully. "I grew tired of hearing my fellow students comment lasciviously on women's forms. As a farmer, I am aware of the importance of the nurturing function. A calf not fed by its mother will die."

"Certainly. But might not breasts serve more than one purpose?" Unbuttoning the first four gold buttons of her bodice, she folded back the two sides. Rob's eyes widened as her large breasts were exposed, thrust high by her linen stays.

She noted with satisfaction that his gaze was glued to her nipples. His cheeks reddened and his chest heaved.

"Does it give you pleasure to look at my breasts?" she asked.

"Vanessa—" his voice died away into silence. He cleared his throat and started again. "Vanessa, I have never seen a lovelier sight."

"Truly, God has made a fine arrangement," she said. "He created women in this form, a form that men enjoy. Men like to touch—and it gives a woman great pleasure to be touched." She drew closer. He stood like a man turned to stone. Gently she took his unresisting hand and laid it on her right breast. "Touch me, Rob."

He needed no second invitation. Grasping her breasts with both hands, he fondled them, rubbing and stroking while her eyes drifted closed. She drank in the delicious sensations. He molded her breasts in his hands, his gentle caresses sending thrills of arousal through her, feelings she knew well.

His breath came fast as he ran calloused thumbs over her nipples. She remembered what Bertrand used to say when he touched her. *"Vanessa, my dear, your lovely pussy is filling with cream."* Somehow his naughty words had aroused her further.

Her pussy was filling again.

Lowering his face, Rob kissed the valley between her breasts, making her shiver with delight. Then he took her right breast in his mouth.

"Oh!" A tiny cry escaped her throat. She ran her hands up and down his back, overwhelmed by pleasure when he worked his tongue all around her areola, then sucked hard on her nipple. Oh, how she'd missed a man's hot mouth on her breasts. His mustache tickled her delicate skin as he sucked, making her nipple swell under his ministrations, then soothing it with warm caresses of his tongue.

"Rob—please—attend to the other one," she said with a gasp. He raised his head long enough to look at what he'd done. Her nipple was rosy and protruding.

"Amazing," he murmured, turning to her left nipple.

Her husband's hands or mouth on her breasts had always served to ready her for his cock. Rob's caresses were arousing the same feelings in her, the hot eagerness in her womanly parts, the intense longing for satisfaction.

Moving her hand downward, she stroked her fingers over the buttoned fly of his trousers. Her fleeting touch was enough to reveal that his cock was hard.

Chapter Two

The act of sexual congress is sacred. Blessed by both our Heavenly Creator and our earthly government, Marriage is an essential first step, the joining of souls a prerequisite to the joining of bodies. Although Literature tells of many who sought pleasure without the Bonds of Matrimony, our best books demonstrate how those who practice immorality invariably come to bad ends.

Professor Woodcock's Guide to Success and Happiness in Marital Relations (1st edition, 1893)

Was she attempting a seduction? It certainly seemed so. Rob felt like a straw buffeted by contrasting winds, tumbling first one way, then another. The temptation was great. He struggled with the excitement that filled him. Should he cling to the hard-won chastity he had kept all these years?

She caught his hand. "Robert." Her voice, by itself alone, had the power to make him succumb. "Further demonstrations will require greater privacy. Follow me."

He allowed her to lead him out of the parlor and through a hallway. Opening a door at the end of the hall, she turned up the flickering gaslight, revealing a small room furnished with an iron bed, a dressing table and a steamer trunk.

"This is your bedchamber?" he asked, surprised at its sparseness.

"Oh, my real bedroom is being repapered," she said. "I am happy to have a roof over my head—now that my husband has passed on."

He embraced her, determined to banish the sadness from her voice. "It doesn't matter. I'm happy just to be here with you." He kissed her, his tongue stroking hers, his hands fondling the luscious curves of her breasts. His member swelled, straining against his trousers until he feared the buttons would burst.

A painting he'd seen in the tavern in Columbus filled his mind—a rosy-breasted, dark-haired woman wearing nothing except corset and stockings, languishing on a bed. How he longed to see Vanessa displayed in the same manner.

And yet, religion and morality spoke against lascivious behavior.

Deftly, she slid his suit jacket off his shoulders. Her quick fingers undid his tie. But when she began unbuttoning his shirt, he put his hand over hers to stop her.

"Is something wrong?" she asked.

"My conscience." He looked into her dark eyes, silently begging her to understand. "Society expects brides to come pure to their marriage beds. Long ago I decided to bring my wife a clean body and a pure heart."

Her eyes widened as she looked up into his face. "You've never made love to a woman? And yet you wrote an entire book about marital relations."

"The topic does not necessarily require personal experience," he assured her. "Aside from my work on Father's farm, breeding animals—"

"Animals are not people," she said.

"*Aside* from that, I researched the subject in great detail." Why had she assumed such a skeptical expression? Didn't she believe him? "I read medical books—spoke to recently married friends—consulted other learned authorities."

"I see. And would you be able to teach another how to ride a bicycle if you had only *read* about it?"

He hesitated, sensing the truth of her words. "My book provides much useful information," he protested.

"Then isn't it your duty as a writer to learn more if you can, so that the second edition will provide even better information?"

"You may have a point," he admitted.

She wound her arms around his neck and gave him a soft, unhurried kiss. "When I first came to my husband's bed, nervous and frightened, it comforted me to realize he was experienced in these matters. I knew he had made love to two wives before me. Men and women view these matters differently, Rob. Women do not necessarily value inexperience."

He had never considered that idea before. Yet now that it was spoken, it made sense. Of course wives required their husband to guide them, to lead them.

While her hands returned to his shirt buttons, she cemented her argument. "I am not advising you to debauch a virtuous young maiden. Or to visit a lady of the evening, who might be diseased. I believe you have found a perfect solution—a lonely widow who cares about you—and misses the embraces of a man."

Who cares about you... His heart thrilled to the words repeating themselves in his mind. She cared enough about him to give her greatest gift...her sweet body.

His conscience silent at last, he let her open his shirt and slide her palms up his chest. He drank in her caresses, his body singing under the silken touch of her fingertips.

He removed his celluloid collar and shrugged off his shirt. Underneath he wore a union suit. Undoing the buttons swiftly, he shrugged out of the top portion and bared his chest.

Teasing his nipples, she pressed her hips into his. His member responded to the heat of her body, her long-remembered scent, her hands that yielded delight.

It is essential to preserve the modesty of both parties during the intimate act of marital congress. A dark room is recommended. Both husband and wife should retain their nightclothes. Although it is regrettably true that men enjoy gazing at the naked female form, they must not subject their wives to this humiliating imposition. Nor should husbands reveal themselves to their wives in a state of tumescence. Such a shocking sight might well give their wives a distaste for future marital relations.

Professor Woodcock's Guide to Success and Happiness in Marital Relations (1st edition, 1893)

Vanessa took a step back, the better to feast her eyes on the sight of Rob's naked chest. She hadn't realized he would be quite so attractively muscular. His shoulders and arms looked powerful, as though he could chop wood for hours or stop a team of runaway horses.

"Shall I turn the gas down?" he asked.

"Whatever for? I enjoy looking at you."

His Adam's apple moved as he swallowed. "You do?"

Reaching out, she placed her hands on his shoulders, rubbing her palms over the muscles. "A man of your age, in the prime of his strength—you could be the model for a classical statue." The hair on his head was a light brown, but his chest hair was a burnished gold. She drew nearer and buried her face in his chest, dropping slow, hot kisses at random. Gripping her waist, he groaned.

"Vanessa... Good heavens, I've never felt like this before."

"Not even with your fiancée?"

A tinge of color rose to his cheeks. "Emily was a pure young maiden. I kissed her bosom once. My forwardness made her cry. We never saw each other unclothed."

His chest heaved as she pressed an open-mouthed kiss at the base of his throat, tickling his skin with her tongue. He gasped, a sound that pleased her. She had always loved teaching, imparting knowledge to receptive pupils. And after his initial hesitation, Rob now seemed receptive indeed.

"Shall I remove my frock?" she asked.

"I wish you would." The sincerity of his tone amused her.

Standing back from him, she unbuttoned the lower eight buttons of her bodice, then slid the gown's top off her shoulders. She pulled down her petticoat and stepped out of it, then pushed the gown past her rounded hips.

He was only the second man who had seen her like this, wearing nothing but stays, drawers and stockings. What would he think of her? Would her unclothed form please him?

"You are perfection itself." He came toward her, moving like a sleepwalker. Wrapping his arms around her, he pressed kisses on her neck and shoulders. The impassioned caresses of his eager mouth made her knees oddly weak. She clung to his waist, her head falling back under his onslaught.

Her pussy clenched, longing for their lovemaking to begin. She wanted to discard her drawers, fall back on the bed and enjoy the delicious thrusts of his cock.

But she reminded herself of her duty. Her goal was more than their mutual pleasure. She needed to instruct him so that his book could be corrected.

"Rob." She put her hands on his shoulders, holding him back. "You must help me out of my stays. I wish to have no clothing between us when we lie in bed together."

Without answering, he pulled her back into his embrace, his hot mouth roving up her jawline. Taking her earlobe in his mouth, he sucked it. Mercy, how could she resist that? She slumped against him, her eyes closing. His lips on her sensitive earlobe stoked the flames raging inside her.

She forced herself to turn in his arms. "Undo my laces, dear."

His fingers fumbled with the knots Annie had tied for her that morning. Although she did not lace tightly, it was always a relief when her stays were loosened. She worked the undergarment over her head.

Private Lessons

When she moved to face him, she saw that his brow was beaded with perspiration. She put her arms around him. "Don't be nervous, Rob. I am quite sure all will go well between us."

"There's something I haven't mentioned. Something I must confess. I suppose I should have told you before I let things go so far…" Despite his words, he held her tightly, as though he couldn't bear to release her.

"What is it?" she demanded. When he hesitated, she softened her voice. "You know you can tell me anything, dear." Lurid ideas arose in her mind, alarming her.

"My-my member. The other boys used to mock me when we swam together."

She hardly dared to ask. Was it deformed somehow? Missing some essential part?

"It's very large, Vanessa." His last words came out in a rush. "I fear you may not be able to accommodate me."

She sighed with relief. "My husband was large too. Now aren't you happy you chose a widow for your first experience?" Whisking herself out of his arms, she went to the bed and reclined upon it.

He remained frozen in place, looking at her.

"Do you know what comes next?" she asked.

Slowly, he nodded. "The act has been described to me by married friends." His voice turning hoarse, he added, "You're so beautiful, it's hard to pull my eyes away. Now I know why the Old Masters always painted nude women. There is nothing lovelier on earth."

"Darling Rob." She reached out her hand to him. "Remove your trousers and join me on the bed."

Keeping his gaze on her, he unbuttoned his trousers and pushed them down. His erect cock swelled against the bottom half of his union suit. He pulled that down too. His cock stood up tall against his lean stomach.

Mercy. He hadn't exaggerated a bit. A phrase she'd learned from her husband, *Hung like a horse,* came to mind.

His ruddy member was not only long but thick as well. She doubted her hand would close completely around it.

She ached to have him inside her, that massive cock dipping deep into her greedy channel. Wetness leaked from her pussy as she anticipated his eager thrusts.

The man should not linger overlong in the act. His wife will thank him for performing quickly and leaving her in peace. Since it is well known that ladies do not experience pleasure the way men do, they should lie still and take their delight in the measure of happiness they provide to their husbands.

Professor Woodcock's Guide to Success and Happiness in Marital Relations (1st edition, 1893)

He stretched out beside her on the bed. He was about to make love to Vanessa, something he had dreamed about for years. Breathing deeply, he noted how her violet scent had altered, growing muskier. His own excitement heightened.

She ran her palm boldly up his shaft. He hadn't expected her to actually touch his member. He gasped with the wonderful pleasure of the caress.

Aching to plunge into her, he restrained himself, waiting for a sign from her.

"I know you're ready to make love, but often the woman takes longer to enter that state," she said. "There are things you can do to prepare me."

He nodded, thinking of what he had learned from his studies. "May I touch you?"

She turned onto her back and raised her knees. "Stroke me with your hand," she murmured.

Although longing to caress her womanly parts, he still hesitated. "Truly?" he stammered. "Your modesty will allow–"

"My husband had a saying, *Modesty stays outside the bedroom door*. When you take a virgin bride, she may know nothing of the marital act. She will follow your lead. *Your* duty will be to show her pleasure."

Her talk of this imaginary female bothered him. He didn't know why — always before he'd looked forward to his future marriage.

"Let us not speak of that," he said. "Show me what pleases *you*, sweetheart."

Taking his hand, she guided it to her nether region. "Do you know what this is called?"

"The vulva. In more common terminology, the pussy." He rubbed her gently, enjoying the springy feel of her dark curls.

She gave a long sigh. "I've always thought it *is* like a little furry cat — happy to be stroked the right away. Mmmmm…" Her breath caught. "That's good. You're touching me just the way I like."

Remembering what he'd read in a medical book, he brushed the back of his hand lightly against her clitoris. She moaned and her hips rose. He did it again, fascinated to see if she would respond the same way twice. She did, except this time her moan held more longing.

"I have read that the clitoris is the seat of female pleasure," he murmured. "And yet other authorities say that ladies have no feelings in this area."

"Now you know the truth," she answered. "I am a lady, yet I love your touch."

He stroked her over and over, thrilled by the way she responded.

Shifting, she moved her thighs parted farther. Her musky aroma increased. "Touch me here," she whispered, moving his hand to her channel. Eager to please, he ventured a finger inside her. He was startled to discover how she felt.

"Your vagina is so wet inside." Truly, this was a time when experience was a far better teacher than a medical book.

"Of course. That means I'm ready to make love with you." Her arms wound about his neck, pulling him closer. She whispered in his ear, "I can't wait until your cock is inside me."

Her words shocked and enticed him at the same time, a potent combination. He moved into position. *Male superior*—the correct position for all civilized humans.

"Start with a slow, gentle thrusting," she instructed. "Then increase your speed as we move together in rhythm."

Doubt shook him momentarily. Would he do everything the right way? Would he seem clumsy and inexperienced?

Then he felt her gentle fingers on his member. She guided him to her slick entrance. He pushed into her in one long hot slide, eased by her wetness.

He thrust deep and fast, greedy for the feel of her vagina stroking him. Her words returned to him through a fog—*start with a slow, gentle thrusting*—but his body demanded otherwise.

He drew back quickly and then thrust again, even harder. She cried out and for a moment he was afraid he'd hurt her, but she tightened her grip on his shoulders and said, "More!"

He took up a fast rhythm, pounding into her quickly. The light slap of his balls hitting her ass stimulated him further. She moved underneath him, her hips arching to capture his member as he thrust inside her. Her moans and cries filled his ears. He plunged into her again and again, wanting to possess her utterly, wanting her to forget everything she'd ever known, except for him.

Her rosy nipples were as hard as tiny pebbles. He sucked on the right one, drawing it into his mouth then circling it with his tongue. Her whimpers increased. Her hands moved down his back then gripped his buttocks, urging him even deeper.

His pleasure swelled and he knew release would soon overtake him.

Crying out loudly, she ceased moving. Her vagina spasmed around his member. He thrust once more and groaned, a noise that felt like it was torn from his throat.

He poured himself into her willing body, knowing he would never be complete again unless he was with her.

Although many positions are possible for sexual congress, the "male superior" position is the recommended method. It establishes the husband's natural order in the household and reminds the wife of her duty to submit and surrender. The husband who allows his wife to take the lead in the bedroom may soon find himself henpecked by a female who has forgotten her place.

Professor Woodcock's Guide to Success and Happiness in Marital Relations (1st edition, 1893)

Vanessa had the oddest desire to cry. Afraid that a weeping woman would disconcert Rob, she turned on her side and pressed her fist to her mouth.

What had started as a casual desire for pleasure had turned into an overwhelming experience. Her entire body felt limp, immeasurably relieved by the cessation of tension, wrung out with the splendid release he'd given her.

She'd never experienced such vigorous lovemaking. Used to her husband's more leisurely movements, she never would have guessed she'd like it. But she had quickly become caught up in Rob's swift, hard thrusts. Lost in the moment, she'd tumbled into effortless, overwhelming pleasure.

Rob shifted, aligning himself along her body, his chest hair tickling her back. His lips moved over her shoulder, increasing her desire to weep.

"Good heavens," he said. "I never knew…"

He ran his palm up and down her arm. Even that simple caress enticed her, made her yearn again for the long slide of his hard cock.

"That was an experience beyond words," he said.

"So you find the real experience more interesting than researching it?"

"Very much so. You were correct, Vanessa. I needed this demonstration. Now I am no longer a neophyte, but seasoned."

"Rob, dear — we've merely scratched the surface."

"Truly? I find myself...completely and utterly astonished."

She turned to face him, unable to suppress a smile. "Now you sound like Professor Woodcock."

"Hardly surprising, as I am he."

"No, you're much nicer. And less pompous."

His mustache brushed her nipple as he kissed her breast. "I will attempt to sound less pompous in the second edition. And I will certainly correct the part about ladies not feeling pleasure."

She ran her fingers down his golden chest hair, taking satisfaction in the way his breath hitched.

"I suppose this is utterly selfish of me, but...do you suppose we might perform the act again?" he asked. "Not right away, of course. Perhaps in a few hours, when you have rested?"

"You must leave at five," she told him. "Annie will return around half-past five to cook dinner. She mustn't find you here."

"What would she do?"

She couldn't repress a shudder. "I cannot say. Perhaps tell my stepfather."

"Do you dislike him so much? With all the money your wealthy husband must have left you, I'm surprised you haven't set up your own establishment. Perhaps with an older lady to chaperone you."

"I have thought of doing that," she said cautiously. "Or I might marry one of the men my stepfather has chosen for me."

She felt his whole body stiffen. "Do you *wish* to marry again?" he asked.

"If the right man presented himself. I do *not* want to marry a gouty man of seventy, nor a red-faced barber with seven children from three previous wives."

"Absolutely not," he said, sounding revolted. "Sweet Vanessa, a woman like you deserves an extraordinary man. A prince."

"The next time a prince comes to Marble Falls, Ohio, I'll be sure to arrange an introduction," she said dryly. Turning on her side, she took his cock firmly in her hand and stroked upward. "Rob, in your book you praise the male superior position. Will you allow me to show you another method of lovemaking that may also please you?"

"Show me anything you like." He gazed at her with his clear blue eyes. "I am putty in your hands, sweetheart."

"Not *putty*, dear. Putty is soft. *You* are anything but soft." Her repeated stroking had quickly brought his cock to a most satisfactory degree of hardness. She eyed it lovingly, remembering how wonderful it had felt, filling her channel.

Straddling him, she lowered herself slowly, fitting herself carefully onto his cock. She sighed as his shaft impaled her, watching his face. He gasped, his breath coming fast as she sank all the way down.

"Do you like that?" she inquired softly.

"It's-it's indescribable." He reached out and grasped her hips. She moved up and down. His expression changed, his eyes widening and his mouth falling open. "My goodness, Vanessa, this is sheer heaven."

Heaven was the perfect word. Was it his size or something more? Perhaps the delight he took in everything she did?

She plunged up and down, feeling her pussy gushing its approval, feeling her climax building. A tiny tickle of pleasure grew and expanded. She rode him without mercy, moving faster when he groaned, when his breath caught, when he palmed her breasts and squeezed. Her climax rose and swelled, centered first on where they were joined, then expanding through her entire being. She closed her eyes, aware of nothing but his body beneath hers and the bursting waves of release flowing through her.

"I don't want to leave you," he murmured. "May I see you tomorrow?"

She opened drowsy eyes. "I fear to invite you back. Annie will grumble."

"I *must* see you again. Can you go for a drive in my rig? I'll buy food and we can have a picnic."

She hesitated, knowing that if her stepfather came to hear of it, he would be furious and arrange punishment. Then her reckless side took over. Where was her life leading her? Soon she would be wed to a man she didn't love. Or if she left Marble Falls, she would be slaving away giving music lessons, living in a tenement in Cleveland or Akron.

All her choices were poor ones. Perhaps this was the last fun and excitement life would offer her.

So she told him where to meet her the next afternoon.

* * * * *

That evening, Vanessa sank into a daydream as Annie helped her undress for bed.

I want to feel his mouth on my breasts again. Mercy, I love how he stroked my pussy, so gently yet firmly. If he were my husband, I'd ensure we made love every single evening. I'd kiss him and love him and help him with his book.

Alas, such a wonderful man deserves a bride his own age. A sweet, demure virgin. Not a woman so much his senior.

"Ma'am, what happened to your corset?" Annie exclaimed. "I am certain I didn't lace you up like this!"

Vanessa drew a sharp breath and let the servant pull the corset over her head. "A lace came undone and I had to retie it myself," she said coolly.

"Ain't never happened before," Annie muttered.

Vanessa moved to her trunk. Opening it, she brought out a pretty straw hat trimmed with a feather dyed blue.

"Annie, I find this hat no longer pleases me. Would you like it?"

The servant's eyes gleamed. "I've always been partial to that hat, ma'am. Thank you."

Vanessa held it just out of her reach. "And you won't tell my stepfather about the professor's visit?"

Annie straightened. "I pride myself on keeping a silent tongue, ma'am."

"See that you do." Vanessa handed her the hat.

Chapter Three

൩

An unchaperoned couple is a disaster waiting to happen. Nature courses strongly through their veins, arousing temptation. In the vast wild of the outdoors, anything might occur. A single sweet kiss turns into unspeakable desire. A lovely white dove flutters from the safety of her cage and returns...soiled! Mothers, guard your daughters' purity!

Professor Woodcock's Guide to Success and Happiness in Marital Relations (1st edition, 1893)

At one o'clock the next afternoon, Rob drove his pair of Clydesdales along the dirt path beside the Cuyahoga River. He wished he had a more dashing equipage—spirited black stallions pulling a phaeton, perhaps. When Vanessa saw his ungainly rig, would she even wish to accompany him?

She deserved the best life had to offer. Elegant clothing, a richly furnished home and fine jewelry. A man who owned no more than a refurbished circus wagon should never have turned his eyes to her.

He considered the words of his favorite poet, *Better to have loved and lost than never to have loved at all.* Was it true? Or would it have been better never to have met her again? The sweet memory of his youthful adoration had been overlaid with their passionate encounter yesterday. When he thought of her after today, it would be with deep regret. He foresaw many sleepless nights, bitterly longing for the beloved who could never be his.

Then he saw a woman standing by the river, clad in a gray walking skirt and a white shirtwaist. A wide-brimmed hat with a veil hid her face, but he was sure it was Vanessa. He knew her by the proud set of her shoulders and the generous curve of her hips, by the way she stood and the way she lifted her head when she heard his rig. Her image was engraved on his heart.

When he reached her, he halted the horses. Aware of the others strolling the park, he gravely tipped his hat to her. "Good afternoon, Mrs. d'Aulaire."

Her dark eyes darted a mischievous glance at him. "Good afternoon, Professor Woodcock. This is an unexpected pleasure. What a fine day for a drive."

"Yes, we are fortunate indeed to have such a fine day. Would you care to join me?"

"Thank you for your kind invitation. I believe I will." She picked up the wicker basket by her side. Grasping the grip on the wagon's side, she stepped nimbly up to the front seat, settling in beside him.

He clucked to the horses, which began plodding along again.

"*Do* find a private spot, Rob." The note of promise in her voice thrilled him. He couldn't wait to kiss those luscious red lips. "I have several delightful activities in mind that require...seclusion."

"I located just such a place yesterday, after our interesting afternoon together," he answered. He wished the horses would move faster, but even slavering wolves would not hurry Patty and Petey.

When they reached the place he'd found the day before, she clasped her gloved hands together joyfully. "Rob, this is perfect! High enough so that no one can approach without us seeing them first. And enough trees to shield us from curious eyes. Not to mention a lovely view of the river."

"I have a lovely view right in front of me," he said, smiling into her eyes. He leaned toward her. "Dash it all, why must women wear these confounded veils?"

"The hat is easily removed," she said, lifting it away from her hair.

Her lips clung hungrily to his. Her tongue glided tentatively into his mouth delicately stroking. Goodness, how he loved the taste of her, the feel of her mouth on his, her breasts pressing against him.

Images filled his mind—the delight on her face and the quivering of her white breasts when his member was deep inside her. The way she'd made love to him, impaled on his shaft, crying out his name as she reached the apex of pleasure.

I must have her again. Soon.

Releasing her, he jumped down off the wagon and stood ready to help her. "Come, I'll unhitch the horses and then I'll show you my home."

"Your home?" she questioned, stepping down into his embrace.

"The wagon, sweetheart. I have no other."

He unhitched Patty and Petey, stroking their soft noses and praising them, then setting them loose to graze.

"You are kind to your horses," she observed.

"They are my only friends on the road." He took Vanessa's arm and walked her to the back of the wagon. Unlocking the doors that formed the fourth wall of the big rectangular wagon, he threw them open.

"I bought it from a circus that went into bankruptcy," he told her, helping her inside. It was furnished like a room with a bed, a table and a bench. Cupboards lined the walls. The wooden furniture was nailed to the floor or walls so that it wouldn't shift as the wagon traveled over rough roads.

"Do you sleep here?" she asked, going to the bed and sitting on it. "Why, the mattress is quite comfortable."

He took an oil lamp out of a cupboard and lit it, then closed the wagon's doors. "You requested privacy, I believe? Now we have it." They exchanged secret smiles.

Private Lessons

"When I come into a town, I sometimes stay at a hotel so I can take a bath," he continued. "But otherwise I have everything I need right here."

"And you can see the country." She sighed. "I am envious. My husband had lived in many of the great European cities in his youth—Paris, London, Vienna. But he was old when we married and no longer had the desire for travel."

"I've visited twenty different states in the past two years," he told her eagerly. "In the summer I visit the Midwest and New England. When the cold weather comes, I will travel to the south."

"It sounds ideal." She gazed around the room. "What do you have in the cupboards?"

"Clothing. Nonperishable food. The printed copies of my book." He grinned. "And many boxes of fine cigars."

"Why, Rob—do you smoke?"

Sitting beside her, he shook his head. "When I began my lecturing, I never dreamt there might be trouble. But occasionally the town fathers have objected to my topic, calling my talks obscene. Now when I come to a new city, I visit the chief of police and the mayor, bringing them a box of fine cigars with a five-dollar gold piece tucked inside. Since then there have been no further objections." *And no more painful beatings from a loutish police captain and his men.*

She gazed up at him, her dark eyes alight. "How clever of you." She stroked his cheek. "Did you think about me last night?"

"I thought of nothing else," he said fervently. He'd lain awake for hours until he'd finally surrendered to lust and committed the sin of masturbation. Twice.

"I couldn't wait for the day to arrive," she said, her voice soft. "What about tomorrow, dear? My parents don't return until the day after. Can we see each other tomorrow as well?"

Pain slashed into his heart when he had to say, "I am afraid not. I leave early tomorrow morning for Akron. I've rented the theater there for two nights and must make haste."

"Oh." Disappointment cast a momentary shadow over her lovely features. Then she smiled bravely. "Well, then we must use the time we have. There is something special I want to do for you, dear—something my husband taught me that he took particular delight in."

His cock swelled at the hint of mysterious pleasure in her voice. "Have I mentioned it in my book?"

She merely raised her eyebrows. "I believe so. Lie back on the bed and undo your trousers."

He took off his jacket then did as she had requested. Meanwhile she stripped off her gloves, laying them on the narrow bed.

"Part your legs," she told him, her enticing voice taking on a husky note. She knelt between his knees and unbuttoned his union suit. His cock sprang up, already half-erect. "In your book, you referred to this as genital kissing. I believe you disapproved."

Holding his member firmly at the base, she bent her head. He looked up in disbelief as she took it into her mouth. Her lips tight against his heated skin, she moved her head up and down slowly, provoking a shuddering thrill throughout his entire body.

And yet, was it right to let his lover perform such an act? He gasped. "Vanessa…truly, I do not expect…are you sure you are willing…"

She raised her head briefly, her skillful hand continuing to give him fast, enticing strokes that were making him hotter and harder than he'd ever been before. "Dear, I want to give you so much pleasure that you'll never forget me."

"As if I ever could," he said.

She took the head of his member in her mouth again, pulled back the foreskin and swirled her tongue over the sensitive head again and again. He closed his eyes, drinking in the intense sensations.

Her curled hand moved up and down, coaxing his member to stand tall and proud. "You have such a beautiful cock," she said, her voice hushed.

The words aroused him even more than her wonderful touch.

Her mouth closed over him again, her tongue teasing his shaft. Her lips sucked on his stiff member, traveling up and down until he thought he'd go mad with pleasure. He clenched his fists and shut his eyes, suspended between anticipation and delight.

"*Good heavens, Vanessa!*"

"Are you enjoying it?" she asked.

He couldn't even form words as she pointed her tongue and teased the slit in the head of his member. A drop of pearly fluid leaked out. She licked it away, then raised her head and moved her tongue slowly over her lips. "I love the taste of you," she whispered.

Sweat broke out on his chest and his breath came in short, labored gasps.

She cupped his balls in her hand, rolling them gently. Everything tightened in his groin. He knew he was close to climaxing.

When her lips stroked him again, his hips bucked involuntarily. Then pleasure overtook him and he plunged into a strong, shuddering climax. She continued sucking. It thrilled him that she savored every drop of his vital fluid.

Finally she stretched out beside him. Drawing her against his chest, he murmured, "That was truly astounding. Thank you a hundred times over, sweetheart."

She snuggled her head under his chin. "It's so pleasant lying here with you. I wish you didn't have to leave tomorrow."

He stroked the side of her face. "I know. I can hardly bear it." His heart ached at their forthcoming separation. "My lectures are scheduled for the next month, but after that—"

Laying her fingers lightly on his mouth, she shook her head. "I would never be able to keep company with you while my stepfather was in town. He wants me to marry one of the men he has chosen. I can just imagine what he would say about you. 'A wandering, penniless ne'er-do-well' would be his most generous description."

"I may be a wandering ne'er-do-well but I am certainly not penniless," he answered indignantly. "My goal is to buy a farm of my own someday—within the next three years, I hope. I have money saved from my lectures."

She sighed. "I admire your ambition, dear."

He wondered if she was thinking the same thing he was. If only he had owned the farm now, he would ask her to marry him and take her there. But how could he ask this beautiful, prosperous woman to join her life to his? To accompany him as another wandering ne'er-do-well?

The admiration he had felt as a stripling had grown into a true love that filled his whole heart. Could he ask her to promise herself to him and wait for three long years until he'd earned the money he needed?

He opened his mouth to speak.

But it wasn't fair to his beloved. She must not tie herself to a man who would take her away from wealth and elegance. He had nothing to offer her—nothing but love.

Bitterly, he concluded that it wasn't enough.

* * * * *

Vanessa stood by the window of her bedroom, dwelling on the sweet memory of her afternoon with Rob. They had picnicked outdoors, frequently pausing to kiss or touch each other, eating the bread and ham and cheese Rob had bought, sipping the champagne she had taken from her stepfather's liquor cabinet. Champagne her husband had imported from France. Her stepfather had claimed it after Bertrand's death.

They had tried to enjoy themselves, but their parting loomed in both their minds, a thundercloud hanging over their joy.

Rob had talked about the farm he wanted to own. Although she knew little of agriculture, his words had convinced her he knew what he was talking about. What a shame his father had lost the family acres.

After eating they had retired to Rob's wagon. The narrow bed became a paradise when they made love. This time he had needed no instruction, touching her confidently, then thrusting into her when her pussy was hot and wet, desperately craving his powerful cock.

Dear Rob. He had always been a quick pupil.

She closed her eyes, playing with the buttons of her lacy nightdress, wishing he were here to make love to her again.

He was so handsome—so intelligent—as well as an excellent lover. What a wonderful husband he would make for some lucky woman. She was sure he would be a prosperous farmer someday, with his clever ideas for new agricultural methods.

The noise of a pebble striking glass startled her. She looked down to see Rob himself standing below the window, the sill at the height of his chin.

"Rob!" she exclaimed.

He held a finger to his lips, then pantomimed that she should raise the window. She did so as slowly and silently as possible, hoping Annie, in her attic bedroom, would not hear anything.

She didn't understand how he was going to get in but he made quick work of it, grasping the sill with his hands and pulling himself up. In a few moments he was inside. Wordlessly he drew her close and kissed her until they were both breathless.

A light went on in the house next door. Alarmed, Vanessa pulled free of his arms and hurried to turn down the gas.

"I hope Old Lady Johnson next door didn't see you," she whispered. "She's the nosiest gossip in three counties."

His shoulders shook with silent laughter. "If she says anything to you, tell her she was dreaming," he whispered back. His expression turned somber. "Sweetheart, I had to see you once more. You mean so much to me."

Rob, take me with you when you go. The words lingered on her lips but she bit them back.

He doesn't need a woman older than himself. I've taught him what he needs to know to have a happy marriage someday – and correct his book. That is my only place in his life.

"I'm so glad you're here," she murmured. "I was longing for you, unable to sleep."

"As was I." His swift fingers unbuttoned the bodice of her nightdress. In another moment he was sucking her right nipple eagerly while his fingers caressed her left. How quickly her body responded to his warm lips. Her pussy pulsed insistently, eager for the thrusts of his cock.

"We shall have to be quite silent, lest Annie hear us," she whispered.

"I understand." Releasing her, he sat on the bed. "Vanessa, undress for me."

She obeyed his command gladly, unbuttoning her nightdress and lifting it over her head. She wore nothing underneath. His gaze traveled slowly over her body, dwelling first on her nipples and then the dark curls between her thighs.

"You're so beautiful, sweetheart. Come and lie on the bed. Let me feast my eyes on you while I undress."

She lay on the bed, her pussy throbbing, filling with cream. He undressed slowly and deliberately, never looking away as he removed each piece of clothing and laid it aside.

She trembled with arousal as his handsome body was slowly revealed—his muscular chest, solid waist and powerful thighs. And his rapidly swelling cock.

"I loved what you did to me today," he whispered. "Now I shall return the favor." Kneeling on the floor, he added, "Move closer to me and part your thighs."

She frowned in confusion. "Whatever do you mean, Rob? Genital kissing is for men only."

He stroked her with his fingers, smoothing her curls back from her entrance. "Why do you think that?"

"My husband told me so."

"Perhaps he knew no better." He smiled. "But Professor Woodcock's research has revealed otherwise." Before she could say anything else, he lowered his head to her pussy and ran his tongue up her nether lips.

She gasped at the incredible jolt of pleasure that shot through her.

When he did it again, a cry burst from her throat. His tongue was warm and wet, providing delight that was new to her. Much though she loved feeling his thick cock inside her, *this* sensation was different and unexpected.

And incredibly powerful.

He licked teasingly around her entrance. She shook and trembled under his ministrations, feeling her climax building incredibly fast. Soon she was lifting her hips frantically, pushing against his mouth, covering her face with her arm to muffle her cries.

All the feeling in her body now centered in one spot, her needy pussy. Her yearning built to an unbelievable level. She moaned like a wanton, whispering his name, begging for more, begging him to end it because the pleasure was more than she could bear.

He wriggled his tongue against her clitoris and she thrashed under his mouth. Reaching up, he grasped her nipples in his fingers and rubbed. Heat flashed through her and a powerful climax exploded within her body.

The strong, pulsing waves of pleasure were still moving through her when he stood, lifted her buttocks with powerful hands and surged into her with his massive cock. Mercy, having him inside her while she was still throbbing with her climax was a miracle of delight. She moaned his name, whispering the naughty word her husband had taught her. "Fuck me, Rob. Fuck me hard."

He thrust into her over and over, tireless, while her pussy pulsed and throbbed around him. She rose to another effortless climax, even stronger than the first. Finally he stilled and groaned, then released while he was balls-deep inside her.

Afterward he lay beside her and gathered her close, stroking her back lovingly. "You had never experienced that before?" he whispered.

"Never."

A smile lingered on his face. "So the pupil has become the teacher."

There is much we could learn together...if only our time were not at an end.

The two climaxes he'd given her had drained her. She fell asleep in his arms.

Sometime during the night, she thought he whispered, "I love you." Then the window opened and he was gone.

Chapter Four

ಸಾ

Too many of our modern-day young people discount love when they search for a partner. Marrying for property or coin is a soulless proposition that leads to unhappiness. The only true currency between husband and wife is devotion. The only true basis for marriage is love.

Professor Woodcock's Guide to Success and Happiness in Marital Relations (1ˢᵗ edition, 1893)

Heavy-eyed and heavy-hearted, Rob rose late. He knew he had to make thirty miles today in order to reach Akron in time for his lecture later in the week, but he lingered as he fed and watered the horses.

Restless, he decided to have breakfast in town before departing. As he tied the horses to a hitching post in front of the Sunrise Café, *Fine breakfasts for two bits*, he saw a woman hurrying toward him. It took him a moment to recognize the seamed face of Annie, the servant at Vanessa's house.

"Professor! I must speak to you!" She clutched his arm.

"What is it?" He caught his breath, afraid of what she would tell him. "Is something wrong with Van—with Mrs. d'Aulaire?"

She nodded, tears shining in her old eyes. "Her parents came home this morning. They received a telegram from Mrs. Johnson next door. She claimed she saw a man entering Mrs. d'Aulaire's bedroom last night."

Rob's heart plummeted. So he *had* been seen. He cursed himself, blaming his selfish lust for their exposure.

"Was it you, Professor?" Annie's gaze demanded an answer.

He nodded, not bothering to deny it. "Is her stepfather angry?"

"Angry! He near collapsed in an apoplexy! Lord above, how that man can rant and rave!" She stared up at him fiercely. "You lusting dog! You've had your way with her and now you're going to leave town, is that right? You menfolk are all alike!"

"You have it all wrong!" he burst out. "I *love* her. But how can I ask a wealthy woman like Vanessa to be my wife?"

Annie drew a sharp breath. "Wealthy!" She stared at him as though he were a lunatic, already certified and headed toward the asylum. "Poor Miss Vanessa has nothing!"

Surely Annie was mistaken. He thought of the expensive velvet gown, the rings and bracelets Vanessa had worn.

"Don't be ridiculous," Rob finally replied. It was too much to hope for, that he and Vanessa were on equal footing. That she would welcome an offer of marriage from a poor man. "I thought her deceased husband was wealthy."

The cook snorted with derision. "He was—once. But he made reckless investments. Lost everything in the Panic." Fixing him with her shrewd gaze, she asked, "Why do you think Mrs. d'Aulaire lives with her parents? They've never treated her good. Her stepfather grudges every mouthful of food she eats, every bit of soap she uses. She teaches piano to children and he takes half of her earnings for her room and board."

Blood pounded in Rob's head. Uncontrollable anger shot through him. He wanted to grasp Vanessa's stepfather by the neck and squeeze until he was dead.

"He took scissors to Miss Vanessa's red gown—the one she wore for you when you came to tea," Annie went on, her mouth quivering. "He cut her only decent frock into tiny pieces. Now he's ranting that she'll marry the barber today or leave the house with nothing."

Rob gasped, unable to believe such cruelty.

* * * * *

"I will *not* marry Horace Bigbee," Vanessa declared. The fury radiating from her mother and stepfather horrified her, but she stood her ground. "I do not love him."

"Wanton strumpet!" her mother snapped. "You should be glad to get any husband after your infamous behavior! Horace may not even take you once word gets around town. We must seal the marriage quickly."

Her stepfather came close, his face red with rage. Vanessa took an involuntary step backward, afraid he would strike her.

"Harlot!" he cried. "Your soul is black with sin!"

How could anything so beautiful be sinful? Oh, Rob, if only I could see you again.

"My only daughter—a fallen woman!" her mother moaned. "I never suspected such vileness."

Vileness? It was pleasure beyond any I have ever known. Pleasure, desire and…love.

Her stepfather pounded the table with his fist. "I won't allow you to drag our good name through the mud. If you won't marry, you will leave my house today."

Vanessa glanced at her mother, wondering whether she would protest her husband's decision. Instead, the other woman gave a firm nod.

"I will leave, then—*with* my clothing and my steamer trunk." Vanessa raised her chin, trying to make her voice sound strong. The money she'd saved over the last eighteen months was hidden in the trunk. Those carefully hoarded coins meant the difference between starting a new life…or utter destitution.

"You own *nothing*," he told her. "You came to my house a beggar and you will leave as one."

Rob, she thought, her heart filled with despair. She was sure he had already left town.

Now she regretted the pride that had kept her from revealing her true circumstances to him. He had viewed her as a prosperous lady clad in fine garments. The adoration in his eyes had pleased and flattered her. The dread of seeing his adoration change to pity had kept her silent.

Her stepfather loomed over her. "I have sent a message to Bigbee. If you will not agree to accompany him to the courthouse and marry today, then you must go to live among strangers and never return here."

"Then I choose to live among strangers," Vanessa said. "No doubt they will be kinder than you!"

"You wound me," her stepfather said. "I am thinking only of your welfare." Stepping to his big oak desk, he unlocked one of the drawers.

Vanessa moved closer, wondering what he was doing.

He held up a black velvet purse, heavy with coins. "I found this when I searched your trunk this morning."

The world was suddenly unsteady beneath Vanessa's feet. "My money!" A savage impulse rippled through her to thrust herself forward and tear the purse from his grasp. "Give it to me!"

Before she could move, he dropped the purse back into the drawer. "I will entrust it into your husband's keeping once you are safely married." His eyes raked over her scornfully. "Bigbee will arrive soon. Go to your bedroom and don suitable clothing."

Vanessa paced futilely around her tiny bedroom, pondering the best course of action. She had thought her money safe. That forty-two dollars would have allowed her to buy a train ticket to Cleveland, to pay the weekly rent in a boarding house, to place an advertisement in the *Cleveland Gazette* for piano pupils.

Without her savings, she was helpless. She had no friends who could lend her money. She had nothing valuable to sell, for her husband's creditors had claimed everything after his death.

She sank down onto her narrow bed, her mind whirling. She needed a plan—and quickly. Yet her thoughts dwelt on Rob. His mouth on her breasts, his mustache tickling her skin. His hands caressing her, arousing her senses. His cock stroking inside her, providing such incredible pleasure.

So much about him appealed to her. When his plans to farm had fallen through, he'd set out with new goals, writing a book and taking to the road. His ambition was admirable. Recalling the way he'd treated his horses yesterday, she smiled. A man who was kind of animals and pleasant to servants would also be good to his wife.

Whoever that lucky woman would be, Vanessa envied her.

She rose from the bed and opened her trunk. Digging down to the bottom, she found "suitable clothing".

The rapping of the doorknocker sounded throughout the house as Vanessa entered the study. She braced herself. Mr. Bigbee must have arrived.

Her stepfather frowned. "Is *that* gown one you deem appropriate to receive your suitor? Your widow's weeds?"

Vanessa smoothed her hand over the black bodice. "Perhaps you should not have been so quick to destroy my other frock," she responded coldly.

The doorknocker sounded again. "I sent Annie to the store two hours ago," her mother said. "Whatever can be taking so long?" She gestured impatiently at Vanessa. "Answer the door, girl. Show Horace to the parlor and let him propose to you."

Feeling as though she were walking to her own funeral, Vanessa went to the front door and let Horace Bigbee into the house. He must have smoked a celebratory cigar on the way over, for the gray ashes decorated his suit.

"Mrs. d'Aulaire, I was overjoyed to receive your father's note this morning." Grabbing her hands, Mr. Bigbee pulled her close. He smelled of tobacco and hair pomade. She turned her head just in time to avoid the press of his thick lips.

"Modest," he said, patting her cheek. "I like that in a woman."

To encourage herself, she thought of Mr. Bigbee's fine brick house on the town square, of his motherless children. Surely marrying him would be preferable to a life of penury, living in a boarding house and teaching piano.

But could she bear to marry a man she didn't love? To live with him for the rest of her life and never allow herself to think of Rob again?

She led him into the parlor, her soul filling with darkness.

With a flourish, Mr. Bigbee pulled a small box from his vest pocket. "My dear little flower, you know I have always held you in esteem. Make me the happiest of men by accepting this ring."

She took the box and opened it. The ruby ring was lovely—and familiar. She had seen it many times on the hand of Mr. Bigbee's third wife.

"I hardly know what to say." Revolted, Vanessa snapped the box shut.

"Say yes," he urged. "My house needs you to make it a home. My little ones cry for a new mama. My dear mother, who lives with us, longs to share the housekeeping duties with a strong young woman." Mr. Bigbee wagged his finger playfully. "Socks don't darn themselves, you know!"

"I am not sure..." She cleared her throat. "Although you do me great honor, I am afraid I must—"

Private Lessons

"I hope it is not the neighbors' unkind gossip that makes you hesitate," he interrupted. "I assure you, my children are *not* evil. Merely jolly and high-spirited."

"I am used to children. I was a schoolteacher before I married."

"That is why I thought you would make an excellent mama for my dear ones." He leaned forward earnestly. "The twins meant no harm when they tied the hired girl up and pelted her with arrows. They love to play at being wild Indians."

"Boys will be boys," Vanessa murmured.

"And Oswald wants to be a naturalist. When he woolgathers, he forgets what he has in his pockets. He didn't *intend* to start the toad infestation."

"I am sure he didn't."

"I particularly wanted to mention that it is *not true* about the cats," Mr. Bigbee continued. "All of their fur eventually grew back."

"What cats?" Vanessa gasped.

Ignoring the question, Mr. Bigbee continued, "And Esmeralda needs someone to nurture her wayward spirit. No matter what the minister says, she is *not* possessed by an imp from Hades."

Vanessa stood, squaring her shoulders. Rather than wed Mr. Bigbee, she would take up residence in the poorhouse.

Before she could speak, the parlor doors opened. Her mother and stepfather entered, their faces like granite.

Vanessa wet her dry lips. "Mr. Bigbee, I am afraid I must refuse your proposal."

Her suitor stared at her in shock, open-mouthed, while her mother put a hand on her heart and rolled her eyes upward.

Her stepfather rushed forward, face flushing. "How dare you! Who else will have you, foolish girl?"

Rob, she thought. If only she'd put her pride away and begged him to take her with him. He wouldn't have had to marry her. Even living in sin with him, as a woman outside society, would have been preferable to marrying Mr. Bigbee.

She was suddenly certain that living in sin with Rob would have been glorious.

The front door flew open with a crash, causing china knickknacks to dance on their shelves and a slender vase to careen wildly. With a shriek, Vanessa's mother caught the vase and clutched it to her bosom, flowers and all.

Rob strode into the parlor. Vanessa's heart soared. An avenging angel sent directly by God could not have appeared more wondrous.

"Sir!" Vanessa's mother stared at him, outraged. "You have not been announced!"

A thrill ran through Vanessa as Rob advanced on her stepfather with flashing eyes and clenched fists. "You, sir, are a scoundrel! I have learned of your abominable treatment of Vanessa. It will cease from this moment on."

Her stepfather's mottled face went from scarlet to puce. "You impudent young dog! Who are you?"

"Professor Robert Woodcock, author and lecturer."

"Was it you who entered my house like a thief in the night?" her stepfather demanded. "Are you the man who debauched Vanessa?"

"I am the man who *loves* Vanessa," Rob answered. "And I am taking her away from here—today."

Mr. Bigbee gasped. "What of my little ones?" he cried. "What of Mother?"

Vanessa hurried to Rob's side. Without looking away from her stepfather, Rob put his arm around her shoulders, giving her a delicious feeling of comfort and safety.

"Take your hands off my stepdaughter, sir!" Her stepfather grabbed Vanessa's elbow and tried to pull her away from Rob. Raising his fists, Rob moved in front of her protectively.

"I hesitate to fight a man who is twice my age," Rob said. "But touch Vanessa again and I will not be responsible for my actions."

Showing prudence, her stepfather released her. Glowering, he said, "You will never leave this house with Vanessa in your possession!"

Vanessa raised her chin. "Oh yes, he will."

*****

"Thank you, Annie." Seated on Rob's wagon, Vanessa blinked back tears as she bade the servant goodbye. "I'm so sorry you lost your position."

Annie tossed her head. "Don't you be worrying about me, Miss Vanessa. I have plenty saved, even after toiling for that miser stepfather of yours. And Mrs. Skylar over on Bay Street has been wanting me to work for her for the last six years."

Rob stowed Vanessa's steamer trunk in the back of the wagon, then came and kissed the old woman's forehead. "Thank you, Annie. I'll never forget what you've done for us."

"Don't you be forgetting your promise, Professor—that's all."

He nodded and jumped up to the seat beside Vanessa. They both waved to the servant as she disappeared back into the house to pack her belongings.

Her soul swelling with happiness, Vanessa asked him, "What did you promise?"

He turned to her with a sly grin. "To name our first daughter *Ann*. Are you ready to head to the county courthouse and get married?"

"Yes, Rob." Tenderly she stroked his cheek.

His expression turning serious, he captured her hand. She sighed happily as his gentle lips caressed her palm. "Are you sure this is what you want, sweetheart? Are you prepared to be a wandering ne'er-do-well with me?"

"I want to be a wandering ne'er-do-well and then a farmer's wife."

He blinked, but continued doggedly, "You needn't marry me out of desperation. If you choose, I will drive you to another town and help you start a new life." His blue eyes darkened as his gaze met hers. "Marry me only if you truly love me."

She smiled. How could she help loving this man who had fearlessly stormed into the house and claimed her as his own? Who had told her parents he was taking Vanessa's trunk and nothing would prevent him? Whose righteous anger had intimidated her stepfather into handing back the money he'd stolen?

"Do *you* love *me*, Rob?" she asked.

"I've loved you since I was sixteen years old," he said, the serious tone of his voice allowing no contradiction. "And I will never stop loving you, Vanessa."

"I love you too—Professor Woodcock." She looked into his eyes, thinking he was everything she'd ever hoped for in a husband.

His passionate kiss made her heart leap with delight.

Sexual congress is one of the most beautiful experiences we humans can know, but it is only part of love. A marriage founded on love is a tiny piece of Heaven. Love that continues throughout marriage is the greatest gift we can receive and the highest emotion we can feel.

Professor and Mrs. Woodcock's Guide to Success and Happiness in Marital Relations (2nd edition, 1897)

RETURN TO XANDER
By Rowan West
ଛଠ

Trademarks Acknowledgement
※

The author acknowledges the trademarked status and trademark owners of the following wordmarks mentioned in this work of fiction:

Titanic: Twentieth Century Fox Film Corporation

Chapter One

The club smelled of excited women and raw men. Mia didn't particularly want to spend the evening surrounded by sweat and alcohol but, as maid of honor, giving the bride what she wanted was part of the job. Her friend Helen had wanted a bachelorette party on Ladies' Fantasy Night at Club Odeon, so here Mia sat, playing with a tiny paper umbrella and trying to make small talk over the pounding music. Although the club usually catered to a male clientele and had female strippers, once a week the tables were turned and male strippers took their clothes off for a female crowd.

So far they had downed three rounds of fruity drinks and been entertained by a pirate named Jack Spear-Oh then Officer Cuffs, the hot cop, and Mr. Grades-Me-Hard, the teacher you would do anything for to get an A. The exotic dancers were young, sexy and good at parting women from their money. Mia had nothing against a fun night out with the girls but she'd had a busy week at work and a lonely month since the end of her last relationship. Okay, maybe six weeks of sporadic dates and lackluster sex were stretching the definition of relationship but that was as good as it had gotten in the last couple of years. At least building her new business made her happy. It wasn't keeping her warm at night but she looked forward to work every day.

"Time now, ladies, for your next fantasy," the announcer broke into her thoughts. "Picture the scene. It's afternoon. You're relaxing on the couch with a book and a glass of wine when the doorbell rings. You're not expecting anyone but you go and answer the door anyway. And who should be there but Mr. Overnight—our special delivery guy!"

To cheers and whistles, out walked a hunk wearing a recognizable brown delivery uniform and carrying a huge box. A cap shaded his face. He started the dance moves that were already becoming familiar at this point in the evening, gyrating around the stage, making certain all the women had a good look at him. And there was plenty good to look at. Tanned and muscular, he must have stood over six feet tall. The low visor of his cap made it tough to see the upper part of his face from a distance but a shadow of stubble covered his lower jaw. Poking out from underneath the cap, his dark hair looked short and wavy, the kind that allowed a man to towel dry and instantly look great. When he ripped off his top, Mia saw that, unlike the other dancers who had gone before him, he hadn't shaved his chest and her eyes were drawn to the smattering of hair and the dark line that arrowed into his brown shorts.

"Come on, ladies. Show our man here some appreciation. Don't you want to see his package?" Shouts of encouragement and waving dollar bills followed that announcement.

"He's the hottest guy so far," Helen said, leaning over and talking directly into Mia's ear.

Mia nodded. He *was* very sexy and it wasn't just his build. It was the air of confidence and power that rolled off him and stood out in a place like this.

Helen waved a five-dollar bill to get his attention. "Let me give you a tip, big boy," she shouted. Mr. Overnight danced over and leaned down to let her put the bill where she wanted. His face still in shadow, he stroked her cheek. Then he turned and glanced at Mia as he was leaving. As he did, a stage light hit his face beneath the cap and she made eye contact with him. *Green.* His eyes were an undeniable "can't-get-it-from-contacts" green. There was only one man with eyes like that. *Xander.*

It wasn't easy standing up smoothly and moving away once he'd seen her. He gave a sly smile to another excited woman, thinking, *Of all the strip joints in the state, she had to walk into mine.* How appropriately clichéd. He was torn between dancing for her to make her uncomfortable or ignoring her to make himself more comfortable. Most nights he did this on autopilot, keeping his mind on the five-hundred-plus dollars that would be his at the end of the evening. He knew how to charm the ladies while he was onstage and a few extra private dances afterward earned him the money he needed to be able to focus on his art for the rest of the week.

With Mia here, it was suddenly different. He felt more visible, more exposed—which was ridiculous considering that his job for almost the entire last year had been to take off his clothes down to the tiniest of skin-colored g-strings. It was even more ridiculous considering that she had seen him completely naked many times. As he had seen her.

While his body moved to the beat of the music, he let memories of fucking her flow through him. Tonight, instead of the crowd's screams, he heard her moans. Instead of their lust, he saw the hunger and delight that shone in her eyes when she climaxed. For the first time since he was dancing, he let himself fully think about sex and, judging from the dollars he was collecting, it was having an influence on his new fans.

He ended his routine sitting on the box he had brought out with him, legs spread, the outline of his hard cock obviously straining the thin material of his thong. The women cheered and waved more money, which he took as he walked around. He was pleased when he saw Mia watching him as he gave them kisses on the cheek while trying to keep their hands out of reach of his body.

"Mr. Overnight will be back in a little while to offer you ladies some private dances so, if you liked what you saw, make sure you call him over to you when he returns."

Putting his clothes and the money he'd collected into the box, Xander tucked it under his arm. He came off the stage, using the side stairs, not the ones behind the screen that led to the dressing area but the ones that led into the crowd. Nearly naked, he walked directly toward Mia. His eyes locked with hers and didn't waver or notice anyone else until he was directly in front of her. He held out his hand and spoke loud enough for the group she was with to hear him.

"I need you to come with me and sign for this delivery."

From the moment Mia had recognized him, she hadn't been able to take her eyes off him. The tingles the alcohol and sex-charged atmosphere had given her were pitched into overdrive. She experienced every single of his sexy movements onstage as if he was making them against her. Suddenly warm, she was grateful she'd chosen a sleeveless shirt. In addition, she was having trouble sitting still. Squirming in the short skirt Helen had encouraged her to wear was also not a good idea since the fabric kept riding up her thighs. Part of her wanted to drag Xander offstage, away from the leering eyes of the hungry audience. Another part of her wanted to run into the night and get as far away as possible from the feelings and memories that were swamping her.

She did neither.

When he made that outrageous request and told her to come with him, she just stood up without thinking, put her hand in his and followed him. She barely registered the catcalls from the other bachelorette party guests but she did hear Helen say, "Go for it, Mia!"

She walked with Xander, winding through the tables toward the backstage area. Once they'd entered it, he stopped at a locker and put his box of tips in it. Then he pulled her into what she assumed was a dressing room since it had a star and the name *Candy Stixx* on the door. He flipped on the lights and she saw that the room wasn't more than an oversized closet with costumes hanging everywhere and a vanity table with lights around three sides of the mirror. The club music faded to a dull beat as he closed the door with a slam and locked it.

Xander turned her to face him. "I wish you weren't here," was all he said before he pulled her against his sweating body, cupped her head and kissed her hard. His heat brought her already warm body to boil. She threaded her hands into his hair and deepened the touch. She had never been kissed by anyone the way he used to kiss her and she had never dreamed she would again. But, oh, how often she'd thought about it in the past couple of years…

Mia moved her hands down his back, loving that he was almost naked already and that she could feel his skin. Hunger and desire coursed through her body. His hands moved down and under her shirt. She had skipped wearing a bra tonight and was grateful he had easy access. Xander played with her breasts, pinching the tips, making her gasp against his lips. When he removed her top, she allowed him to break their connection, but only for an instant. Then she returned to touching him, raking her nails over his back, giving *him* reason to gasp. Xander bent to suck on her nipples and she arched her back to press herself against him.

"Damn it, I want you," he said against her breasts, anger and passion evident in the words.

"I want you too," Mia answered. She was willing to let him know that bit of information but not how much she had been wondering about him, fantasizing about being in his arms again as well as apologizing for the way she had left him. That information she would keep hidden beneath the need she felt at the moment.

His hands traveled lower and found the edge of her skirt. He hiked it up and moved directly to her crotch. The thong she wore had a little more material than his, but not much. His fingers teased the skin at the edge of the triangle that covered her pussy. The slow movements were such a contrast to the fiery kisses she felt a flood of wetness drip from her.

"I need… I need…" She was unable to say anything else.

"I know," he muttered and swiftly slid his fingers under the fabric and into her pussy. Mia moaned and her head fell back involuntarily. His mouth found the exposed skin of her neck and he kissed what she offered to him. She breathed deeply, taking in the smell of his body, sweat and heat. It made her even wetter.

Without warning, Xander stopped kissing her and let go of her. He brought his hands up to her face and forced her to meet his eyes. "I will give you a choice," he said, his voice husky with emotion. "Turn around and face the mirror or leave now."

Mia didn't kid herself about what he meant. Either she could end things now. Or she could stay…and he would fuck her.

She turned around, bending slightly and bracing herself against the vanity table. The well-lit mirror revealed eyes that were glassy, lips that were swollen. She had never seen herself looking this passionate, needy, ready. The image made her feel too exposed so she looked at his reflection as he stared intently at her naked breasts then moved his eyes down her body. Mia was aware of every sensation as her skirt was lifted over her hips. She felt the tug as he ripped her underpants off. He did the same to the scrap of fabric he wore then pulled her back against him to play with her breasts. His erection rubbed against her ass, making her juices drip down her thighs. She let her head fall back against his shoulder but couldn't take her eyes off the image of the two of them in front of the mirror. It was a fantasy come vividly to life.

She reached behind to run her hands over his tight bottom while he began to grind against her, mimicking the way he had danced only minutes earlier. His body was perfect, so right for her. Nothing and no one had gotten her this excited since the last time she had been with him.

"Lean forward so I can take you," he whispered hoarsely into her ear. She did as she was told. He covered her body with his while reaching over to open what looked like a candy dish in the corner of the vanity table. When he lifted the lid, Mia saw an array of multicolored condom packages. He grabbed a black one and she heard the telltale ripping sound. A moment later he was nudging her legs apart with his. His erection pressed against the entrance to her pussy and she instinctively arched into him to give him complete access. With one forward movement he was filling and stretching her. This time her response was louder than a moan. She experienced a split second of clarity, thanking the crowd and the music from the stage that would probably drown out any sound they made. Then they started to move together and her thoughts were only for Xander.

She didn't realize she had closed her eyes until he said, "Look at us, Mia." Again she did as he asked and fully took in their reflection. His hands were on her hips. Her hands were digging into the vanity so that she could push against him. She saw the passion in his eyes and it matched the look in hers. The intensity, the desire was all there, clear as if spoken of aloud. *Please only let him see the need, not the regret*, she prayed silently. It was hard enough being exposed to him physically. She couldn't show him more tonight.

His cock felt so right inside her and they knew each other's bodies well. She allowed herself to get carried away by the sensation of being truly fucked. When Xander got into a rhythm, Mia felt one of his hands leave her hip and move down toward her pussy, aiming for her clit. He found it immediately and she let out a small scream. "Oh God, yes." Now she moved as if she were the one stripping onstage, grinding herself against his shaft, letting him finger her.

"Tell me," he growled as her breathing sped up.

"I'm on the edge, Xander. I'm going to come."

"Then watch," he said and her eyes met his in the mirror. He started working his finger faster on her clit and his cock deeper into her pussy.

"Yes, yes, that's it," she said breathlessly, knowing that her climax was gloriously close. And then it was there, surrounding her. For the first time in her life, she could see her face as she came and saw the satisfaction in his eyes. Despite the lights, her pupils were dilated. Her mouth opened to release a series of loud moans, her skin shiny with sweat.

"My turn," he whispered and she felt him move faster behind her, touching her deep inside. In this position it was easy to meet his thrusts and she did, aching to return the pleasure he had given her. His hands tightened on her waist before he moaned, "Oh yes." She stared into the mirror so she could see the familiar look that told her he was coming. It was an expression she hadn't seen in so long…too long.

As quickly as it had started, it was over. He pulled out of her smoothly and grabbed a tissue to dispose of the condom. Then he looked at her as if he wanted to say something but he decided not to since he remained silent. He moved to the door, ready to leave, not bothering to put any clothes on. When his hand reached the doorknob, Mia stopped him.

"Xander?"

He turned his face to her, keeping his body turned toward the door. "What?"

"I'm sorry."

"Of course you are," he said and left her there to get dressed.

Chapter Two
༄

After years of trying to put him out of her mind, Mia couldn't stop thinking about Xander. It was very helpful to have Internet search engines to locate people. Men's last names didn't change and Xander Alessio was an unusual enough name to find him easily. Mia stared at the headline. *Artists Make a Home & Living in Lowell Lofts.* The article discussed the different artists who had moved into a cooperative in Lowell, Massachusetts, where they could live and work in their own space, having open studio hours every week at posted times. Most of the artists who were interviewed had other part-time jobs to help pay the rent, an arrangement that let them focus on their art the rest of the time. Xander's extra job wasn't mentioned. She had spent the week trying to forget the hunger he had created in her but she couldn't help picturing his naked body every time she closed her eyes.

She probably shouldn't be searching for him, she told herself. But what had happened at Club Odeon wouldn't leave her mind. The rest of that night had been a blur for Mia. She had left the dressing room and found her way back to the bachelorette party where there'd been some good-natured teasing from Helen's friends who didn't know her and questions she didn't want to answer from Helen, who had recognized Xander once he'd taken off his cap. She'd been relieved that Helen didn't press her for explanations. Making some excuses, she'd told Helen she'd call her and gone home. There, she had dropped her clothes on the floor and slipped into bed naked, her skin still sensitive from her encounter with Xander.

During the next days, she'd tried to forget about what had happened but in her dreams she remembered it all—every night they were fevered and vivid. Her mind conjured up the same images when she was awake. It had been hard to concentrate at work or at home. Seeing him again had brought back too many memories, both good and bad, and for the last week she hadn't been able to focus. The only thing clearer to her than their encounter in the dressing room was recalling the way she had ended their relationship.

She'd been a second-year associate at Norris, Jensen and Lyons on the fast track to making partner when he'd walked into her office with a delivery of papers she had been waiting for. Normally she didn't notice the bike messengers who were constantly coming and going from their firm but his eyes had made her do a double take. And the double take had made him smile. She'd flirted with him for a second while signing for and checking the contents of the package, after which she'd forgotten about him. A few days later she'd seen him again when he made another delivery. The next time he'd left her a coffee at the front desk. It had been a fun but sporadic flirtation until she'd found him waiting for her when she left work and he asked her to dinner. Mia wasn't sure what had made her say yes, but she did.

What was supposed to be nothing but fun and sex had become the closest and most emotionally intimate nine months she had ever spent with someone. Maybe it was because she believed it could never be anything long-term that she'd opened herself up to him. He in turn had showed her a world of creativity and color, far away from the billable hours and deadlines that made up her days. It was also a world of sexual discovery for Mia. She finally understood why so many of her friends loved oral sex and she had been deliciously surprised at being introduced to the pleasures of anal sex. She would never forget the first time he teased her ass while he licked her. Her reaction had been so strong he'd made it a regular part of their sexual play until finally one night when she'd begged him to take her that way.

She'd fallen in love with his art, his passion and him. While they'd been together, everything had been wonderful but when they'd been apart, doubts had crept in, fed by friends and coworkers. The career-driven part of her had agreed with them when they said he was inappropriate and not successful enough for her. When she'd decided she couldn't take him with her to her cousin's wedding, she had also decided to end their relationship. It had been a horrible fight.

"Art isn't a way to make a living, which makes you a delivery boy," she had finally shouted.

"And what are you?" he had yelled back. "A robot in an expensive suit, following a path that has nothing to offer you but an ulcer and high blood pressure."

"I want to be with someone who understands my decisions, my commitments."

"Then you're right. We don't belong together, because I could never understand someone who actually *wants* a limited life."

Mia had left and spent weeks crying, certain that moving on was the right thing to do, no matter how much it hurt. A year later, she had started to date again and then six months after that, her mentor and boss had almost died.

Ruth Ann Lyons was a legend in the Boston legal world and Mia had been thrilled to work for her. When Ruth had suffered a nearly fatal heart attack, both their lives had changed. Mia had visited her regularly in the hospital, turning her room into a mini office. One day Ruth had said to her, "Don't make my mistakes, Mia." Mia had stopped what she was doing and waited. "Two divorces, no children and a partnership to keep me company at night. A lopsided success, don't you think?"

"It was harder for your generation to have both a career and a family," Mia had answered.

"Don't kid yourself. I stopped doing that a long time ago. I never let a man be more important to me than my job and both of my husbands knew it. They couldn't compete. The firm always came first. I hate to think I would have put the firm before children but it's possible. I have loved many things about my life but some of the consequences have been tough."

"I've never understood that marriage and kids are all that great," Mia had said. "My mom had no career besides getting married and having kids." She'd thought of her three stepfathers and two half brothers and half sister. Men who cheated with younger women or drank instead of having any connection with their family. What was so wonderful about that? To make Ruth happy she'd said, "I'm sure when the time is right I'll find the right man."

"That's a crock. The time will never be right. You'll keep finding excuses. You'll focus on your work, because you know how to succeed there and you'll avoid relationships, because there is risk and uncertainty." Mia had looked down at her hands. Ruth knew her well. "Even your female friends will disappear over time as their lives change and yours doesn't. If I had a daughter, I would want her to be like you. And I would tell her to find a way to have love *and* work and as few regrets as possible."

Those words had rattled in Mia's thoughts for weeks. Ruth had returned to the firm part-time and had agreed, after years of turning them down, to join the staff at Harvard. Teaching had brought her new joys and her students were the kids and grandkids she would never have. Ruth's happiness had helped Mia make the decision to start her own business, something she had thought about for years but feared because of the risk. She continued to be part-time at the firm, which meant *only* forty hours a week, and then at night she worked to build her new company.

Her business Forget-Me-Not had grown out of the insane schedules she saw her friends and coworkers keep. She helped busy people remember important dates, including birthdays and anniversaries. Mia e-mailed clients a week before the date as a reminder and then offered several services to go along with the reminder, such as mailing cards and shopping for and sending gifts. It had proved to be a profitable and fun job that she was able to start with very limited capital.

Normally she looked forward to stepping into her home office and working on something that was hers to create, but she had done nothing but the basics since seeing—and fucking—Xander.

Now, as she was staring at the computer, his face was on the screen with a picture of his loft in the background. Scanning the article again, she read that Xander had studio hours on Sundays from one until four. Maybe if she visited toward the end of that time, it would be long enough to explain to him why she had apologized at the club and to make a quick getaway. Then she could be done with him. He'd be out of her system once and for all, which was of course what she wanted...right?

The next Sunday, Mia kept wondering about the truth as she drove to Lowell from her apartment in Boston. For some reason she had been thinking of Xander for months, before she had even seen him again, and not only because she was lonely and sexually frustrated. It was because she knew she had lost something special from her life when she'd left him three years ago. She had never been as happy or close to anyone before and since. Mia regretted what she'd said on that last day. Today she hoped she would be able to fix that.

Lowell was easy to get to but hard to navigate and by the time she was buzzed into his building, it was a quarter to four. She signed the guest book at the table staffed by one of the other artists from the building. When the elevator opened directly into his loft, another couple was waiting to leave. They nodded to each other in passing.

"You're in for a real treat, dear," the woman said. "His work is fantastic."

"Thank you. I'm sure it is," Mia answered.

She stepped into the loft, the thick heels of her boots echoing with every step. The space was open and light, with exposed beams and poles throughout. Some of the poles had been used to determine where divisions between rooms would go. "Hello?" she called.

"Back here," said a familiar voice. "By the windows. You're kinda late. Studio hours are almost over but you're welcome to stay for a little while."

"Thanks," she said, now standing a few feet behind him. He turned quickly, almost knocking over the can of brushes next to him.

"Mia," he said coldly.

"Hello again, Xander." The bright light coming in from the wall of windows should have been harsh and made him look less sexy. It didn't. He was working and his passion for his art shone in his eyes and was evident in every line of his body. He was wearing jeans, an old t-shirt and was barefoot. Something about that was very provocative, that trace of bare skin that should have been covered. She fisted her hand in the pocket of her dress slacks to hold back the desire to reach out and touch him. "This is quite a place you have here."

"It suits me."

"It's a huge improvement over your old studio apartment."

"Yes, well, any place where the kitchen and the bathroom are more than two feet apart and I don't have to deflate my bed for the day in order to work is an improvement. How did you find me?"

"Online. The article on the new Lowell artists."

"Of course. You always were resourceful. Resourceful, hardworking and focused. That's what you pride yourself on, isn't it?"

"It was." He didn't seem to notice her use of the past tense.

"Looking to buy something for your office wall?"

"I always loved your work." She nodded to the oversized canvas on the easel. "That's beautiful. Stormy."

"It's part of a series I'm doing on the elements."

She stepped closer to the painting, taking in the vibrant details. "This one looks like fire."

"It is." He shook his head as if to clear it. "I can't do small talk with you, Mia. Why are you here? I'm certain you weren't accidentally in the neighborhood or didn't have a sudden need to see my latest painting. Did you come to gloat?"

"Gloat? Why would I do that?"

"First I'm a messenger boy, now I'm a stripper. I haven't amounted to much, just as you predicted."

"You're painting, creating. I assume working at the club is a way to make ends meet in the meantime, right?"

"You always were a smart one."

She chose to ignore his sarcasm. "It's clear looking around here that you are doing well and doing what you love."

"Yes, but it's been three years and I'm still not a success as you would define it, so you can sleep soundly knowing you made the right decision in leaving me."

"To be honest, I haven't slept well since seeing you at the club."

Xander put down the brush he was holding and wiped his hands with a cloth. "Well, that kind of honesty I don't mind hearing…and certainly wasn't expecting."

"You deserve that from me."

"I got a lot from you last week."

Mia blushed to the roots of her hair. "We did get carried away."

"Well, I always was good for a fuck, wasn't I?" She flinched but didn't answer. In addition to the other things she'd said when she'd left, she had claimed that the relationship for her had been all about the sex. It had been a way to push him away. "When you left the dressing room you said you were sorry. What was that about? Sorry for what we had done?" he asked.

"No, I was sorry for the past. For the way I ended things between us. I wasn't kind."

"You were a cold bitch who wouldn't give me a chance either to ask questions about why you were leaving me or to change your mind."

No arguing with that. She had been cold, felt that she needed to be. "I didn't want my mind changed."

"That was clear. You made the decision and I had to live with it."

"I had to live with it too," Mia said, taking a step toward him. "It hurt then and it hurts now. I was…" *Scared of getting too close*, her mind completed the words she couldn't say.

"So convinced we didn't suit each other."

Better he thinks that, she thought. "I know. You were different from everyone I spent my days with."

"Was that a bad thing?"

"I thought it might be. It made me uncomfortable and I couldn't afford to be distracted from work then."

"Yes, your precious career. More important than anything—or anyone—else."

"I couldn't see a way to make you fit into my life."

"Because you couldn't accept who I was, who I am."

"Because I couldn't think clearly when we were together."

"So you made sure you stayed in control and ended it."

"Is that what you want by way of an apology from me? You want me to give you control?" The words were out before she had a chance to fully appreciate their meaning. She knew she was in trouble the moment she saw the grin start on his face. When he stepped forward, she stepped back. He looked predatory.

"It would be a good start."

Chapter Three

❧

"It has possibilities, you know," he said. Xander closed the distance between them until he was directly in front of her. He took a deep breath, giving himself time to consider her unintentional offer. Her scent, familiar and intoxicating, filled his senses. He was torn between kissing her and throwing her out on her tailored ass. What made the decision for him was the thought of having her in his control. It was intriguing, exciting—and making him hard.

When she'd announced the end of their relationship three years ago, suggesting it had been about sex and nothing else, he had been devastated, although he'd refused to show it at the time. He had offered her his love, maybe not in words but certainly in actions. She had walked away from it and made it look easy. He, on the other hand, had hardly been able to breathe from the surprise and pain of the loss. Now she was offering him the opportunity to get even. How delicious…

He had been distracted by thoughts of her for the last week and it was beginning to impact his work. He had a gallery opening to get ready for in a few months and images of her as he fucked her had kept him from making progress. Having her here at his beck and call might get her out of his thoughts *and* provide some new inspiration. It could be a perfect chance to build an inventory for his show while he could treat her the same way he had been treated—giving him the advantage on both accounts.

He could see her now, posing for him, spread out in various stages of undress, calm and yet vibrant, her energy transferred onto the canvas. He would start with her fully dressed in those appallingly drab clothes she was wearing and then allow her to be slowly revealed. His fingers itched to grab her, a canvas and a brush—in that order.

"Yes, definite possibilities," he repeated.

"What does?" she asked. He liked seeing the uncertainty in her eyes.

"Buttoned-up Mia Belmont—the lawyer turned artist's model."

"What are you talking about?"

"You want to apologize. I need a model for the next part of my work. I was going to use a recommendation from one of the other artists who lives here but this is much better. You never agreed to let me paint you when we were together. You can make up for that now. Call in sick. You'll stay with me for the week and you can leave knowing you apologized for the shitty way you ended things."

"Model for you? How?"

"What do you mean, how? I'll put you in a pose and you'll hold it for as long as I tell you. Think you can sit still for that long?"

"Of course I can," she said, rising to the bait. "I meant, wearing what?"

"Whatever I choose. I have a few ideas in mind," he said, walking around her, taking in the possibilities she presented. "I can see where your thoughts are going. Yes, some of them may be nudes. It's not as if I haven't seen you naked, Mia." Truthfully, he hadn't thought of doing any nudes for the exhibition but now that she was here he wasn't going to miss the opportunity. He would find a way to make them work into the overall theme of the show.

"Naked in bed and naked while you paint are different."

"True. Are you saying no to the proposition?" Xander enjoyed the pause, her obvious discomfort. He was counting on her predictability. He was presenting her with a challenge and he knew Mia never walked away from one.

"How recognizable will I be in the paintings?"

"Your expressions only, not identity. Your coworkers will never know it's you." He saw her square her shoulders. *Got her*, he thought.

"When do we start?" she asked.

"We start now," Xander said, grabbing a pad.

A week with him. It hadn't been twenty minutes and already sparks of anger and passion were flying around them in equal measure. What would happen if she gave him what he wanted? She could make the time at the firm since she had plenty of leave saved that Ruth Ann had been encouraging her to take. She could do Forget-Me-Not work from any computer with Internet access. But her true concern was deeper.

Having him stare at her, see her. Mia had left him because she'd felt too exposed. He had seen and understood her so clearly when they'd been dating. The one thing she'd always said no to had been his requests for her to pose for him. He had asked repeatedly but she'd never agreed. Accepting his suggestion now would show him she was sincere about her apology. It was a risk of course. She already knew that being near him tempted her and made it impossible for her to think unemotionally. Could she be with him constantly for a week and then leave?

Xander broke her out of her thoughts. "I want the first picture to be one of you looking buttoned-up and lawyerly. Then I'll unveil you." She flushed at his words. "Put that satchel you call a bag down over there and stand by this pole." He pointed to the one near the window. Mia walked over and he arranged her with her back against the pole, arms behind her, hands threaded together. The position forced her to arch slightly, her breasts thrusting forward. "Keep your head back, chin up and look at me."

She did. The coolness of the metal of the pole seeped through her shirt and chilled her heated skin, making her aware of how easily and how completely she'd agreed to this arrangement. It was out of character and natural simultaneously. "It's hard on my arms."

"Let me know if it gets too uncomfortable." He walked back to his chair and stared at her. Finally he said, "Good. Stay in that position while I do an initial sketch." He picked up a charcoal and got to work.

"Sounds like you've thought about this."

"It shouldn't be a surprise. I always wanted you to pose for me and you've been in my thoughts since our…" he paused, "encounter. You know me—when I think, I think in pictures. Now you're here, so I am going to make use of that."

She didn't like the sound of "making use" but she couldn't blame him for choosing those words. Thinking about their time in the dressing room, Mia remembered a question and asked, "I've been wondering about something. Who is Candy Stixx?"

"She works at Odeon on regular nights."

"And how did you know she had condoms in the candy dish?"

"Locker room talk among the other dancers."

"So you never took advantage of their availability or hers before?" Mia asked, arching one eyebrow up.

"I like that brow up. Can you keep it like that for a bit?"

"If you'll answer my question."

"I don't typically go to the club on nights when I'm not working, so, no, I never enjoyed Candy. Not my type. She's a blonde with a few too many enhanced body parts. I prefer cool brunettes who make me work to get close to them."

"Now wait a minute—"

"Get rid of the scowl, please."

"I let you get very close…"

"Back against the pole, Mia."

"Said the stripper." She smirked and did as he said, although she added a shimmy.

"Stop moving your body and your mouth." Xander looked down at his sketch then back up at her. "The scowl, Mia. When I want to paint something called *Attitude*, I'll ask for that look."

This was going to be harder than she'd thought. When Xander got into a project, he was single-minded. It was something they shared. However, she had never been the object of that focus before and it unnerved her. She had never watched him work for any length of time. In the past, he'd finished for the day when she came over or he'd started as she was leaving. Now she had an opportunity to see his concentration and she found herself mesmerized by his intensity.

His eyes were like green glass, focused and grave. His hands moved rapidly, his body hardly at all. She had no idea how long she stood for him. It must have been over an hour, because when he put down the sketch pad, she saw that the light in the room had changed and the sun had gone down significantly.

He walked over to her and stared into her eyes. What was he thinking? What was he seeing?

"Good job. Thanks." Not the words she'd been expecting. He didn't move.

"You're welcome." She matched his stare with her own.

"You can let go of the pole, Mia." She did and groaned as her muscles ached in protest to the sudden movement. "Ah, a hazard of the modeling trade. Come over to the couch and I'll give you a massage."

The thought of his touch on her skin sent her blood surging to places other than her muscles. She had no control, only reactions where he was concerned.

Xander took her hand, which produced another moan. "Poor baby. Go sit down over there while I'll get some lotion."

He gestured to a futon in an area of the loft arranged for socializing. She sat down and realized that her legs and feet hurt as well. She had already dropped her boots on the floor when he returned.

"Take off your shirt and lie down."

"We're going to need extra room if I'm going to do this right," Xander said, putting the lotion bottle on the table. He walked behind the futon, lifted a latch and the back came down gently, creating space—and a bed. "Scoot over." Mia did and grabbed a pillow to put under her head. *She looks so content*, he thought. Even after staring at her for nearly two hours, he could hardly believe she was here with him. Sketching her had felt almost like touching her. Or so he thought—until his slick hands wrapped around her shoulders. There was no heat in a sketch. There was in a touch.

"Harder," she demanded.

"What?" he said, startled. He'd been lost in the moment.

"Your hands. A little harder, please."

He smiled. "As you wish." He increased the pressure on her shoulders and back and moved down her arms, pressing his chest against her as he did. She sighed softly.

"Do you do this for all your models?" she asked.

"Yes." She tensed under his hands and he smiled again. "I paint abstracts, Mia. You're the first live model I've used."

"Oh," she said, and he could feel the relief as she relaxed again.

Her skin felt wonderful under his hands and he loved the small sighs of pleasure she made when he did something she liked. It was time to do something *he* liked. He unhooked her bra and moved the strap away from her back. He worked the area then slid lower. Xander smiled when he saw her hips move in a sensual rhythm against the couch, a rhythm he'd like to feel against him.

What was it about her that made him ache with desire? He usually didn't go for high-polished women but the first time he'd seen her smile—her real one, not the one she gave the delivery man—he'd known there was more to her than the front she presented. No one could have such a sexy open smile and be truly reserved. All he'd done was bring her a cup of coffee and he'd been rewarded with a flood of warmth and possibility.

Warmth and possibility... He wanted that now but he knew it wasn't a good idea. She was his for the week. He could wait. Xander moved his hands down her back and into her pants, massaging the top of her ass. The moan he received changed his decision. No more waiting.

"Take off your pants," he ordered.

Mia heard his request as though it came from far away. She had been floating on the feelings his hands were creating. Without thinking, she responded by rolling over, raising her hips and allowing him to undo her pants and pull them off along with her underwear. It wasn't until she felt the couch beneath her naked skin that she was fully aware of what she had done. She shut all thoughts out and didn't argue...didn't want to.

His touch was wonderful. Her body had hungered for this attention and when he moved his hand down her stomach and trailed a finger toward her pussy, she willingly let her thighs part. His fingers moved lower and teased the lips at her entrance. Heat became wetness as she responded immediately to the caress.

"Does that mean you need more, my star?" he asked huskily.

My star... She hadn't heard that in so long. It was the endearment he'd given her, because he'd said she glowed from within. It melted her as much as his attention. "Yes. More." And that was what he gave her.

He adjusted the position of his hand so that one finger entered her pussy while another found the hard tip of her clitoris. Mia lifted her hips to give him better access. Sensations flooded her and she gripped the material of the couch as she started to grind on his hand. She couldn't believe how completely she responded to his touch.

Xander's body covered hers as he bent over and whispered in her ear, "You want even more than this, don't you?"

"What do you mean?"

"This," was all he said.

"Oh God!" she screamed as his finger moved from her pussy to her ass and sent heat coursing through her. The awareness of her own desires had been his gift to her and no one had ever been able to excite her the way he did. With his fingers still creating their magic, she didn't notice his weight shift and was surprised when she felt his mouth on her entrance.

Mia was lost. Her body was a mass of nerve endings. She surrendered to her reactions until she knew she wanted one more thing. "I want... I have to..." She couldn't finish the sentence.

"Tell me," he growled against her pussy.

"Touch you. I need to touch you."

His mouth moved away from her mound but his finger continued teasing her ass. She heard him getting out of his clothes completely one-handed. *Thank God for his work as a stripper*, she thought.

Xander settled his body over hers, his cock above her face. As she took him into her mouth, he rolled them both over so that she was on top. He began to lick her pussy again.

As she breathed in his masculine scent, her mouth became reacquainted with his cock. Mia cupped his balls with one hand, ran her tongue around the tip of his penis and was rewarded with his gasp of pleasure, which she felt on her pussy lips. His tongue and fingers were working together to bring her to a rapid climax. Not wanting him to be left behind, she increased her attention, fingering his ass gently. Their moans blended as they pressed their bodies together for deeper contact.

Soon she reached that almost magical point, the point where her muscles were contracting and climax was beginning. She couldn't hold back any longer. Mia took him deeper into her mouth to signal her near-orgasm and knew he understood when his fingers moved faster and his hips rocked, matching her movements. His free hand grabbed her waist and pulled her even closer. Her hand around his balls, she felt him tighten. Thrilled to know he was as close to coming as she was, she intensified her sucking motions and heard him groan "I'm coming!" against her pussy before he pressed closer to her mouth. She eagerly swallowed his cum and then her own climax hit in endless waves. Her cries were muffled by his cock but the experience was no less powerful.

When she stopped shaking, Mia rolled off him, boneless, satisfied and unable to speak. Her mind had wanted to move on from her past with Xander but clearly her body wanted to be with him. Her heart was beginning to feel torn between the two. After a time, Xander turned around so they were face-to-face. He cupped her chin and kissed her.

"That was…" she started.

"Yes, it was," he finished, running his fingers gently up and down her arm. "Muscles more relaxed now?"

"Definitely. The perks of modeling are much better than lawyering. You may not get a lot of work done if this is how all of our sessions are going to end." Mia wasn't sure what she had said that hurt him, but his eyes became cautious and he pulled away.

"Let me worry about my work." Xander sat up, looking for his clothes. "You can sleep here during your stay. I'll get you some bedding and call in for Thai food for dinner."

She nodded her response as he walked away. Mia had no doubt that she would want to be close to him again in the heat of the moment, but after the intensity of their passion passed, she was left with more questions than answers. She was going to have to do something about that.

Chapter Four

✹

"Wake up, time to get going."

"Mom?" Mia said groggily.

"Not quite. Here's coffee. Drink, put on this t-shirt and get up. The light's perfect for what I want to do next."

She did what Xander said—in the order he'd said it. It was Monday morning and she'd slept on the futon. While slipping on her underwear, Mia made a call to the office to let Ruth know she would be out this week then shuffled sleepily to the dining space of his loft.

"Sit at the table, please."

"Do I have to give up my coffee?"

"No, which I say is lucky for me since you look as though you'd do bodily harm to anyone who tried to take it from you."

"Damn right," she grumbled.

"This picture is going to be called *Waking*, so you only have to sit at the table as you normally would and read the paper. There's a bagel too, so feel free to eat."

"That's exactly what I can handle. Am I allowed to turn pages?"

"Yes, but try to go back to the same position after."

Mia sank onto the seat with one foot on it, her knee bent, elbow on knee, head in her hand. She was comfortable and soon relaxed. She had finished half the mug of coffee before she realized Xander had made it exactly as she liked. He remembering this detail hit her hard. He'd always noticed the small things and it had pleased and unnerved her. It still did.

It didn't matter that she was wearing clothes. She felt exposed again.

One of the things she appreciated about her work as a lawyer was that it required her to keep an emotional distance from clients and be professional with coworkers. She was good at façades. She had been ever since the first school counselor had asked if things were all right at home and she'd been able to answer "Yes" with a convincing smile. No need to tell anyone that her mother had been having an affair with her boss and was now heartbroken and unemployed. No reason to show them how tired she was from being the adult in the family.

In her new business, she rarely had to meet her customers since most work was done by e-mail or phone. Now sitting here with Xander staring at her made her feel far too vulnerable, even more than during sex where the sexual haze gave her cover.

"Bad news in Boston?" Xander's question interrupted her thoughts. She looked up and noticed his pencil had not stopped moving.

"No, why do you ask?"

"Your face. You look very serious and troubled."

Mia tensed, realizing she couldn't even drink her coffee without him noticing what she was thinking. She consciously schooled her features into a relaxed pose. "Same stuff, different day. I have to admit it's been a while since I've been able to sit and read the paper without being interrupted."

"Busy at the firm?"

"Nothing extraordinary. But I'm fairly certain I've kept still more in the past twenty-four hours than I have been in the past twenty-four months."

"And you don't like that." It was a statement, she noticed.

"It's not that I don't like it…"

"Oh, come on. Remember that trip we made to the Berkshires? Two nights to get away in the off-season, time to catch up on books we wanted to read, a chance to relax. Make love." He dropped his tone suggestively at the end. "You were practically pacing. You'd read for an hour, make notes for work for a while and then try to find a way to get Internet access."

"I had some ideas for a case we were working on that I didn't want to forget."

"You badgered the innkeepers."

"I did not badger." Xander gave her a steady look instead of a verbal response. "Okay, maybe a little but it was my first time away from the office in ages and it was tough."

"You had books, the great outdoors and me. Couldn't that be enough for a weekend?"

Mia looked at him and wisely, she thought, stayed silent. She was thankful when he went back to the canvas. She didn't have an answer for him and found that she couldn't stop thinking about what he asked.

She remembered that weekend clearly, remembered looking forward to it for weeks. He was right. She hadn't been able to sit or allow herself to relax. It was as if she had forgotten how. Assuming she had ever known. She had always been a doer. It was how she lived her life, the only way she knew to keep things in control. He was asking her to just…be and she didn't know how to manage that request.

Three weeks later she had ended their relationship which, she now realized, answered the question about whether he'd been enough. She shuddered at her actions.

"Are you cold?" Xander asked.

Mia took a sip of coffee to delay her answer. "No, trying to wake up."

"Never something you particularly liked."

"Nope. I'm still more of a night owl. I don't understand anyone who wants to get out of a nice warm bed. Someday I'll have a job that lets me sleep in every day."

"That will be an unusual law firm."

"Maybe it won't be law." She waited for him to look at her— He didn't.

"Yeah, right, Mia. Like you'd walk away from all the hours you put in at the firm of Work, Work and More Work."

"I might for the right reason," she said.

"Sorry, can't imagine it." He sounded so sure of himself. She decided to eat her bagel instead of answering, which wasn't easy with the lump that had appeared in her throat. She knew that he still believed she was a workaholic. For the first time, it bothered her.

* * * * *

Wake, eat, pose, eat, pose, work for Forget-Me-Not while he napped, eat, read and sleep. The following days had a lazy and predictable quality to them. Xander told her what he needed and she did it. Mia found herself enjoying having so few responsibilities. There was only one thing that was not going well.

It had been four days since he had last touched her. Technically they were sleeping in the same room since the loft was one big space, but she slept on the futon, he in his bed. She wore his t-shirts and boxers when she wasn't modeling since she had no other clothes than her conservative ones with her but that was the only part of him that was close to her skin and it was driving her insane.

Each day's poses left her physically and emotionally exhausted. She had never thought she was capable of sitting and doing nothing for such long periods but it was wonderful to be so close to him as he created. He would work long past the time she would stop modeling and she spent that free time reading. Every day while he was resting—having a "creative nap"—she was busy catching up on calls and sending out reminders for Forget-Me-Not. She hadn't found a way to tell him about the changes in her career, even though they spoke about nearly everything else.

Sometimes they talked when he worked, at other times music was the only sound in the loft. Xander usually stopped for a break around dinnertime and they'd eat whatever they could find or have something delivered. Since her arrival, she hadn't had any direct contact with anyone other than him—and surprisingly she didn't miss it at all. She loved being the focus of his attention. That was the most unsettling revelation of all.

"Are you going to invite your family to the opening of your show?" she asked over a late dinner. That evening's pose required darkness, so they had gotten a delayed start on the day and Xander had called the club to say he wouldn't be in that night.

"Absolutely. They've always supported me, even when they worried I might end up homeless and starving. Or worse—a lawyer." Mia laughed at the face he made, knowing that the ribbing was meant to make her smile. "What about you? Think your folks would want to see what their daughter's been doing for the past week?" he asked.

"I thought you said I wouldn't be recognizable?"

"You won't be but you could always tell them it's you."

"I could tell my brothers and sister, but my mom? No way. She's not interested in any event that's not about her. Unless you plan on painting her, don't expect to see her at a gallery."

"From your tone I'd say I hit a nerve. Sorry, I didn't mean to. You still don't want to talk about her or your family?"

Mia shrugged. "My mother wasn't the best role model when it came to mothering or relationships." She stopped poking at her food, looked at Xander and since he looked like he was waiting, continued, "Mom was either taking care of her newest husband or herself, so she could attract a new husband.

No one stayed in her life very long when it came to men. Her choices were terrible. As soon as I could get out, I did."

"You never said… How many siblings do you have?"

"Two half brothers and a half sister. I'm the oldest."

"And the responsible one."

Mia nodded. "Didn't ask for the job but someone had to do it."

He took her hand and kissed it. She was grateful for the touch and the lack of additional questions.

"So," he said finally, "if you're done eating, are you ready to get naked?"

* * * * *

Mia lay on Xander's bed completely nude, lit only by candles, surrounded by and leaning on pillows. She'd known when this week had begun that he would ask her to pose naked. She'd struggled with the idea at the time but tonight shedding her clothes felt natural, comfortable and, more surprising, it was exactly what she wanted. She wanted to be bare, heart and body, for him.

The setting gave her the sensation of floating. She could almost believe she was alone since Xander was hidden behind his canvas. Like many women, Mia had found the movie scene in *Titanic* with Jack sketching a naked Rose highly sensual and romantic, but it couldn't compare with how she felt now — knowing Xander was looking at her constantly and transferring what he saw onto the canvas. There were times when Mia swore his pencil and brush were stroking her skin, making her aware of every part of her body…including her heart.

Without her noticing, it had happened again. With every picture sketched, joke shared, meal prepared, her love for him had returned and grown stronger. She could completely relax and be herself with him — even complain when she was tired. It wasn't only that she didn't have to keep up a front for him, it was that she didn't want to. Three years ago, even with Xander, Mia had always looked for distance in her relationships, because she refused to be hurt or left. Being with him now was showing her that, by not risking the pain, she had also rejected the possibilities of deeper pleasures.

She wasn't aware that her emotions were so close to the surface until the wetness hit her ear. Being undressed didn't make her feel half as vulnerable as falling in love did. Days of sitting still stopped her from wiping her cheek and she thought that the darkness would keep her crying private until she saw him get up from behind the canvas. He walked over, sat on the bed next to her and passed his hand over the tear.

"Is everything okay, my star?"

She turned her face fully into his hand. "Everything is just right."

"I didn't believe it was possible," he said softly, "but I'd forgotten how deeply beautiful you are. How you glow." Xander leaned in and tenderly kissed her. His lips covered hers and her entire body softened. She hadn't enjoyed a touch this much since leaving him and didn't know how she had longed for such tenderness until this moment.

Mia reached out and threaded her fingers through his hair, deepening the kiss. He tasted so good, familiar, yet in this instance, new. She needed more and she wanted it now.

"Touch me, Xander. Please. I need to feel. I have to feel you, feel connected," she whispered against his lips. She was afraid he was going to ask her questions when the last thing she wanted to do was talk. Instead he kissed her again and she was grateful she wouldn't have to explain herself. *Not yet.*

"This is a nice switch," he said against her neck as his kisses moved lower.

"What is?" she murmured.

"You're naked and I'm completely dressed."

"Not for long, I hope."

"Definitely not." He shifted to his knees and pulled his t-shirt off. Then he reached for the button on his jeans but she stopped him.

"I'll do that." Mia gave him a playful push. He fell back against the bed pillows and stretched his legs out, allowing her to take off his jeans and boxers together. When she looked up, she smiled at the sight of him naked and hard, lit only by candles and the moonlight coming through the windows. "Now *this* is an image that makes me wish *I* could paint." She slid herself up his body, stopping to lick his cock and play with his balls.

Xander allowed her to touch him in this way for only a little while before he put his hands on her shoulders and moved her mouth away from him. "Oh no, you don't. Not tonight. Tonight I want to be inside you."

She smiled, moved up on the bed and straddled him. "Then be inside me." With no other warning, Mia took his cock halfway into her. She was wet and ready. Her reward was his groan of pleasure. Gyrating slightly, she allowed his shaft to sink a little deeper. She could stand the gentle contact for only a moment before she moved down on him in a rush, completely sheathing him inside her. His hips lifted off the bed in an obvious effort to be as deeply in her as possible.

"God, you feel so good, Xander." She moaned at the intense sensation.

"So do you, my star," he said, holding her hips, bringing her closer. Suddenly he stopped moving. "Shit, Mia, I'm not wearing a condom."

She leaned down, pressing her breasts to his chest, and ground herself against him again. "Then you'll just have to come in my ass instead." She knew it would be safe with him. Xander grabbed the back of her head and kissed her hard, giving her no chance to think about her boldness.

"If that is what you want then that is what I will give you." Staying inside her, he rolled them over. He placed her beneath him and within reach of his nightstand from which he took a familiar-looking little bottle. Moving slowly, he put his hands behind her bent knees and pressed her thighs back, forcing her hips up and exposing her ass.

He slid out of her pussy then, still facing her, repositioned his cock at the tight entrance of her anus. He squeezed the lube onto his fingers and gently circled her bud. The coolness of the gel teased her skin. When he put more on his cock, her breath caught. It had been so long since she'd had anal sex. Only with Xander had it ever been this pleasurable. He entered her gently but steadily, stretching her to accommodate him. A flash of discomfort came and went swiftly. Then all she was aware of was how filled she was, how close she was to him.

Once she completely surrounded him, they began to move together, meeting each other's thrusts and needs. Mia ached to touch every part of him. Her hands were first on his chest then raking down his back. She arched up as he bent over her to suck one of her nipples into his mouth. When his hand slid between them and found her pussy lips, she knew she would climax soon.

"Mia, love, you are so wet, so responsive."

"It's what you do to me," she said in his ear. "What you have always done to me."

"My body remembers the feel of you so well."

"Mine missed yours." She gasped as his finger moved faster. "God, I'm so close. Are you?"

"Very. Keep moving like that. Let me come with you." He leaned back slightly and rubbed his finger directly onto her clit.

Mia moaned loudly with the intensity of the pleasure. "That's it, Xander. Now. Please. More... Yes."

His hips slammed into her faster, matching the pace of his fingers circling her nub. When he screamed out her name, she knew he was coming too. Wave after wave of sensation broke over her and she pushed herself against him, wanting as much contact as she could get.

After a while, bending his elbows, Xander leaned forward, kissing her as they both tried to catch their breath. His skin was hot and sweaty and she was thrilled to feel his heart hammering against her chest. He shifted gently away from her body and rolled to the side.

"That was..." she said.

"Perfect," he completed.

Mia turned and looked at him "Are you always going to finish my sentences after we have sex?"

"Only if you insist on talking after."

She smiled and lay back in his arms, happier than she had been in years. It was amazing how she was able to simply turn off her thoughts and respond with her emotions around him. Nowhere else in her life had she been able—or willing—to do that. Was that the real reason she'd walked out on him? Had she been afraid to be that vulnerable? Was she really a coward? Mia wondered if after this week she would find herself taking new risks in other parts of her life but she was too tired to think about that tonight.

"Sleep here," he said. "Stay in my bed."

She answered with a kiss.

Chapter Five

Mia knew from the shadows in the room that she had slept late. Stretching to look at the bedside clock, she saw it was nearly eleven. She couldn't remember when she had last slept this late or felt this good. *That's not exactly true*, she thought. She knew precisely—three years ago. She had to admit that she was enjoying this casual living. Time had become more fluid during this week with Xander since everything was determined by light, not appointments. Walking over to the coffeemaker, she found a mug laid out for her with a note. *Gone to get supplies. Back in a bit. X*

She poured herself some coffee then, sipping her drink, strolled over to where his most recent painting of her stood. From the fresh smell of the paint, she gathered he had gotten up early and done work on it already. Sitting on a couch near where the canvases had been arranged, she looked at the images of her Xander had created. Although she had enjoyed being covered in sunlight—and clothes—for her initial poses, the new ones he had done at dusk and at night were becoming her favorites. She had never known anyone who painted by candlelight. It had been very sensual. Then again, everything in the past few days had been. Mia relished being awash in passion, creativity...and love. God, she was completely in love with Xander again. Assuming of course she had ever really stopped loving him.

Her week with him was almost up. They'd never left the loft and had eaten almost all the food in his kitchen. She'd be happy to never leave, to stay and be sustained on sex. Mia smiled, thinking there was nothing she craved. Well, maybe some chocolate.

Chocolate, shit!

Mia jumped off the couch. Mr. Howard's, one of her first and best customers, anniversary was next Monday and she was supposed to send a box of chocolates to his wife. It was one of his traditions on her birthday and their anniversary. Mia grabbed one of Xander's shirts that was lying on the floor, threw it on and headed for the computer. A couple of quick clicks and the order would be placed and in Mrs. Howard's hands on time. Then she could go back to being in Xander's hands.

And hopefully come up with a way to be in his life.

* * * * *

Xander had left Mia dreaming when he went out to get more acrylics—and condoms. He hoped she would still be sleeping when he got back. Images of kissing her awake filtered through his mind along with an idea for a picture of her asleep in his bed. He would call it *Sated*.

He'd had the best—well, worst—intentions when this week had started. He'd expected to paint her, fuck her and throw her out when he was done. The first two items on that list had gone smoothly, very smoothly, but the last would be impossible. There had to be a way to show her that they were meant to be together. If she could see how she had relaxed and smiled in the last few days, he knew she would stay. He would bet that she hadn't been this happy in a long time. He had to admit he hadn't been either, even though he had told himself he was fine. He would tie her to one of the poles if that was what it took to convince her that she belonged with him. That image made him smile.

The smile disappeared when he came into the loft and found her at his computer. She was deep in thought and didn't hear him come up behind her. He could see over her shoulder and knew she was online. She had at least three different windows open simultaneously. Accessing work, e-mail and who knew what else, he thought angrily. It was an all-too-familiar sight.

This was what she had done most of the time they had spent out of bed. Once the sex was done, the work began. And here she was again. Nothing had changed and nothing could ever take her away from that world. At the end of the week, she was going to leave again and he would be left with a pain so fresh it would be hard to breathe.

"Checking to make sure the firm can't do without you?" He couldn't keep the annoyance out of his voice and was too disappointed to care.

"Yes... No... Wait, let me explain." Mia was clearly startled, probably upset at being caught. She may have been enjoying her time with him but playtime clearly had its limits.

"Don't bother. I said you had to stay with me for the week. I didn't specify that you couldn't be in touch with your office, so I guess you haven't broken your word. Don't let me interrupt you." Xander turned and started to walk away. Damn, he was an idiot for letting this happen to his heart a second time.

"Don't walk away, Xander." He kept walking. "Please, it's not what you think," she called after him.

Xander stopped, turned and crossed his arms. The look in his icy green eyes made her shudder. It was terrifying because, if she couldn't warm him up, she knew she would lose him again. He spoke before she could gather her thoughts.

"Go, Mia. Run. Hide behind your cases and your motions and your future partnership. I hope you enjoy their company. I hope they keep you warm because as long as they are more important to you than a relationship, I won't be the one in your bed."

Mia cringed. That was the tone he'd used the day she arrived in his loft. She hadn't liked it then. She liked it even less now. "Xander, please listen." She breathed a sigh of hope when he uncrossed his arms and put his hands in his pockets. "I left the last time. You deserve to be the one to leave now and

I will accept it if you do, but I'm asking you to hear the truth from me first and not leave because of an incorrect assumption."

"I'm listening." She tried to read him but he was still closed to her.

"Everything you said about me that first day was true. My career was my whole life. I wasn't able, wasn't willing, to make you more important or even as important. Then I almost lost a good friend who had made similar choices and regretted them deeply. I decided to make a change. I am still with the firm but finishing up. What you saw me doing was work for my own company, where eventually I will be able to make my own hours and have a life outside my job."

She thought she could see her words sinking in. "No partnership?" he asked.

"Nope, turned my back on that possibility months ago. You were right. I was living without any real connection and I missed that terribly after you were gone. I didn't have a great example of what a good relationship looks like and there are times when I am still scared. But I'd rather be out of control with you than in control without you." Mia looked at Xander, trying to discern his reaction. Were his arms starting to relax? Did his legs seem less stiff? She hoped with all her heart he was hearing her.

"You've always been able to see the truth in me. See it now, Xander." She slowly unbuttoned the shirt she was wearing. "Please look at me." She let the shirt fall to the floor and stood there naked. "Please see me."

He closed the space between them faster than she thought possible, scooped her into his arms and carried her to his bed.

They both fumbled with his clothes, moving feverishly in their shared need to feel each other. As soon as he was naked, he kissed her hard, passionately, his mouth open. Mia responded by giving him all the love she had for him and taking all he gave in return.

Xander moved away from her mouth and kissed his way down her body, stopping to stroke her breasts, lave her nipples. Her muscles softened at every touch. He continued to sink lower until he got to her navel.

"Open for me, Mia. Let me see you, taste you."

"Yes, see me." She closed her eyes in pleasure, letting the sunlight swirl images inside her eyelids. His tongue gently sought her skin, a whisper of contact, as he traced the lips of her pussy. Her body flooded in response. Nothing was as torturously wonderful as the flicker of touches she was experiencing. The lightness was maddening and out of proportion to the intensity of her responses.

Mia had not thought it possible she could enjoy the thrill of his mouth on her more than she had in the past, but now that she had surrendered to her emotions, her body was surrendering as well. Every response was heightened, the depth greater than she had ever experienced. It was as if love had deepened her ability to feel pleasure.

Xander moved his tongue quicker and inserted a finger deep inside her. A moan escaped her as her hands grasped the sheets. She had a fleeting thought that she might shred them in her fervor. Then the flat of his tongue was against her pussy and she considered nothing beyond what she was feeling. Everything was sensation and every sensation came from him. Too soon and not soon enough her climax began.

"Xander, oh yes, I'm coming. I can't wait, can't stop."

"Then don't, my star. Show me your passion." If he said anything after that, she didn't hear it as she screamed out her orgasm. Every muscle in her body experienced the release. Control was an illusion and she was happy to have it shattered.

When she came down from her peak, only one thought was clear. "I need more of you. Closer. Now," she said.

"You have to wait while I get something," he said and she heard him running to the other side of the loft. He came back opening a box of condoms and had one on before he joined her in bed again. Without hesitation, he buried himself inside her and she lifted her hips to welcome him completely.

"God, yes," she sighed with pleasure. Mia looked into Xander's eyes, loving how he was so close he filled her vision. They moved together. There was no space between them. She wanted contact with every part of him—especially his heart. Thoughts of how much she loved him flooded her.

She touched him as if it were the first time, as if she was only getting to know his body, and she was rewarded by finding new places where he was responsive. The nape of his neck, the small of his back, the curve of his ass all received her attention. She was thrilled to hear him gasp when she found another sensitive spot. Never had she gotten so much out of pleasing another person.

"Mia, love, what do you do to me? I can't be deep enough inside you."

"I want you as close as you can be, in all ways."

Xander stopped moving and Mia smiled, hoping he could see the truth in her eyes. His mouth dropped to hers in the most tender of caresses and she responded fully, putting all her ardor into that kiss. Then she wrapped her legs around him, using them to pull him closer to her. When he began to move inside her again, it was faster, more intense than before. She knew he was building up to his climax and her body quickly responded in kind.

As always, he read her perfectly. "Come with me," he demanded. "Kiss me." She did both, letting him swallow her screams as she came again. His orgasm was close behind. His muscles were tensing beneath her hands. Mia pulled Xander closer and let him collapse onto her, loving his weight against her. They stayed that way until their heart rates dropped to safer levels then he rolled off her, drawing her into his arms.

"That was…" he said.

"Love," she answered and turned to face him.

"Guess it was your turn to finish the sentence. Do you enjoy turning the tables on me, my star?"

"Absolutely. I would never want you to be bored."

"I can't imagine that happening." They lay in each other's arms. "Do you mind if I keep working at the club to make ends meet?" he asked.

"As long as you stay out of dressing rooms with anyone other than me."

"That's a promise." He smiled at her.

"Do you mind if I stay at the law firm until my company is doing better?"

"As long as you don't let it take over your life. You deserve more than that. I love you, Mia. I love your focus and drive and how you let yourself go with me."

"And I love you. Your passion and vision and how you share it with me. I love how you see me."

"You are worth seeing." Xander kissed her. "Tell me you aren't going to leave."

Mia pushed herself up on her arms and looked into his beautiful green eyes. "Tell me you want me to stay."

"I want you to stay."

"Then I am never going to leave."

SORCERER'S SONG
By Cindy Spencer Pape

ಐ

Dedication

This one is dedicated to my husband and sons who put up with a phenomenal amount of weirdness. Without you I'd be lost.

Acknowledgements

Thanks to my wonderful editor Helen for her help and encouragement, and to the friends who helped me polish this manuscript on short notice – Judith, Janet, Anny, Steven, Sarah, and Christine. Thanks for being there when I needed you. And finally to my guys, for all the times they have to say, "Mom, can you move the computer so we can eat dinner now?"

Chapter One

Cian stood, taking his leave of his grandparents at the end of their holiday dinner. His grandmother smiled, spry and bright for all her twelve hundred years.

"The time has come," she told him. "Within the year you will have a mate."

With as much affection as duty, he bent down and kissed her pale, lined cheek. "If the Fates so will it, Grandmama. But I wouldn't get your hopes up yet. There aren't too many women out there willing to take on a family like ours."

"You'll see." She squeezed Cian's hand. "But you'll have to work for it, my lad. Yours won't be an easy love."

A chill passed down Cian's spine. He liked being single. He didn't want to hear that his carefree bachelor days might be numbered at the relatively young age of three hundred and six. But he'd never known his grandmother's visions to be wrong. He tried to return her smile.

She winked. "Ah yes. These old bones will dance at your wedding, before next Yule. Now go on with you. I'm an old woman who needs her rest."

* * * * *

From the balcony of his penthouse apartment, Cian looked out over the city. Waves crashed and rolled on the Lake Ontario shore. He loved Toronto, this young but vibrant city. It was a good headquarters for his various companies and charity foundations as well as his mystical research. Lately though, he'd been restless—almost as if there was something he was missing or something he was supposed to do. Maybe it was time to pay a visit to the family home in Ireland. Or even take a vacation, perhaps somewhere warm and sunny.

He listened to the waves and sipped his drink. His grandmother would have a fit if she knew he favored Scotch. She believed that nothing good could come from those barbarians across the Irish Sea. Cian considered himself a true son of Erin, but he wasn't about to give up his aged single malt. Not even for Grandmama. Barbarians the Scots may be—at least in her eyes—but they sure knew how to brew whisky.

Thinking of Grandmama reminded him of her prediction last New Year. He glanced down at the Celtic tattoo that banded his upper arm. Entwined in the knotwork was his sorcerer's mark. When that mark appeared on another, and his own turned red to match, he'd know he was mated. It was still green and black. So far, so good.

A whisper of sound brushed against his ear. Was it music? His better-than-human hearing focused in on the beach. There was something out there. Something almost…calling him.

"Black is the color of my true love's hair…"

A voice. Possibly the most hauntingly beautiful voice he'd ever heard. She was singing a song he'd heard back in Ireland as a child. It was a love song, but his mother had altered the lyrics to sing to him as a baby, in honor of his dark curls. The voice singing now, however, was seductive rather than maternal. It was strong, pure and richly feminine.

"His smile is like the roses rare…"

A deep powerful need filled his body, hardened his cock. He didn't understand it, but he had to find the woman who was singing. He had to see her with his own eyes and touch her with his own hands.

"He has the sweetest lips and the strongest hands…"

Closing his eyes, he raised his hands to the night sky and summoned his power. There was a blinding flash. Moments later the world re-coalesced around him and his bare feet touched the cool sand of the beach.

* * * * *

"I love the ground on which he stands."

Lyra lounged on the rock, her face turned up to the stars as she sang. She leaned back on her hands with her legs stretched out in front. She didn't know why she'd chosen this song, one she hadn't sung in probably a hundred years. It had simply emerged from her throat when she'd perched on the rock in the moonlight to sing.

She'd waited too long this time, easily a year since she'd last answered her body's call to summon a lover. Her breasts were swollen, achy with need, while her cunt was wet and wanting. She poured her heart into her voice and let her song soar to the heavens like a prayer.

She'd grown so tired of this existence, of her body's insistence on the meaningless cycle of song and sex. She'd tried other ways to find a lover—even dressing in human clothes and going to a singles bar—but it hadn't satisfied the demand. The siren's destiny required that she sit on the rocks in the spray of the waves and sing until a lover responded. Nothing else could calm the raging need that gripped her body and soul. She'd even appealed to the river god himself, Achelous, the father of the siren race. He'd dismissed her as if she was an adolescent and told her to solve her own problems.

As one song ended, she began another, letting all the longing she couldn't suppress infuse her voice. She rubbed one hand through the slick cleft between her legs, trying to assuage the pain of emptiness, but her own touch only made it worse. Gods, she hoped that a lover answered her song and soon. Someone with the skill and patience to make the most of an anonymous moonlight tryst. If the Fates were kind, he'd also have a really nice, hard cock. Her own pleasure wasn't required for the energy absorption magic, but it would be nice to enjoy herself while she was about it.

There was a flash, almost like lightning off to her left and Lyra glanced over her shoulder to see the cause. Her breath caught in her throat and her voice actually stopped.

She hadn't heard any footsteps. Where had he come from?

Standing barefoot in the sand was a man. And oh, what a specimen.

His hair was dark and worn in short curls close to his head. Silver moonlight glinted off the sculpted planes of broad shoulders, muscular chest and rippled abdomen. A narrow line of dark hair bisected the abs and disappeared into a pair of low-slung dark silk lounge pants. Lyra blinked as her eyes continued downward. Tenting the front of those pants was the most impressive erection she'd seen in decades, if not longer.

"Who are you?" His voice was strong, brusque. He'd succumbed to her call, but this was no meek spineless sailor. For the first time her song had brought her a *man*.

She wet her lips and pressed her thighs together to quell the ache which had grown worse at the sight of him. "My name is Lyra. And yours?"

He stepped closer to the rock, close enough for her to see his eyes. They were bright, almost luminous in the moonlight and they narrowed as he raked his gaze across her. He gave a single crisp nod. "Siren."

She bowed her head, wrapped her arms around her knees and let her hair fall forward to curtain her face. "Yes." He had to be a magical being himself to know of her existence. Moisture seeped from her core onto the rock as her need intensified. She'd never had a supernatural lover. Usually her song summoned only the weakest-minded of humans.

"Why have you called me?"

Unwilling to look up and meet his piercing gaze, she merely shrugged. The very fact that he was questioning her meant that he was not properly enthralled. She had no idea what to do, or how this had come to be.

Cian stared at the siren, trying to ignore the persistent throb of arousal. Even while his gaze took in the phenomenal body that reclined on a flat boulder and the flowing platinum hair that cascaded down her back, his magical senses spread out, looking for trouble. He'd made more than a few enemies over the years. This could easily be some sort of trap.

Nothing.

None of Cian's senses showed any trace of a third being braving the chilly fall air on the darkened beach. There was magic aplenty, but it all belonged to either him or the naked temptress. Even now that she'd stopped singing and lowered her head to her updrawn knees, he could feel the power swirling through and around her. It was almost as seductive as the sheen of her ivory skin gleaming in the moonlight.

An involuntary step drew him closer to her perch. He knew at once that he'd erred as her musky feminine fragrance tickled his nostrils and his cock stiffened even further. He'd never encountered a siren before, but his studies had given him a basic understanding of their nature. She was an immortal being who needed sex the same way humans needed oxygen and vampires needed blood. Or the way sorcerers needed magic.

But he'd never heard of a sorcerer being vulnerable to the siren's song. So he asked again, "Why have you summoned *me*?"

"My song summons whomever it wishes. I don't control it." Her words were spoken softly, almost as though whispered on the breeze off the lake.

He was inclined to believe her, but he was too horny to completely trust his own judgment. "Who does?"

Her pale shoulders shrugged and she raised her face to look up at him. "The magic controls itself, I suppose. It never occurred to me to wonder."

Cian took another step and brought his hand up to cup her chin, forcing her to meet his gaze. Looking into the soul of another being was dangerous, even for a sorcerer of his power, but it was one certain way to determine whether she told the truth.

He could feel her body tense at his touch and he could smell the thread of fear that warred with her body's obvious arousal. But she opened wide pale eyes and met his gaze.

Cian almost forgot to breathe. Staring into Lyra's soul was perhaps the single most intimate moment of his life. As he'd expected, she was a carnal creature, but there was no malice or cruelty in her makeup. She needed a man, but she would give pleasure in return rather than simply taking. She hadn't lured him here to his death. And she hadn't called him specifically. He could read the confusion in her mind as clearly as he saw the desire that coursed through her body — desire so powerful that if left unsatisfied it could literally mean her death.

There was something else there too. Something as thin and delicate as a gossamer thread that stretched between them. He could feel the loneliness of her existence and it called to something within him. For the first time he felt the solitude of his own existence and at the same time he felt a powerful need to protect and care for this woman who was so sad, so complex, so desperately in need of love.

She gasped and he knew she'd seen into him as well, though probably not as deeply since she wouldn't be familiar with the process. Before that changed, Cian broke the link and let his eyelids droop. He studied her lush mouth that quivered with every breath and he couldn't help but envision those plump pink lips wrapped around his rigid shaft.

"You want me." Her small soft hand caressed his erection through the thin silk of his trousers, making him even harder than he'd already been. Her quiet breathy voice was just as musical even when she panted rather than sang. "Will you take me then? Please?"

He heard the urgency in her tone. She needed this to survive and damned if Cian didn't feel almost the same. For all of about two seconds he thought about resisting. Losing control of his desires was anathema to him, but he knew he was going to give in. Instead of answering with words, he dropped his lips to hers and replied with a kiss.

Her broken cry spilled between them but was cut off as their lips fused. He slid his tongue along the crease between her lips and tickled. She opened eagerly, sucking on his tongue when it entered her mouth. He stroked deep, tasting, exploring and staking his claim. She tasted of the sea—salty and sweet and rich with life. Her tongue fluttered alongside his own. The teasing little touches only served to inflame him further. He retaliated by thrusting his tongue in and out in a blatant imitation of what he would soon be doing with his cock. Her hand clenched on his erection, squeezing him through the fabric, which he could feel growing damp where it rubbed against his leaking tip.

His own hands wrapped around her waist and drew her up to stand before him on the sand while his mouth continued ravaging hers. She leaned into him and rubbed her heavy breasts against his bare chest in an open display of want and need. He groaned and pulled out of the hot cavern of her mouth then bent lower to capture one of those luscious globes with his hand and lips.

"Yes," she cried out when his mouth closed over her tightly beaded nipple. Her breasts were generous and full. While the silky white flesh spilled over his hands, her nipples were dainty and petite. Hard as a pearl, the tiny bud fit perfectly on the tip of his tongue. He circled it until it was damp, then gently nipped with his teeth.

"Please!" She started to sway, caught herself by grabbing his shoulders. "I need you. *Now*."

"Not yet." He knew from the soul-gaze that she wasn't in imminent danger, as long as she fed sometime tonight. Cian was nowhere near done playing. For some reason it was crucial to him that tonight be special, meaningful for both of them, rather than just mindless sex. He leaned her back against the boulder and dropped to his knees in the sand. "Spread your legs."

Small but strong fingers threaded through his hair and gripped his scalp as she obediently widened her stance and let the rock bear the weight of her ass and lower back. Cian rewarded her with a leisurely lick along her gleaming cunt. She was as wet as the lake behind him. Thick cream coated his tongue and glistened on the skin of her upper thighs. Her pussy was smooth, with just two small tufts of damp silvery hair guarding her slit. He used his tongue to toy with the tiny curls and the edges of her puffy lips. Even in the moonlight he was somehow sure that like her nipples they were normally a pale shell pink.

"I could eat you all night," he murmured. He blew a gentle puff of air along her heated flesh and she writhed, more warm wetness trickling onto his tongue. Ravenous for the taste of her, he licked along her opening. His tongue probed deeper with every stroke. Finally, he speared it up into her channel.

Lyra screamed and her thighs tightened down around Cian's head. He smoothed them with his hands to ease them back apart. His tongue kept up the onslaught, thrusting rhythmically into her snug pussy. Every third or fourth stroke he paused to circle her erect clit. The tender nub poked free of its protective hood and hardened further with each moist swipe.

He knew she was close. Tremors began to course through her taut muscles. Her breathing was rapid and fractured and her cries had dissolved from words to whimpers. He slid his hands over the firm flesh of her thighs and used the tips of his fingers to part her pussy lips while both thumbs slipped into the entrance of her cunt. She was so tight they barely fit. He breathed in the heady fragrance of her musk and groaned. "Let go, Lyra. I want to watch you come apart for me." His lips closed around her clit and he sucked at the same time he stroked inward with his thumbs.

"Goddess!" Her scream filled the night, crashed right along with the waves as she came. Her vaginal muscles clamped down around his thumbs and her hips bucked beneath his face. He maintained the suction until the ripples of her orgasm had faded then he soothed her with a series of slow, thorough licks. Gasping raggedly, she sagged against the rock. "Thank you. Now please—I need more."

"Oh, we're nowhere near through yet, *leannan*. That was just the beginning."

"Your turn?" She stretched and made a sound that was nearly a purr. "I want to make sure you have fun too."

"I have been," he told her honestly, somewhat to his own surprise. He was never a selfish lover, but he'd never felt like this before—that his partner's pleasure was far more important than his own. "Watching you respond to my touch is a pleasure." That was an understatement. He'd nearly come in his trousers like an untried lad.

"Cian…"

He started, then realized she must have learned it during the soul-gaze. There was enormous power in a man's name, so he rarely gave his real one to the women he slept with. *KEY-in.* She pronounced it with just the right Gaelic inflection. The syllables sounded musical when she whispered them. Suddenly he couldn't wait another moment to be inside her.

He reached for the drawstring of his lounge pants, but she leaned forward and brushed his hands out of the way. The top of her head brushed against his stomach, making him gasp in a breath. He knew that she drew energy from her partner's climax, but that it wouldn't damage him. The siren's seduction was only deadly if she chose to use it that way. So why did it feel like she was reaching inside him to grasp his very soul? Something shifted in his chest. He didn't want to think about that. Not right now.

His pants dropped to the sand and he kicked them away from his feet. Warm soft lips brushed against the head of his cock and he gasped again. He reached out with one hand to brace against the rock behind her.

The sight of that pale head bent before him was the most erotic thing he'd ever seen. When her tongue darted out to lick the tiny drop of fluid from his tip, his eyes closed of their own volition. The groan he heard over the crash of the waves had to be his but he didn't remember uttering it.

"You are beautiful," she murmured between pressing exploratory kisses up and down the length of his erection.

He managed to bark out a rough laugh. "I think you've got that backward, *áilleacht*." Beauty. It described her perfectly—inside and out.

She traced her tongue up the ridge of his shaft then circled the flared head. "Magnificent, then. Is that suitably masculine?" He heard the smile in her tone and was unaccountably gratified that she could tease him even in the middle of mind-blowing sex. A warm feeling of contentment washed over him. Instead of warring with the sexual pleasure, the sweetness somehow made it even stronger.

"If you say so." He wasn't modest but she was a siren. She'd been with hundreds if not thousands of men. If she was exaggerating to stroke his ego, he didn't want to know.

"Mmm." She teased with a flicker of her tongue down into the weeping slit. "I do." Then she stopped talking to open her mouth and take him inside.

Cian couldn't have spoken if his life had depended on it. All he could do was push against the rock with one hand to hold himself upright and tunnel the other one through her thick wavy hair.

She drew him deep into the recesses of her mouth, surrounding him with wet heat. Her tongue toyed with the underside of his cock, right where the head met the shaft. Meanwhile her talented little hands were busy driving him to the very edge of control. One cupped his taut sac, massaging gently, while the other circled the base of his penis, sliding up and down in the same rhythm as her mouth. She sucked strongly, letting him feel the muscles at the back of her throat clench when she swallowed.

"I thought you wanted me to come inside you." He wasn't going to last much longer if she kept up this delicious torture. He could already feel his balls tightening, getting ready to explode.

She purred—there was no other word for it this time—around his cock, then pulled free with a loud slurp. Her hand tightened on his shaft, letting him know she wasn't done. "Oh, I think you're good for more than one round. I'm willing to take that chance."

Far be it from him to argue. With her he thought he could probably go all night and still get hard again. He threw his head back and clenched his teeth around a groan. Not only had she engulfed him in her hot little mouth again, she slid her index finger back away from his balls to press firmly against the sensitive nerve endings of his perineum and anus. With one deep breath she pulled him in farther, until he felt himself at the very back of her throat.

Stars burst through his vision. He couldn't tell if they were in the sky or his eyes. Sparks rocketed through his body from his testicles along every nerve all the way to his fingers and toes.

He called her name and then screamed his pleasure to the skies in Gaelic and Latin and whatever else occurred to him. She drank greedily, swallowing every drop of his seed as he jetted down her throat. The climax rolled on and on, until Cian wasn't sure he'd be able to hold himself upright when it was finally over.

Chapter Two

Lyra licked the last droplets of semen off Cian's only slightly softened cock. The bitter salty tang left her hungry for more. She could feel the warm pulse of energy under her skin, energy she'd absorbed from the force of his climax. And for the first time ever, it wasn't enough. Her need for sustenance was met, but she wanted more. A tightness like a fist closed around her heart. She was very afraid that she would always want more of this man—and in ways she'd never wanted another.

She cupped his balls in her hand, enjoying the feel of the soft crinkled skin and crisp hairs. Her tongue traced a circle around the fat flared head of his penis. To her immense delight he was nearly ready again. "On the sand or on the rock?"

His fingers trailed through her hair, then he hooked both hands under her arms and lifted her to stand. She leaned into him, rubbing her belly against the thick ridge of his shaft.

"Does it have to be here?"

His rumbled question took her by surprise. She tilted her head to gaze up into his ruggedly handsome face.

"Can you leave the beach?" He trailed his hands down to her waist then around to clasp the globes of her ass. Strong fingers dug into her flesh and pulled her more tightly against him.

"Well, yes, if you want me to. For a few hours at least." She was so lost in the warm glow of his touch that she had to think about her answers. "I need to be in the water before the sun reaches its height tomorrow." Half a day was the longest she'd ever been able to stay ashore without repercussions.

She'd never wanted to spend the entire night with a lover, though. Until tonight.

"Will you trust me?"

She gazed up into his eyes and saw nothing there to fear—just the promise of satisfaction and maybe—something more. "Yes."

He took both her hands in both of his and lifted them to the sky. He whispered a word in Gaelic and Lyra felt the sand fall away under their feet. Blackness shot with starbursts swirled around them and it felt as if all the air had been sucked from her lungs. Before she could gasp for breath however the sensations ended. The swirling stopped, the blackness receded and soft carpeting kissed her toes.

Cian's grip on her hands steadied her wobbling legs as she regained her footing.

"What an interesting way to travel." Her laugh was a little throaty until she caught her breath. She looked around at a luxuriously appointed living room. Leather sofas were grouped near the huge stone fireplace, a grand piano filled one corner and a wall of windows looked out over the city skyline. She stepped over to the window and gazed out toward the lake. "So this is how a modern sorcerer lives."

"As much businessman as wizard in this century." He stepped over to a bar built into a wall and lifted two stemmed crystal glasses down from a rack. He appeared utterly unconcerned that both of them were naked. "Do you drink wine?"

Lyra nodded. What was she doing here? Back there, on the beach, going home with Cian had seemed like such a good idea, but now she was not so sure. Just being near this man was a more intense, more intimate experience than she'd ever had before. Standing with him here in his home was almost overwhelming. She'd been in palaces before but it had been many, many years and so much in the world had changed since then. And she'd never been with a man like Cian. Tiny goose bumps prickled on her arms as she thought of the raw power she'd seen in his gaze and felt on his skin.

He was even more beautiful now that she could see him clearly, and after the soul-gaze they'd shared, she knew that beauty went all the way to his heart. His eyes were a brilliant emerald green, full of life and intensity. His chiseled face was a work of art and his body was magnificent. Tall and strong, he was a sculptor's dream. Even in moderate repose his cock jutted proudly away from his narrow hips. A tattooed band of bright green Celtic knotwork circled his upper arm, and even from a distance she could see what appeared to be black magical runes worked into the design. He uncorked a bottle and poured unexpectedly moderate amounts of the ruby fluid into the goblets. Then in a few long strides he crossed the room to stand by her side. She took the glass he offered. She was glad her hand trembled only slightly.

"To tonight." His voice was a soft caress that demanded nothing and promised everything.

She touched the rim of her glass to his and smiled. "To tonight." Why did she feel like she was saying "Forever"?

He gazed out into the night as they each sipped.

"How is a siren here in Toronto? I'd have thought you required salt water."

"No. Just a large body of water that connects to the open sea. My race originated in the Mediterranean area, but we lived in the rivers of southern Europe as well. Now we're spread all over the globe. Just like Irish sorcerers."

The corner of his lip quirked upward for just a second before his thoughtful expression reasserted itself. "And you live beneath the waves?"

Lyra took a sip of her wine and nodded. "Most of the time. I've tried living on land, but it's awkward at best. Being out of the water in human form takes a toll. It's easier to stay underwater rather than to have to run back and forth every day."

"What about when the lake freezes?"

She turned to face him, leaning her shoulder against one of the cool chrome window frames. Did he care where she would be several months from now? The thought made something tingle deep in her chest. "I hadn't intended to stay in Toronto that long. But I could live under the ice for a few months if I had to. I can take the form of a fish. I don't need to breathe air."

"Woman, fish or halfway between, correct?"

"Yes. The mermaid form is more or less my natural one, if I have any such thing. And you forgot this one." She set her glass on a small table and willed herself to change. She saw the look of surprise on his face as he looked down at the small white bird now sitting on his carpet. She laughed as she changed back into her human guise.

"A gull."

"Mmm hmm. Can't do the halfway step there though. The bird-woman thing belongs strictly to the harpies." Lyra picked her glass up and took another sip. The rich mellow taste flooded her mouth and warmed her throat.

An impish grin quirked at Cian's lips and she couldn't resist returning the smile. This man was appealing on so many levels. "You're not the only one with a few tricks, *leannan*." He gestured and his glass floated over to rest on the same small table she'd used. Then with a flash, the man was replaced by a raven with laughing green eyes.

She clapped carefully around the stem of her glass. "Bravo. Very nice."

He dipped his head in an avian interpretation of a bow and grinned again after he transformed back into a very handsome, very naked man. Then he looked into her eyes and the laughter in his gaze was replaced by heat. "Perhaps sometime we can fly together."

"That would be nice." It would be a thrill to soar with him. A wave of longing crashed in her belly. What would it be like to stay with one man, this man? Maybe even...forever?

"Would you like to go out on the balcony?" His voice dropped to a suggestive growl. "Or would you rather see the rest of the apartment?"

It was astonishing to know that the heat in his eyes had nothing to do with her song, and everything to do with the unique magic that seemed to have been created when their souls had touched. He knew what she was. He'd looked into the deepest corners of her heart and mind, and yet he gazed at her with that heady mix of desire and tenderness. She'd felt physical desire before, but never this gut-wrenching longing for one specific man. It was beautiful and horrifying, and she didn't intend to waste it. For one night she would know what it felt like to be treasured. She raised her eyes to meet his gaze and licked her lips. "The apartment, please."

He held out a hand and she slipped hers into it, enjoying the heated tingle that coursed through her at his touch. They each carried a wineglass in the other hand, and as they passed the bar, he caught up the bottle as well. He muttered a syllable or two and the lights behind them dimmed and went out as they stepped into a wide hallway, lined with artwork and small benches.

"Quite a collection." She recognized some famous names on the paintings, but she was too focused on him to pay much attention to the art. "Have you been at it long?"

There was a faint rumble deep in his chest. "Are you trying to subtly ask my age, madam?"

Her answering chuckle was brief but genuine. Laughing with a lover—that was a sensation as new as the tenderness and longing. "I suppose. Though I'm quite used to...er...seeing...younger men."

"I'll bet." He stopped at a door and nodded for her to precede him through. The muted glow of a dozen fat white candles sprang to life as he waved his hand, and a fire began to crackle in a small stone hearth. "I turned three hundred and seven at the autumn equinox. And you?"

She gaped in shock. She knew sorcerers lived longer than typical humans, but he looked no more than thirty.

He used the tip of one finger under her chin to close her mouth. "Surprised, my dear?"

"Quite." She shook her head. "Well, I am a bit older, but not very much. My race isn't the best at keeping track of time, but I was born just a couple of years after Catherine I of Russia—so toward the end of the seventeenth century."

"Then you're a very well-preserved antiquity."

"Likewise." She gave him what she hoped was a flirty wink.

Without her even realizing it, he'd drawn them up next to the bed. It was huge with carved wooden posts and a fluffy duvet covered in gold velvet. Red and gold velvet-covered pillows were mounded against the gleaming dark wood of the headboard.

He set the wine and his glass on the table beside the bed, then drew back the duvet to reveal creamy linen sheets. Lyra swallowed hard. Being here with Cian, in his bed, was very different from an anonymous fuck on the beach. There was something new here—something more than she'd done or felt before. Then she looked up into his eyes and forgot every one of her reservations. There was no room for doubt, not in her mind or her heart. There was only room for him.

The bed was high off the ground, and Lyra wasn't very tall by human standards. Cian solved that problem by placing one hand on either side of her waist and lifting her to sit on the mattress, which proved firmer than she'd expected, but with a soft downy layer on top. She drained the last of the wine from her glass, then handed it to Cian who set it on the table and moved to stand between her legs.

The crisp dark hairs on his thighs rasped against the soft skin of hers, but she didn't mind. She trailed one hand through the hair on his chest while the other reached up to rest on his shoulder.

"You're even more beautiful in my bed than you were on the beach." His voice was a deep rumble she could feel vibrating in his chest. "I wish I could keep you here for more than one night."

How she wished that too! At the moment though, she was too far gone to reply. Then words became unnecessary as he bent his head and took her lips in a kiss so passionate she nearly forgot her own name.

She'd been aroused before she'd started singing—that was part of her siren's nature. When Cian had appeared, she'd gotten even hotter, and what they'd done on the beach had only left her wanting more. Her nipples were beaded into points rasping against his firm chest. Her pussy was wet and clenching with need. As Cian's tongue stroked possessively into her mouth, seeking, exploring, claiming, she tightened her legs around his, drawing his hips closer to her aching flesh.

The height of the bed was perfect, she discovered. His massive erection prodded her lower belly, and she knew that with just a small shift, it could be right where she needed it. She wriggled helplessly, wanting his cock, but unwilling to give up the drugging glory of his kiss. She wrapped both arms around his neck and ground her pelvis into his.

Cian's lips finally left hers, trailing down to nibble at the sensitive tendons of her neck. Lyra cried out as he nipped softly. His talented hands slid up from her waist to cup the sides of her breasts, and she drew back just enough to allow him to grasp her nipples between his forefingers and thumbs.

"Oh, Cian." The sensations speared from her nipples to her womb. She pulsed her mound against his penis, begging for more.

"Soon, *leannan*." Then he dipped his mouth to her breast and laved one pebbled bud with his tongue before drawing back to blow on it softly. He shifted his hands and treated her other breast to the same attention, following the warm puff of air with wet, hungry kisses.

When he drew the tortured peak deep into the hot recesses of his mouth and suckled strongly, Lyra moaned and fell back against the sheets. Her hands fisted in his hair and drew him with her. He didn't even pause in his ministrations, just braced himself above her with one strong hand.

Lyra's head tossed from side to side. Her back arched up to lift her breasts into his touch and she held his head close with both hands. He shifted back to the other nipple and feasted on that one for a moment. His cock poked straight ahead, now poised right where Lyra needed it. The fat bulbous head grazed her slick, swollen lips with each upward pulse of her hips.

"Please." Her request came out as a fractured whimper. "Please."

"Tell me what you want, *áilleacht*." He swayed his pelvis so that his erection brushed more firmly against her mound, but not hard enough for her to take him in. "Tell me and it is yours."

"I want you," she gasped, straining to capture his cock with her weeping cunt.

"How do you want me?" His own tone was dark and thick with arousal. "Tell me you want my cock, Lyra."

"I do. I want it so badly I can barely breathe."

"Say it."

"I want your cock. I need you to take me, Cian. I crave the feel of your rod inside my cunt. Filling me. Fucking me." The words were nearly as erotic as his touch and she felt a fresh trickle of moisture seeping from her already drenched slit.

He groaned and gave her nipple one last lick before moving back up to kiss her mouth. "Thank you." He levered his upper body back into a standing position and used one hand to rub the head of his cock around her entrance, wetting it even further with her juices. Then with one powerful flex of his thighs he drove inside, sheathing himself to the hilt in her passage.

Lyra screamed. She'd never felt so stuffed in all her years. No man had ever filled her so completely, so perfectly. Her muscles clenched around him greedily, as if she could hold him inside like this for all eternity. She knotted her hands in the bedclothes and felt the wet trace of a tear trickle down her cheek.

"Perfect." Cian held himself balls-deep in the snug heat of Lyra's pussy and let the pleasure wash through his body. He'd had plenty of women in the last three centuries, but none had ever made him feel like this. It was as though their bodies had been made specifically to fit together. More than that, sliding into the warmth of Lyra's body felt oddly like coming home. It felt right, in more ways than his sex-hazed brain could begin to process. He knew—in the tiny corner of his mind still capable of thinking—that he could stay like this, buried in her body, for the rest of his life.

He slid one hand under each of her knees and pulled her closer to the edge of the bed, allowing his cock to nudge just a tiny bit deeper. He didn't know if the groan he heard was hers or his. Her legs wrapped around his waist and he gripped her soft full buttocks in his hands. He'd never get tired of this, of her. He truly wished tonight never needed to end.

Eventually however his body demanded that he move. As slowly as he could, he pulled back out of Lyra's channel, until only the tip of his penis was lodged inside. She whimpered, bucking her hips as if in protest, but he held her in place with his hands. When her motions quieted, he rewarded her and himself, by pushing back in as far as he could go. Her eyes closed and her head lolled against the sheets.

Her flesh was slick and wet but her inner walls gripped him tightly and made him feel every bit of the incredible friction as he slowly stroked in and out. Lyra's breathy cries broke over him with every thrust, urging him on.

"You're so wet, so tight, so warm." One hand came around to slip between her lips and find her tautly budded clit. "Your pussy fits my cock like a custom-made glove."

"Fuck. Me. Cian." He'd pushed back the hood of her clit and started rubbing the tiny beaded nub in counterpoint to the rhythm of his cock. He was thrilled that she had to pause and gasp between each word.

"I will, *leannan*. All night, and all day." He refused to utter the words "until you have to leave".

He picked up speed, unable to stop himself from pounding into her harder and faster. She dug her heels into his ass and strained into every stroke.

He felt his balls tighten as they slapped against her ass. They were ready to burst, so full he wasn't sure he'd survive the blast. Lyra's pussy began to twitch as her spine tightened in preparation for her own climax. He leaned down and took one shell-pink nipple between his teeth at the same time as his fingers pinched her clit. She screamed her pleasure, calling his name over and over as he slammed his cock into her one last time, feeling every pulse of her muscles. Her channel gripped and milked his shaft hungrily, pulling the seed up out of his balls with explosive force. He held himself deep, letting her clasp him close while he filled her over and over with rivers of hot fluid.

When the orgasm finally subsided, he discovered that Lyra continued to pant and pulse around him, aftershocks coursing through her limp, sweat-sheened body. He eased himself down on top of her, then rolled, bringing her to rest on his chest. His penis was semi-erect inside her heated core.

"All right, beautiful?" He kissed the tear away from her cheek.

"Marvelous," she hummed. She snuggled her head down into the hollow of his neck. "Thank you."

"Once again, I think you've gotten it backward. Thank you."

She didn't reply, so Cian touched her cheek, hoping he hadn't offended her. "Lyra? *Leannan?*"

Again, no answer. Then he heard a faint sniffle that could almost have been—no, it was, there was no doubt about it—a snore. She'd fallen asleep cradled in his arms, his cock nestled in her pussy.

Cian smiled and waved a hand, dousing the candles and the fire with one motion. Another slight gesture brought the duvet up around them both as he rearranged them to rest properly on the bed. She'd said she'd be fine until noon. Might as well let her get some rest before he wore her out all over again.

He curled his arms around her and wondered what it would be like to be able to hold her like this every night for the rest of his life.

Chapter Three

෩

Lyra awoke to the most wonderful sensations she'd ever felt. Her body was cocooned in soft silky warmth. The source of the heat lay close to her right side and it felt like a pair of agile lips were caressing the underside of her breast and toying with her nipple.

Her eyes shot open as she realized that she'd been exactly right. She was in a human bed mounded with covers and pillows, and burrowed beneath was a very big, very warm man—who was licking his way around her already swollen and needy breast.

"Cian?"

He responded with a warm chuckle from under the bedding. "I should hope so. Otherwise he's going to be very angry to find another man in his bed."

Lyra rolled her eyes but allowed him a tiny laugh. Teasing while lovemaking was a novel experience—it didn't often go with anonymous quickies on the beach, and a warm happy emotion flooded her heart. "Is it morning yet?"

Cian detached his mouth from her flesh and moved to join her against the pillows. A few of the candles flickered to life, illuminating his face. His dark curls were tousled from sleep and exertion, but she didn't think any man had ever looked better. "Only in a technical sense. It won't be dawn for several hours yet."

"So why are we awake?" She couldn't keep the smile off her face while she teased. Even now his hands were busy caressing her waist and thighs under the covers.

"I was hungry."

Goddess, she loved that deep seductive growl.

"I assume you have food in this house." A tiny giggle escaped her lips as he gave her a fierce mock glower. Then he winked and shot her a wicked grin.

"As a matter of fact…"

He sat up, dislodging the duvet from around their shoulders. Lyra moved closer to Cian's heated skin to replace the missing warmth. What was he up to now?

Cian muttered a word under his breath, igniting more of the candles. A crystal bowl appeared in his hand, full of some mud-colored substance. After another word, two silver spoons glinted on the bed.

"What is that?" Lyra sat, the chill air forgotten in her curiosity.

"Just a little snack." He spooned out some of the muck—it really did resemble mud—and held it to her lips. "Taste."

She'd trusted him this far, and been rewarded beyond her wildest dreams. If he wanted to feed her mud, she'd at least give it a try. Obediently she opened her mouth and took a tiny taste.

Oh! It was the sweetest most delicious mud she'd ever encountered. When the mouthful had melted away, Lyra practically wept. "Ambrosia! What is this?" Eagerly she took the other spoon which Cian held out. She scooped up as much as the spoon would hold and sucked it into her mouth, then used her tongue to lick every last particle off the silver. She squeezed her eyes shut to better savor the rich creamy sweetness.

Cian made a noise somewhere between a strangled groan and a laugh. "That, my dear, is chocolate mousse. My grandmother was here for lunch yesterday, and she has quite a sweet tooth. My housekeeper likes to indulge her with a variety of goodies."

"Your housekeeper could be a chef to the gods." She inhaled another bite. "This is the most wonderful thing I have ever tasted." She'd heard of chocolate, of course, but she'd had relatively few opportunities to sample human cuisine. Now she understood why women craved the stuff.

She had demolished at least a third of the bowl before she noticed he was not eating, but watching her with a fondly amused smile on his handsome face. She paused with the spoon halfway to her mouth.

"Are you not having any?"

He licked his lips. "When you're finished I'll have my share. I've a mind to eat it from something other than the dish."

"What do you mean?"

His smoldering gaze made her breath catch in her throat. "Like this." He took the spoon from her unresisting fingers and turned it toward her chest. Then very carefully, he daubed the rich chocolate cream on the tips of each of her breasts and set the spoon back into the dish.

"Oh." The mousse was cool and thick. Her nipples hardened instantly at the sensation.

With slow deliberation he set the bowl aside and turned back to Lyra. Her body had frozen in expectation.

Cian lifted one of her heavy breasts and cradled it in his hand, then slowly lowered his mouth to the coated peak. With long, leisurely flicks of his tongue, he cleaned the confection off her nipple, leaving it wet, beaded and aching for more. Then he turned his attention to the other side, laving it with just as much care and precision.

Lyra whimpered at the exquisite beauty of his gentle touch and braced her hands behind her on the pillows for support.

"Ummm—you're right," he murmured. "Perfection." He snaked one long arm back to scoop up a dollop of the mousse on his finger and rubbed it onto her lips. She parted them to lick the creamy treat inside, but before she could, he was there, nibbling the chocolate from her mouth and rubbing his tongue along hers to share the taste.

Distracted by his kiss, she didn't notice he had stripped the covers completely back and collected even more of the mousse until she felt something cool and wet filling her navel. She tore her lips from his to gasp, but barely had time before he was using his finger to paint a chocolate line down her belly straight to her mound, which he covered with a thick chocolaty coat.

"Mmm. Chocolate mousse has never tasted so good," he murmured as he moved down. His tongue dipped into her bellybutton, scooping out every drop and tenderly bathing her skin. "Nearly as delicious as you."

"Be my guest." She let herself fall back to the pillows and gave herself up to the pleasure he created with his talented hands and mouth.

By the time her mons was completely cleaned, she was whimpering and writhing, desperate to have him touch her even more intimately. Her body's need for the sustenance of sex was completely absent—he'd more than taken care of that the night before. What she felt now was simple desire for *him*. Not just for sex, but for Cian. She wanted him in a way she'd never wanted anyone else. It was almost as if— No! It couldn't be. Sirens didn't fall in love. It wasn't allowed. Focusing back on the physical, she lifted her hips off the mattress to meet the first swipe of his tongue between her moistened labia.

"Need more chocolate, right here." He dipped his finger once more into the bowl and ran it down the seam of her lips, just barely darting inside to flavor her cunt as well.

"Yes," she moaned.

He knew exactly what she needed—where to touch and when and how hard. He licked away the chocolate, then his tongue delved inside for several long slow tastes.

"Come for me, *leannan*. I want to watch you this time in the light." At his words the candles flared to a greater brightness, illuminating the room almost as if it were day. She looked down to see his intense green eyes sparking up at her from between her legs. Then he cast her that wicked smile of his and bent to capture her clit between his lips and suck.

Her orgasm burst so suddenly she hadn't even felt it coming. Every muscle clenched and fireworks exploded in her body and mind. She cried out his name and tugged at his hair with her hands, desperate to bring him up to kiss her, to bury his rod in her channel. She needed to feel him inside her almost more than she needed to breathe.

Cian must have understood. With a featherlight kiss on her mound, he moved up to cover her, sliding deep into her core with one smooth thrust. He took her mouth in a wet carnal kiss but otherwise held himself motionless until she stopped spasming around his cock. Then he began to move in short powerful strokes. She wrapped her legs up around him, locking her ankles about his waist. Her arms wound around his broad chest and her fingernails dug into his skin as she kissed him back and met him thrust for thrust.

The steady pulse of his strong body into hers drove her higher than she'd ever been. This time she felt the climax beginning in her fingers and toes and coiling into a solid mass at her center. The universe contracted down to include nothing but the two of them and this raw, primitive act. He stretched her to the point of pain, pounded deep and hard against her womb, but she didn't care. There would be time to be sore tomorrow. The only thing that mattered now was reaching that elusive peak before she expired from sheer sensory overload.

Then the swirling vortex finally sucked her in and time itself ceased to exist. There were no words to describe the rush of raw ecstasy that burst from the core of her and sent her hurtling out to the stars. She thought she heard a shout—it may have been in Gaelic. She may have heard her own voice screaming. She couldn't be sure. She did feel the hot wet splash of Cian's seed as he poured his essence into her, claiming her, marking her as his own.

She also felt the warmth of his arms as they enfolded her and rolled her to rest against his chest. She heard him murmur a few words and the sticky chocolate mousse disappeared from sheets and skin. She kissed his shoulder and snuggled her head more comfortably against his neck. For just a few moments as she drifted off, she allowed herself to imagine what it would be like to fall asleep in his arms night after night—and to wake with him beside her every dawn.

* * * * *

It was late morning when Cian woke again. He immediately felt something lacking but for that first hazy moment he couldn't get a grip on what.

Lyra. He'd spent half the night lying beside her watching her sleep. Hour after hour he'd pondered how to bridge the gap between their worlds. After only a few short hours she'd become so important that he couldn't imagine just letting her go without a fight.

So where was she? Her absence was an almost physical pain.

Golden sunlight streamed through the opened drapes and he blinked hard. Ah. Lyra sat on the waist-high marble windowsill, wrapped in his black silk bathrobe. His world settled back into place. She hadn't left him. Even in the light of day she was stunning. Her eyes, the clear blue-gray of the sea on a cloudy day, gazed at him with an expression both troubled and fond.

"Good morning." His cock hardened instantly at the sight of her. He inhaled her rich scent which clung to his sheets and his skin.

"Good morning, Cian." A trace of humor touched her smile. "I take it you slept well."

"I did." He rolled to his feet and was by her side in a few quick strides. He pulled her into his arms for a brief but ruthless kiss. They were both breathing hard by the time he stepped away. "I'm sorry if you didn't."

"I slept beautifully," she corrected him. She trailed one finger across his lips then fingered the lapel of the robe. "I only woke a few minutes ago. You seemed so peaceful and the sunshine was too lovely to resist. So I helped myself to the robe."

"You're welcome as long as I get to take it off you." He checked the clock and was relieved to find they had almost two hours left before noon.

"Last night was not enough?" From the way her breathing quickened, he didn't think she was finished either.

But right now he wanted to be serious for a moment. He leaned against the windowsill took both of her hands in his, then waited until she raised her eyes to his. "Last night was…amazing. And unless I'm very, very, wrong it was out of the ordinary for you as well." He wanted to say more, but knew it was too soon. He couldn't possibly have fallen in love during one night of nonstop sex. Except that he had.

She met his gaze and the intensity of her emotions was more blinding than the morning sun. "It was more than extraordinary for me. Nothing, ever, has come close. Thank you."

"My pleasure. And I mean that literally in this case." He squeezed her hands and maintained the eye contact so she would know he was serious. "Last night was a wonderful beginning, but it was only a beginning. I want to see you again." Which was perhaps the greatest understatement he'd ever uttered. He needed to see her again — needed it more than he needed to breathe.

"But…"

"I know it will be complicated. We are neither of us easy creatures. But I'm willing to make the effort. If you'll have me,

I'll meet you at the rock again tonight. Perhaps we could fly somewhere."

"Oh, Cian." Tears welled up in her sea-colored eyes. He could sense her hesitation as she processed all the reasons why they both knew this relationship could never be. And yet, he saw something that looked like hope in her expression. He prayed that she wanted there to be a future for them, that she'd fallen as he had. She shook her head and opened her mouth but no sound came out. Finally she sniffed and nodded. "Of course."

"Thank you." Relief rushed through him and weakened his knees. Now at least he would have time to convince her that they could find a way to bridge the gap between their worlds.

He drew her to her feet and into a kiss no less passionate than any that had gone before, though it was infinitely more tender and sweet. Love, he noted in the back of his mind, had a very strange effect on a man, sorcerer or not. "Would you like breakfast or a shower first?" Or sex, though he left that one unspoken, much to the dismay of his cock which prodded against her hip.

"I saw your bathroom," she admitted, slanting him a flirtatious grin. "The shower has definite…possibilities."

"It most certainly does. To the shower then." He bowed and gestured for her to precede him. She dipped a playful curtsey then sashayed into the master bath.

"This reminds me of Rome," she said, gesturing around at the travertine marble columns that bordered the whirlpool tub. Matching columns formed the stanchions of the glass-walled shower.

"Intentionally so. I love the Roman baths, but don't tell my grandmother. She thinks poorly of anything that isn't Irish." He stepped to the control panel and set the temperature and pressure he wanted then turned to ease the slippery silk robe down her equally smooth shoulders.

"You are close to your family?" She leaned back against his chest, rubbing her lush little ass up against his crotch.

It was an odd time and place to be discussing family, but his need to know Lyra and to have her know him was almost as powerful as his need to make love to her. *Aye – make love to her*, he admitted silently. *Not just to fuck.*

Out loud he replied, "To my grandparents. There are only the three of us left. My parents were never true mates, so my mother only lived a short human lifespan. My father died in a wizards' duel some hundred years ago now."

"I never knew my father." Her words held a trace of regret, but no real devastation, for which he was glad. He hated the idea of anything hurting her. "He was just some anonymous sailor. My mother remains among the living, I think. We haven't seen one another in decades. Sirens very rarely form lasting family attachments."

"I'm sorry to hear that." Sorrier than he could say. But she had said rarely rather than never. He could work with that.

She shrugged and turned in his arms, lifting her face to his. "Don't be. You can't miss what you've never known. I'd like to meet this grandmother of yours someday, though. She sounds fascinating."

"She is. And I'm sure she'd love to meet you. Grandfather as well." He couldn't help thinking of Grandmama's words from last Yule. "I'll dance at your wedding within the year." A lump of emotion caught in his throat. In the course of one night he'd gone from scorn and trepidation to desperately hoping her prediction was accurate. Now all he had to do was convince Lyra, and pray that the Fates would smile on the union and prove them to be true mates on a mystical level.

He opened the shower door and turned her in his arms to enter the steamy chamber. She squealed with delight at the many nozzles that sprayed water from overhead as well as up and down the walls of the shower. After she'd played with the controls for a moment, Cian teleported in a bar of rosemary-scented soap and began to lather her skin with the fragrant suds.

When he turned her to soap her left side, he swore and dropped the soap. It couldn't be! Not so soon.

"Cian, what is it?" She whirled to face him, almost slipping on the soapy tile floor. "What's wrong?"

"Wrong?" He shook his head, willing his voice not to crack. His fingers traced the green Celtic knot tattoo that twined around the milky-white flesh of her upper left arm—a tattoo that had not been there last evening. Small ruby-red runes were worked into the green band. "Nothing is wrong. In fact, something is very, very right."

"What?" She followed his gaze down to her arm and yelped. "Where did that come from? Did you…"

"No." He shook his head. "Not consciously anyway. But look at mine."

She touched gentle fingers to the runes on his arm. "The markings are red. Yesterday they were black. Now it looks…just like mine."

"When a sorcerer finds his one true soul mate, the other half of his being, the Fates place a mark on each of them. If they reject their destiny and go on with their lives as if nothing had happened the marks will eventually fade. If they choose to embrace the mating they swear promises to one another and the bond is formed. The two individuals truly become one being."

"But I'm not a sorceress. I'm not even human."

A short bark of harsh laughter escaped his lips. "That doesn't seem to matter."

"I have to spend at least half of every day in the water."

"The Fates never promised it would be easy. I had already decided I was willing to do whatever it took to make our relationship work. And that was before I knew about this. All I knew was that I had fallen in love with you last night.

This..." He bent and kissed the mark on her arm. "This is just a gift. But it's up to you whether we accept or reject it."

"I want to." She looked up at him, her eyes clouded with doubt and fear—and maybe, he thought—with a tiny kernel of hope. "This mating, this melding of lives—why have I never heard of it?"

"It is seen as a weakness among many sorcerers. After all who wants your enemies to know that by killing your mate they can kill you too? Once the joining is complete, our lives would literally be as one. We would die within minutes of one another, whether that happened next week or centuries from now."

"That's why you said your parents weren't true mates. Because your mother died and your father didn't."

"Yes. If they'd been fated to be together, she would have gained the lifespan of a wizard, like him. Instead he had to watch her age and die." He was thankful that he wouldn't have that experience with Lyra. Even if she rejected the mating, as a direct descendant of the gods, she'd almost certainly outlive him.

Lyra's arms crossed over her chest and she tilted her head to one side as another thought seemed to occur to her. "And if we choose to ignore the offer, will you eventually find another mate?"

"No, my love. One mate to a customer."

She looked so agonized that his heart clenched in his chest. He sat down on the marble bench built into the wall and drew her down onto his lap and into his arms heedless of the water pouring around them. "There's no rush," he assured her with a kiss on the top of her head. "You can take as much time as you need to think things over. It's a big decision." The biggest.

"I do love you, Cian." Her words, muffled against his chest, made his heart sing. "But I live in the water and feed off anonymous sex. I just can't imagine how we can be together. And it's breaking my heart."

Chapter Four

It took every bit of strength he possessed to let her go. After they made love in the shower, he fed her breakfast, then teleported both of them to a secluded area near the beach. Once there, he watched her walk into the waves without a backward glance.

Had it only been yesterday he'd wondered what was missing in his life? How the world could change in less than twenty-four hours.

He spent the day in his office, trying to ensure that his various business and charity ventures would survive if he had to take a sudden leave of absence. He sent a long email to his grandparents. Then he started reading, arming himself with every bit of information he could garner. Now, as the orange orb of the sun began to sink behind the city and paint watercolor hues on the lake, Cian waited on the rock. He had no idea what the hell he'd do if she didn't appear.

It was well past sunset when she finally arrived. The beach was utterly deserted except for Cian but suddenly he knew he wasn't alone anymore. He didn't need to see her rising from the waves. He could feel her presence by the sudden lightening of his heart.

Lyra didn't hesitate but walked directly into his outstretched arms. Cian wrapped her in his embrace and held her close, breathing in the scent of woman and water and life. Long minutes later, she gulped in a big breath and took a step back.

"I missed you." He tucked a tress behind her ear then leaned his forehead against hers.

"And I missed you." She sighed heavily and some of the weight on Cian's heart returned.

"Will you come home with me again?"

Her smile was beautiful and tragic. "Of course."

He teleported them directly to his bedroom this time. Their feet had barely touched the carpet before they fell on each other like a pair of hungry tigers. This mating was brief and furious, nearly frantic. After one voracious kiss, Cian turned her and pushed her torso down on the bed. Lyra complied eagerly, widening her legs and wiggling her pert little ass in the air.

"Take me, Cian!" Her panted words were muffled by the sheets, but Cian heard.

"Oh, yes, *leannan*. You—" He paused to position his turgid cock at her weeping entrance. "Are." With one hard shove, he pushed inside, seating himself to the hilt in her core. "Mine!"

"Only yours, Cian," she vowed. "My heart, my love, only yours."

Her body, too, he added silently. One way or another he'd find a way to have that for his own as well. He thrust inside her, deep and fast. Her spine arched, allowing him to penetrate her fully, claiming every inch of her heat as his own, just as she'd branded him as hers from the moment they met. The Fates had given her to him, and he was determined to protect and cherish that gift for all time.

Her climax came quickly and hard. Her muscles clamped down on his cock, milking him fiercely even as her musical screams rang in his ears. Cian bellowed his own satisfaction, spurting furiously into her, wave after wave of white-hot pleasure. When it was finally over, he rolled to the side, collapsing beside her on the bed.

They lay there for moments, both gasping for breath.

"Oh!" Lyra's pleased exclamation roused Cian enough to make him lift his head and gaze into her beloved face. "I feel...full. As though I'd fed. Cian, this is wonderful. It means I may not need to find a stranger to feed. At least, not every time!"

"Not ever, if I have any say in the matter," he growled. But he was more than pleased, and he squeezed her in his arms. "I have been doing research today, my love. I have a surprise for you, I believe."

"Oh? Is it as delicious as the chocolate?" She tickled his ribs with her fingertips.

"I think so." He pulled her into his arms and teleported them to another place.

Lyra blinked and looked around at the room. It resembled the Roman-style bath in Cian's apartment, but was much, much larger. Several lounge chairs clustered around two pools, one large and one small. The small one bubbled and gurgled. She looked up through windows in the ceiling to see the stars.

"This is the swimming pool for my building," he told her. "I changed the water today for lake water. It took a fair amount of magic, but I wanted to see if that would satisfy your needs."

"What a wonderful thought!" She threw her arms around his neck and kissed him soundly. Hand in hand, they stepped down into the water. "It feels...right," she told him, her voice filled with wonder and hope.

"I'd like you to come here tomorrow, instead of the lake. If this works, we'll know we're on the right track."

"Thank you, Cian. It means more than I can say, that you've gone to such trouble for me." She blinked the unfamiliar tears out of her eyes.

"Don't cry, my love. I told you I would find a way. If this isn't it, we'll simply keep searching until we find another."

They swam for a while, touching and sliding along one another's bodies as they did. When the temptation grew too strong, Cian lifted her and carried her to one of the cushioned lounge chairs. This time the lovemaking was so sweet and tender it brought fresh tears to Lyra's eyes.

"I love you, Cian," she whispered, holding him tightly. His shaft remained embedded in her channel and his powerful body pinned her to the chair.

"And I love you, Lyra." He gazed into her soul with those vibrant green eyes. She didn't hesitate this time, just opened herself to him and gazed right back. With an almost physical click, their souls merged and mingled. Everything was open between them. Every hope, fear, passion, and dream. Lyra couldn't breathe, the experience was so overwhelmingly beautiful.

"I would say the words, my love." His voice was low, rough with love and vulnerability. "In my heart you are already my mate. Please let us say the vows that will seal the bonding."

"I want that more than I have ever wanted anything in my life." She had to speak the truth. While they lay locked in the soul-gaze, there was no possibility of a lie between them. "Without you, I am afraid I would die, one way or the other."

"I know I would," Cian replied. He linked both his hands through hers and spoke reverently in Gaelic—or some similar ancient language.

Through the soul-gaze she understood the words. She repeated them in ancient Greek, her own ancestral tongue. "Cian, my mate. You to me. Me to you. Two as one. One from two. For this life and beyond."

Time froze as she felt the bond snap into existence between them. She felt his heartbeat as her own, felt the power that coursed through his veins as if it were in her own. She felt stronger, safer, more complete than she'd ever been.

Cian flexed, and she felt his cock surge back to life inside her. She cried out at the pleasure, which was even more powerful now that she felt his as well as her own. "Cian," she cried.

"Lyra!" He pumped into her with strong, sure strokes. "My mate. My love."

She knew what he was going to say next and she said it for him. "My heart."

* * * * *

It was evening the next day before she felt the gradual weakening that told her she'd spent too long out of the water. Lyra was curled in a big leather chair in the book-lined library at Cian's home, reading about current world events while Cian studied an ancient magical tome.

"I need to swim," she told him.

He closed the book at once. "Will you try the pool?"

"Of course." They met in the middle of the room and clasped hands, so Cian could teleport them to the swimming area. It was empty again, and Lyra looked around. "Does no one else use this pool? It seems large for just one man."

His smile was a bit chagrined. "My employees normally have use of this area. For the last two days, I've had it closed. They believe it is being repaired."

Lyra held her breath as she descended the marble steps into the pool. The warm, silky water lapped around her. When she stood up to her waist, she smiled widely at Cian, who waited on the edge. "It is good," she told him happily. "I can recover here. I will not need to spend the winter under the ice of the lake."

"And it is almost six hours past noon," he added with a grin. "I had hopes that the bond would extend your endurance."

Her gaze flew up to the skylights and she saw the colors of the sunset tint the sky. She had been out of the water for nearly a full day, and was only now beginning to suffer. "It is a miracle!"

Cian laughed and dove cleanly into the water. "A miracle of love, *leannan*. I promised you we would find a way. And together we shall."

* * * * *

He wasn't smiling a few days later. Apparently the pool was only an interim solution. By the third day, he felt the tug of her weakness on the bond between them. He was able to lend her some strength, but soon it wasn't enough. He needed to get her to the lake.

"I am sorry, my love." Lyra's voice was full of unshed tears.

Cian took her hand. "Don't be sorry. We are not defeated yet. I'm taking you to Ireland. You'll like the castle, and I can make my headquarters there as easily as here. The ocean doesn't freeze over, so we can live there in the winter."

He teleported them to the family seat—a rambling stone manor atop a wild, windswept hillside. They arrived in a small cove, where waves crashed onto a rocky shore, but within sight of the castle.

"It is beautiful," she agreed. She was looking at the water instead of the house. Cian held her hand and walked with her into the surf. When he was up to his knees, she kissed him sweetly, then pulled away and dived beneath the waves.

He watched for several minutes as she swam and splashed. Then she swam up to him and stood. "Go. I'm sure you have work to do, and this is mine. Come back for me at sunset."

Reluctantly, Cian agreed. He had research to do. He couldn't stop until he'd found some way to be with her completely. And the spell he'd been working on was nearly complete. With one last look over his shoulder, he walked up the rocky path to the house. He saw her silver tail flash in the sunlight, and then she was gone once more, disappearing under the waves.

* * * * *

When sunset arrived, Cian was waiting by the shore. He smiled widely as Lyra approached. His research had been successful. He couldn't wait to show her what he could do.

"Cian!" She called his name excitedly as she transformed her lower body and stood in the surf. "It is wonderful here. Only a few hours and I am fully restored."

"And I have a surprise for you." He waded out to meet her, taking her in his arms for a kiss. While their mouths were fused, he fell back into the waves, pulling her with him. As he fell, his lower body transformed. Instead of legs, he now possessed the muscular, gray-skinned tail of a dolphin.

"Cian! What have you done?" Lyra broke free of his embrace and stood, chest deep in the cold waves. She stared at his altered form, biting her lower lip.

Cian changed back, just to reassure her that he could. "I learned a new shape, my love, that is all. I can only maintain it for an hour or two, but that is a little more time each day that we can be together."

"Oh, Cian, I love you so much!" She tackled him there in the water, kissing him until they both came up sputtering and splashing. Then her eyes grew wide and serious and she gripped his hands hard. "I have…done something else, as well. Something that may change our future forever."

"What is it, *áilleacht*?" His heart thudded in his chest, fear condensed in his stomach.

"I have made arrangements with one who may be able to help us."

"Oh? And who might that be?"

"His name is Achelous."

"The river god." Cian knew the legends.

"Yes, though he can move in the sea as well. He is my great-great-grandfather and the ruler of my race. The original sirens were his daughters by Terpsichore, one of the Muses. If anyone can grant us the chance to be together, it will be him."

"Then why do you look so frightened?"

She sighed. "He is not an Olympian, or one of the most powerful gods, but..."

"But what, *leannan*?"

"But he *is* a god, my love. And that means he is more than a little unpredictable."

"I understand."

"Do you?" Her lovely voice went shrill with worry. "If he is in a good mood, he could choose to make us both aquatic — or to alter my body so I can live on land. If he is angry though, he could simply kill us both."

"He will not hurt you, *áilleacht*. Not while there is breath in my body."

She shook her head. "What do you think I meant by kill us both?"

Cian refused to consider that possibility. "When do we meet him?"

"Soon. He said he would come here as soon as it grew dark."

"Then we wait." Cian perched on a rock and held out a hand. "One thing first."

"What?"

He waved his hand and held out a simple silk slip dress, one he'd purchased for her in Toronto. "I would have you dressed when we speak to another man, even if he is your ancestor."

She took the garment and slid it on over her head. "Thank you."

Cian flashed himself a pair of loose trousers, then they sat on the rock and waited. Cian kept one arm firmly around her waist while he studied the water. Lyra gazed out as well, finally pointing to a tall bearded man as he rose from the waves.

She stood and dropped into a deep curtsey. "Grandfather."

Cian made a polite bow, never letting go of Lyra's hand. "River Lord. Thank you for meeting us."

"So you wish to marry one of my sirens." In human aspect the god was tall, powerful and imposing. In the reflected moonlight Cian could see that his skin was the pale tan of river rocks while his hair and eyes were slate gray.

"I do."

"You wish me to make her able to live on land so you can take her away from all she has ever known."

Cian shrugged. "Or change me so I can live with her in the waves."

The god raised one eyebrow. "And if I do not?"

Cian gestured up toward the castle atop the craggy hill. "Then this will be my home and we will make the most of whatever time we spend together each day. I promise she will never want for anything, not as long as I live."

"I see you have at least taken time to think," the god acknowledged. "What if I were to say that in return for this boon you must give me that castle?"

That was a no-brainer. "Done. I have other houses."

"What if I demanded those as well? And your corporations and foundations. You see, wizard, I have done my research."

"I would prefer not to take a wife while destitute, but I will find a way to support her, whether in the water or on land. All of my assets are yours if you so require."

The gray head dipped in grave acknowledgement. "What if I said you had to fight me for her hand?" His voice rose to a thunderous roar. "Would you be willing to challenge the wrath of a god?"

Lyra gasped in fear. Cian sent her a reassuring smile. Then he pushed her behind him and stepped away to summon a ball of fire and hold it in his hand. "I'd say bring it on, old one. But I'd ask that you sever the bond between us if I die, so the siren will not be harmed."

There was a flash of light on the beach, and Cian turned to see his grandparents standing tall and proud on the shore, hands linked. "I will fight in his stead," called Cian's grandfather.

"It is my fight," Cian replied. "And how did you know..." His voice trailed off. Of course they knew. His grandmother was a seer. He suddenly felt like an errant six-year-old. He was encouraged, though to see his grandmother immediately open her arms to Lyra.

Achelous watched the spectacle and laughed. "You interest me, sorcerer. I have discovered a few things about you this day. Your corporations are among the greenest in the world. You sacrifice profit to reduce harmful impacts on the lakes, rivers, and oceans. Your foundations donate heavily to environmental causes. Why?"

Cian let the fireball fade away. "Because this planet needs all the help it can get. Most humans exist in such a short span of time that they have trouble seeing the big picture. I have that advantage, so I do what I can. Power brings responsibility."

"Very true. But not every mage believes that."

"He was taught well," Cian's grandfather commented dryly.

Cian chuckled. "Aye, so I was."

Lyra moved back into the surf to stand proudly at Cian's side. "I love him, Grandfather. That should count for something."

The god's lips twisted into something that resembled a smile. "In truth, it counts for much. I've a mind to reward you, wizard, for both your stewardship and your courage."

Feeling the first rush of hope, Cian reached out for Lyra. They joined hands, bowing their heads in front of Achelous. The god put one hand on each of their shoulders. "Daughter of the waves, I bless your union with this man."

"Thank you, River Lord." Cian spoke reverently to the god. "I will care for her with my life."

"I believe you, wizard." He turned to Lyra. "You have already discovered that you can feed off him exclusively, so you needn't worry about that."

Lyra nodded.

The god continued. "You have both proven to me that you are devoted to one another and resourceful. I believe that between you, you can come up with ways to deal with your dependence on the water."

"Yes, my lord." Cian's heart sank a little, but he knew they would eventually prevail, now that they would have the chance.

"And I assume you can arrange for all the proper papers so she can walk in your world?"

Cian nodded. Identification paperwork was the least of his worries. What magic couldn't handle, money and connections could.

The god smiled at them both. "Very well, you have my blessing. I'll expect to be invited to the mortal wedding posthaste." With that he turned and strode back into the rippling black water. He stopped with just his head just above the surface, and threw an object at Lyra. Cian snaked out his hand and intercepted it. The small shell on a gold chain sloshed as if filled with liquid. "This should help. Consider it a wedding present." Then he disappeared into the inky depths.

Lyra took the pendant. Her eyes widened as she studied it. Cian wrapped his hand around hers and felt the power that radiated from the object. "It is...the essence of the sea. When I wear this, it will be as though I am swimming."

"Aye," Cian agreed. "I'll never take you from the water for long, but this will buy us time if the need arises."

"A perfect wedding gift." Lyra draped the necklace around her throat. Together, they staggered to the shore.

Cian's knees gave out, and he sat down heavily, drawing Lyra down into his lap. He ignored the sharp poke of the rocks beneath his ass. It was done. He didn't know whether to shout with joy or weep with relief.

Lyra felt tears of happiness trickle from her eyes.

"I'll start the wedding preparations." Cian's grandmother hugged each of them, as did the older man who looked so much like his grandson. "Welcome to the family, my dear." Then there was a flash and the older couple was gone.

"I love you." Lyra wiped her watery eyes and clung to Cian for all she was worth. Then she pulled back one hand and smacked his shoulder. "I can't believe you offered to fight a god over me. What were you thinking?"

"That I love you and that I'd do anything to be with you."

How was she supposed to be upset about that? Lyra did the only logical thing she could do. She kissed him.

Seconds later she was flat on her back in a big soft bed. Their clothing had vanished and Cian loomed above her. His rock-hard erection prodded at her already wet and swollen entrance.

"You are mine, Lyra. For the rest of our lives and whatever lies beyond."

"Of course I am." Her heart was full to the point of overflowing. "I love you."

He slid into her body, claiming it as surely as he had already claimed her heart.

WHITE VALLEY
By Lacey Thorn

ಐ

Dedication

For PKP. Thanks for being there for me on every step of life's journey...my sister, my friend.

Trademarks Acknowledgement

The author acknowledges the trademarked status and trademark owners of the following wordmarks mentioned in this work of fiction:

Animal Planet: Discovery Communications

Playgirl: Playgirl Key Club, Inc.

Chapter One

Dakota walked slowly through the thick trees. There was a stitch in her side and her breath was coming in short pants as she struggled to fill her lungs with air. This was supposed to be a nice relaxing weekend away. Just her and nature. It was a way to step back into the past, to a time when she had a family to do things with. Before the accident that took her mom, dad and baby sister away. And it had been until she awoke this morning and got the bright idea to go hiking in a different part of the forest. If she had it all to do over again she would have ignored the voice that kept calling to her and urging her in this direction. Well, no, she wouldn't have, but it was a nice thought.

Where she was going she had no idea. At least she had thought to grab her backpack from the tent this morning, so she had a few bottles of water and a box of granola bars along with a flashlight and first-aid kit among other odds and ends that she carried with her.

All she knew was that she had to keep going. Something was urging her on. She felt compelled to keep going, like she would know what to do when she got to the right place. She blew out another breath and switched her backpack to the other shoulder. Was she crazy? What the hell was she doing out here by herself? And hiking on an unknown trail alone? What was she thinking?

She came to a clearing in the middle of the forest and realized that she had no idea where she was anymore. This valley wasn't on the topographical map, at least not any that she remembered seeing and she had been coming here since she was twelve. She stumbled along looking for some familiar landmark that would help her figure out just where she was.

But no matter how hard she looked, nothing seemed familiar. She heard the sound of water and followed it until she reached a cool brook. Continuing along beside it, she soon found herself in what appeared to be a lush garden complete with waterfall and a base that seemed deep enough to swim in. Or if she was lucky, bathe in.

"Hello?" Dakota called though she didn't know what she would do if anyone answered. "Hello?"

Thinking herself alone, she tumbled to her knees and began slowly taking off her shoes. She just wanted to wash the dust off and maybe the memories of what had driven her to take this trip by herself this weekend. The memory of walking in on her fiancé while he was with another woman. The same fiancé who thought it was so important that she remain a virgin before they were married. Because he wanted their wedding night to be so special. Please. She was a gullible, stupid fool. She just wanted to wash it all away and go back to the way things used to be. She shook her head with disgust. No, she didn't. She couldn't lie to herself. She wanted to forget what's-his-name ever existed.

Why fate had stripped her of people who had loved her completely and unconditionally and then put her in the hands of such a jerk she would always wonder. She'd never made friends easily and now that she had severed her tie with him, she was truly all alone in the world. When would she find a family of her own? People to love and comfort her? When would it be her turn for happiness?

The water seemed to call to her as if it would give her exactly what she desired. With renewed energy Dakota began peeling her clothes off with only one thought. Submerging in the crystal blue water before her.

Dimitri and Sebastian Cordova followed the sounds to the bridal pool and stood hiding behind the lush foliage to watch the woman undress. Her hair was a cascade of sun-kissed brown curls that reached nearly to the small of her back. Her breasts were high and full, her stomach concave. The flare of her hips called to man and beast alike urging them to take and mount her. Her buttocks were creamy and smooth and it was all they could do to control the wolves that sought to howl inside them. She was sheer perfection and the brothers wanted her.

Who is she? Sebastian asked through his link with his brother. *Have you ever seen her before?*

Never, Dimitri answered. *She cannot be from the Valley.*

But she bathes herself in the bridal pool. Sebastian stated that fact as they continued to watch her frolic and splash in the water. *It is only for those who are preparing to mate. You know what the water will do.*

Dimitri's grin was carnal. *Yes, we do. But I'm guessing that she doesn't.*

Sebastian laughed softly. *Good thing that we are here to see that she does not suffer needlessly.*

You are saying that you want us to claim her? Dimitri asked just to be sure that his brother was thinking the same thing that he was.

We have reached our twenty-fifth year. It is time that we claim a mate. Sebastian turned to look at Dimitri's face. *Tell me you do not want to mount her right now. Tell me that your wolf is not howling for release.*

You know that it is, Dimitri told him.

It won't be long now. The waters will work their magic soon and then she will be ours. Sebastian glanced back at the woman and almost groaned when she stood from her play. Water dripped from her pebbled nipples. It clung to her body and he wanted to lick every inch of her skin before placing her on her hands and knees and claiming her in the way that his wolf demanded.

Soon, Dimitri murmured, his eyes glued to the woman as well. Soon all three of their lives would change. The bridal pool would ensure it.

Dakota stepped from the water and frowned. She had been so sure that the water would cool her off but it felt like her body was on fire. She groaned and lifted her hands to her breasts. A thousand tongues seemed to be licking over her body, exploring her. She gasped again and one hand slid down to her curl-covered mound. She could feel the moisture slipping from her vagina to mix with the water on her thighs. She burned there, deep in her center with a need for something she had never known before.

Her hand tentatively went to her clit, so swollen with need that it protruded from its hiding place, begging for attention. She brushed her fingers over it and cried out at the pleasure that so small a movement sent through her. Her nipples were on fire and she took her other hand up and pinched one of them as hard as she could handle. And came. Her orgasm rippled through her womb and spiraled out until she felt it in her fingers and toes as well.

She collapsed onto the plush grass at her feet and lay back, eyes closed, panting. The orgasm should have helped, but if anything, it had only made things worse. Her nipples were even harder and her empty channel was clenching, trying to grasp something that wasn't there. She cried out as her body's demands grew more and more intense. What was happening to her?

"Oh, God, what do I do?" she cried. "How do I make it stop?"

"You don't," a voice spoke softly from just above her and Dakota jerked her eyes open. "We do."

She didn't realize that she was holding her breath until her vision started blurring. She let it out with a whoosh and inhaled again, filling her lungs with more than just air. She could smell the sexual musk of the two men standing over her, undressing. Undressing! Oh my God, they were undressing and they looked even better without clothes on. Sweet merciful heaven, if this was a dream then she didn't want to wake up.

The two men were almost identical in every way. Both had long dark hair that hung in waves to their necks. Two sets of bright green eyes were busy looking their fill of her splayed body. They were maybe six feet tall with long, lean muscles that made her think of runners' physiques. As the clothes continued coming off she caught her breath again. Each chest was covered with crisp black curls that tapered down a washboard abdomen to what lay below. And there was a lot below.

As they stepped out of their jeans she could see just how excited they were. Both cocks stood to attention. They were mouthwatering, like the cocks displayed in the *Playgirl* magazines she often looked at. They weren't overly long, but the width was almost as thick as her wrist.

"I'd like to do that for you," one of them said to her and when he nodded at the hand buried between her legs she was startled to realize that she was fingering herself. She had been so wrapped up in watching them that her body had taken over. But now that she was aware she felt the enormous pressure building inside her, the violent clenching of her vagina.

"Why is this happening to me?" she found the strength to ask.

"You bathed in the bridal pool," the other one answered and they knelt on the grass, one on either side of her. Their cocks bobbed up from their laps, begging for attention, and Dakota really wanted to give it to them. More than anything she wanted to experience everything that she had been denied with her fiancé. She wanted to touch and explore. But most of all her body was screaming for sex. That pool of water seemed to have ignited her hidden hunger into a raging inferno that only the act itself could satiate. What had they called the pool?

"The bridal pool?" Dakota was lost again or maybe she just couldn't focus.

"It is where our women bathe when they are preparing for the marriage bed. It aids in the first time," the one on her left said and he gently ran a figure down her arm to where her fingers were still busy tugging at her nipples. "You do not know of the pool?"

"No," she whispered, "I'm not getting married." Not anymore, she added silently.

"But it is law," was the reply from her right. "You cannot break the law without being punished." His hand trailed her arm to where she had two fingers moving in and out of her desperate flesh.

"Punished?" she moaned.

"We will not let you be punished," was the promise before her fingers were pulled from her nipple and replaced with the rougher, calloused ones.

"How," she managed to force out as the fingers moved to her other breast and lips began to gently suck on the first one.

"You will form a marriage bond with us," she was told and a thicker finger joined with her two, stretching her virgin channel.

"But, but…" There was something she needed to say but for the life of her she couldn't think. What came out instead was, "Both of you? I don't even know your names."

"I am Dimitri Cordova," said the man with his finger in her pussy. She glanced at the other brother but it was Dimitri who continued talking. "And since he is too busy enjoying your bounty to introduce himself, that is my brother Sebastian."

"I… You can't marry two men," she whispered and almost laughed at the absurdity of this conversation. There were so many other things that she should be saying. Like, "I don't talk to strangers much less fuck them". Like, "I've never had sex with one man much less two". Or what about, "Where are the condoms because I don't see any lying around in the grass"?

"It is the way of our people for one woman to mate with two men," Dimitri told her. Then he used his other hand to tug her fingers free and bring them to his mouth where he sucked greedily on them. They both moaned with pleasure. "You are so hot and wet, gripping my finger with your pretty cunt. Your taste is better than the sweetest wine, spicy and rich. I could eat you forever."

"I'm Dakota," she whispered. "Dakota—"

"Dakota Cordova," Dimitri said, interrupting what she had meant to say. "From this moment on you will be Dakota Cordova."

Sebastian finally released her nipple with a pop. "From now on you will be known as ours." His eyes seemed to glow as he spoke. "From this moment on you will belong in White Valley as the sacred mate of the Cordova."

"White Valley?" she questioned with the last shreds of nonsexual awareness she had.

"That is where you are, love," Sebastian informed her. "White Valley, home of the weres for too many generations to count. The last true oasis for our kind."

There was something so wrong with that sentence but she couldn't put her finger on it at the moment. The heat was too much, the desire to be filled taking precedence over anything else. "I need," she groaned and cried out when the finger pushing in and out of her channel was joined by anther.

"We'll give you everything that you need, Dakota," the promise was whispered in her ear as teeth nibbled along her neck and shoulders. "You have only to say the words."

"What words?" she demanded, her body screaming for relief.

"All you have to say is that you choose us. Just say that, Dakota, and we'll make it all better." The promise came from her other side and Dimitri's fingers began pushing harder and faster, his thumb strumming over her distended clit. "Just say, 'I choose Dimitri and Sebastian Cordova as my mates'. Only by freely accepting us and our desire to claim you can we aid you." He lifted a hand and waved it over her body. The debilitating desire seemed to vanish for a moment so that she felt herself once more. Oddly, she missed the desperate burning ache from moments before.

She looked up and was lost in the deep green eyes staring into hers. With no thought to the consequences the words left her mouth. "I choose Dimitri and Sebastian Cordova as my mates." And the all-consuming sexual need raced through her body once more.

She cried out at the feel of sharp teeth biting into her shoulder where it met her neck. It was like a dog's bite, sharp and painful. Then a rush of euphoria went through her and it was better than any man-made drug. She felt boneless, like she was floating on clouds instead of on her back in the grass with two aroused males bending over her.

"You bit me," she moaned as he licked over the mark he had left on her flesh. "Why did you bite me?"

"I marked you as mine," Sebastian told her. "My saliva will help to relax you more and prepare you for what is next."

She was mesmerized by his hand stroking the length of his thick cock up and down. She licked her lips, bringing a groan spilling from his lips. "What is next?"

His face was a mask of carnal intent that took her breath away. "Fucking. Next is fucking."

"Yes," she breathed the word, somehow knowing that her whole life would change in the aftermath of what she experienced next. But it wasn't fear that she felt. It was anticipation and desire. She was most definitely ready for the fucking.

Dimitri could barely hold himself back from what his body wanted, what his wolf cried out for. He wanted to plunge his swollen cock as deep in her hot cunt as he could get, filling her with his seed. That was the only thing that would appease the beast inside and allow him to keep from letting the animal take over. She already bore his brother's mark on her shoulder and soon she would have his as well. It was time to ensure that she was marked by their seed, ensuring that any other male who came upon her would know that she was claimed and mated.

Women were scarce in their band of wolves and thus the need for two men to share one mate. It was one way to ensure that their species continued to exist. Or maybe it was just a way to ensure that death was not an everyday occurrence as men fought in both human and wolf form for the few women single and old enough to claim. No matter the reason it was working and they were continuing to thrive.

He thanked the goddess Enuba, sacred mother of the White Valley for bestowing the gift of Dakota on him and Sebastian. She was everything that the brothers could wish for in a mate. In time they would come to know her better, obtain the intimate thoughts of her heart and mind. But for now they must continue the claiming of her body, ease the fires the water had set burning in her treasured places.

He and Sebastian exchanged glances, communicating what they desired to do next.

You wish to mount her now? **Dimitri questioned.** *She bears your bite already.*

I wish to taste the sweet nectar clinging to your finger. I need to bathe my tongue in her essence, washing away all tastes that have come before her. Sebastian's moan filled Dimitri's head.

Dimitri slowly removed his finger from Dakota's pulsing channel and lifted it to his mouth for another taste. *She is indeed a tasty treat.*

Sebastian groaned out loud and quickly positioned himself between her thighs, burying his face in her curls and inhaling deeply of her sexual musk. He ran his tongue over the plumped lips of her sex, nipping them with his teeth and sucking them with his lips until she bucked against his face in a demand for more. He heard her sharp cry fill the air and knew without looking that his brother was eating at the ripe fruit of her breasts. They were enough to satisfy even the pickiest of men. Only when he could wait no longer did he part her folds with his finger and thrust his tongue into the weeping portal of her pussy.

Her taste washed over and through him and his wolf howled with pleasure as he fed from her juicy cunt. He couldn't work his tongue deep enough, couldn't lap fast enough at the nectar that flowed so freely. She was the sweetest ambrosia just as Dimitri had promised. Spicy and hot, she filled his mouth and overflowed his senses. He would love to dine on her for hours, for days, but the pulsing of his cock was a brutal reminder of other pleasures that he could and would find with her.

I can't wait any longer, he warned Dimitri.

Then don't. Dimitri's pant filled his mind. *Claim her fully that I might begin my claim as well. I can barely hold my wolf back either.*

Wasting no more time, Sebastian came to his knees between her thighs and lined his hungry shaft up with her opening. He could tell from her taste, from her clean smell that she had known no other before him. She was pure, untouched by the seed of others and this made her a special gift indeed from the goddess. A gift that he and Dimitri would treasure for the rest of their days.

She was as tight as a fist, her sheath fighting as he pressed inside her. He fought against the wolf's need to thrust violently inside, to claim as an animal in heat. He was not just the wolf, but a man as well and it was the man who she needed this first time. It was the man who would be the first to claim her, to mate her. Slowly he worked his cock in and out of her pussy, gaining a few inches with every stroke. So slowly he moved inside her, coating his shaft in her spilling juices until he was buried to the balls in her wet heat. It was sheer pleasure and total pain as man and beast fought for control. Sebastian fought desperately to hold on to his wolf, to keep it inside him. But the wolf wanted to claim its mate as well and it was a desperate battle. With a shudder he regained the control he would need to take her slow and easy this first time.

A slow glide inside until his balls pressed firmly against the rounded cheeks of her ass and he held still for just a moment, enjoying the feel of her snug heat. He pulled out, groaning at the tight clasp of her pussy on his shaft and her body's reluctant release of him. She was sheer perfection and this slow fucking was surely going to kill him.

I won't last long, Sebastian cried out to his brother.

I pray to the goddess that you don't. I'm not sure how much longer I can manage to hold back either. Dimitri's groan of torture was just the push Sebastian needed to regain his focus.

Slow and easy, he worked his cock in and out. Her cunt dragged along his length with each thrust, unwilling to let him go, then just as reluctant to accept him back. He hooked her knees over his elbows and spread her wider, enjoying the view of his cock tunneling into her flesh. There was something so carnal about watching his cock, coated in her juices, working in and out of her pussy. It was the most beautiful sight that he had ever seen. His arms shook with the effort to hold back, to keep the beast at bay. And he succeeded for a moment.

"Yes. God, yes. Make the ache go away. Yes." Dakota's cries tore his control away and what was meant to be a slow and easy mating became something so much more. She wanted more and the wolf was ready and willing to ensure that she got it. With a shudder of release he uncaged the wolf and let it merge inside him so that the spirit of the beast could enjoy the first mating as well as the man.

His thrusts became rougher, his hips slamming into her as he rode faster, plunged deeper into her womb. The wolf howled its pleasure as his balls swelled with seed. His grunts joined her cries and just before his seed exploded from his body, Sebastian leaned down and bit once more where his mark already lay upon her flesh. She bucked beneath him, but his pumping hips kept her firmly in place. He could feel the rhythmic clutching of her pussy and knew that she had reached her pinnacle with him. The sharp contractions of her channel nursed and sucked at him, pulling him headfirst into the best orgasm of his life.

Not holding back any longer Sebastian rammed his cock as deep as it would go and filled her with his seed, marked her completely as his mate. He felt the wolf's pleasure and happily joined with him, throwing his head back and giving voice to the howl inside. Dakota was his now, completely. The next thing was to ensure that she became his brother's as well. Just as soon as he regained the strength to move or, better yet, to breathe.

Dakota heard the howl as if from a distance. It seemed to fill the air, almost as if she could feel the sound vibrating over her skin like a ripple of water. The cock buried in her channel continued to pulse hot jets of cum deep inside her. She knew that she should protest. She wasn't on the Pill and he obviously hadn't used a condom. But then nothing seemed to be as it should be here. She felt as if she were Alice who had fallen into the rabbit hole and came out in some alternate time and place. These two were definitely not the white rabbit though. And damn it, she would probably cry if she woke up like Alice and realized that this was all a dream.

The grass was lush and fragrant beneath her back and though she had just had the best and only sex of her life, she could already feel the need building within her again. They had said something about the bridal pool and that bathing in it was what had caused this. But surely that wasn't possible. How could a pool of water cause her body to burn with such an erotic desire to have sex? No, to fuck and be fucked. That was a better description of how she felt. It was as if an animal was coming awake inside her and with it other desires and needs were awakening. The only explanation that made sense was that she must be dreaming. In what realm of possibility would there ever be two gorgeous men set on pleasuring and claiming her as their own. It was definitely a dream.

Sebastian rolled them so that she was on top of him. His spent shaft eased from her vagina, leaving her empty and hungry. She started to protest but rough hands clasped her hips from behind, urging her to her knees astride Sebastian's big body. His hands soothed her shoulders, slipping between them to fondle and pinch her breasts and nipples.

She felt a hand push gently at the small of her back and then the thick shaft of Dimitri was there probing for entry. His cock ran along the puffed lips of her sex in short, quick thrusts and groans drifted from both her and him. The tip of his cock butted against the swell of her clitoris with each rub and the tension coiled tighter inside her. It wouldn't take much to push her over the edge again into oblivion. Her body craved it, hungered with an intensity that was terrifying in its newness. How was it even possible to want this again when she was pretty sure that what she had just experienced with Sebastian had been mind-blowing? She might not have experienced it before but she'd read books, watched movies and overheard enough that she was almost certain she'd just engaged in earth-shattering sex. Yet here she was, anticipating the feel of Dimitri inside her, of him fucking her 'til she screamed anew.

She arched her back further and with the next quick glide, Dimitri's cock slid deep within her pussy, already stretched and wet with both her need and his brother's seed. He held completely still, buried to the balls in her and it was the most amazing sensation. She could feel her sheath clasping and squeezing every inch of his delicious cock. Her pulse seemed to be centered there. It was sheer torture and yet one of the greatest pleasures she had ever known.

When she couldn't take it anymore she pushed back against him, forcing him deeper still, and panted out, "Fuck me. Please fuck me." She glanced back over her shoulder at him and locked her gaze with his, allowing him to see just how hungry for him she was.

He held still for just a moment longer but then it was as if her words, the look in her eyes, had shattered his control. He slammed in and out of her so hard and so fast that she could barely stay on her knees. She swung her gaze forward again. If it wasn't for the hands of Sebastian who still lay beneath her and Dimitri's firm grip on her hips she probably would have collapsed. But neither man would allow her anything less than the pleasure they were so eager and willing to give her.

Dimitri pushed on her lower back again while shifting so that her knees spread even wider. Then with the next inward thrust of his cock he seemed to hit a spot inside her that was the center of her pleasure. One more thrust against it and she was exploding around him, screaming her ecstasy at the top of her lungs. He continued his parry and retreat, not allowing her to come down, instead forcing her higher and higher 'til the pleasure mixed with pain and she couldn't see, smell, taste, hear or feel anything but him, them, and the raw animalistic mating that consumed them.

Dimitri leaned over her and he bit down on her flesh close to where his brother had bitten. His teeth sank into her skin and he sucked wickedly on her, holding her in place for his continuing thrusts. His cock jerked inside her and the hot splash of cum filled her womb and dripped from her channel. She felt the warm splash of liquid against her belly and knew without looking that Sebastian had come again as well.

She collapsed on top of Sebastian, unable to manage her body weight any longer. She was jelly, boneless and wobbly. Lethargy seemed to fill her as she continued to gasp for breath. She could still feel Dimitri against her back, his knees outside hers, his cock still snuggled inside her. He was licking over the tender spot that he had made on the base of her neck where it met her shoulder and she would swear that he was growling with pleasure.

She felt Sebastian's lips along her temple and heard him whisper to her.

"Sleep now, Dakota Cordova. Your mates will watch over and protect you. For now and for always. Never shall you walk alone again."

For now and for always, she repeated in her head. *I like the sound of that.*

As do we, my love. As do we.

She thought the words were spoken in her head but she was too tired to care. She let the peacefulness of sleep overtake her, pull her under and give her the rest she craved. She had been mentally exhausted for days after running circles in her head playing the "what-if" game. Now she had the blissful physical exhaustion that would allow her the respite of sleep. She knew that it had been an amazing dream and she didn't want to leave it or these two amazing men behind. She wanted to stay in this mystical White Valley as the chosen and desired mate of the Cordova. She wanted it more than anything she'd ever desired before. She fought for only a moment against the darkness, unwilling to slip from the comfort of her lovers' arms only to awaken to the reality she had left behind.

"Don't leave me," she mumbled, reaching blindly with her hands for the feel of their warm flesh. And she would swear that she heard two voices assure her that she would never be without them again.

Chapter Two

Dakota awoke with a start, sitting straight up in bed. It took her a moment to focus and realize that she had no idea where she was. The room was rustic, a cabin of sorts, which made sense since the last place she was had been somewhere in the forest. The bed she lay in was big enough for an entire family and took up most of the space. A fireplace lay across the room and she was startled to see a cheery fire already burning there. She could just make out a door that led to what she prayed was a bathroom and another one that might go to a kitchen or something. Her stomach rumbled with hunger but it was her bladder that was demanding the most immediate attention.

When she swung her legs out from under the covers she was no longer able to deny that she was indeed naked. As she didn't remember taking her clothes off she didn't want to think about how that happened. She grabbed a quilt up and wrapped it around herself before darting to the door she prayed was the right one. Relief flowed through her when she discovered she was right and after taking care of her more pressing need she turned to the mirror and gasped out loud. There were twin bite marks marring the flesh where her neck met her shoulder and her dream came back to her with vivid clarity. She reached up to touch the tender bite-marked flesh. Was it a dream?

There was a shifting inside her, as if something were coming awake and stretching beneath her skin. It was a weird sensation. Like she was sharing her body with someone or something else. But that made as much sense as everything else at the moment. It made her wonder just how old the bottles of water in her backpack had been, and if it was possible for water to go bad.

She remembered the pool of water and the two men who had been there when she exited wet and achy with need. Her thighs tightened and she felt the tenderness between them. She had tried to pass it off as only reminiscing from her dream but there was no denying the proof before her eyes. Someone had been with her, bitten her and somehow managed to get her to this cabin. So what was the dream and what was the reality? Where was she? And most importantly where was the person—or persons, if she went by her dream—who had brought her here?

Dimitri and Sebastian Cordova. The names ran through her mind along with her saying the words that she chose them. It hadn't really happened, had it? She couldn't really be mated to two men straight out of a sex dream. What did it mean to be mated anyway? Wasn't that something that one watched on Animal Planet? She leaned down and turned the water on, splashing it over her face and neck before looking back into the mirror. The marks were still there. They hadn't been a dream or a delusion after all.

"Oh, God. Where am I? What have I done?"

She gave a squeak of fright when the door pushed open behind her and one of the men she thought she'd dreamed stepped in behind her.

"We moved you to the mating lodge while you slept. We will spend the next week here getting to know one another better before we take you to meet the rest of the people of White Valley." His hands wrapped around her waist, pulling her snugly back against his groin and the thick shaft there. It seemed only natural to relax against him, to absorb his warmth and revel in the comfort of his arms.

"I... Who are you?" she whispered though her head whispered the name Sebastian.

"Yes, I am Sebastian. It pleases me that already you can tell us apart." His lips whispered over her hair, nuzzling against her. "It was not a dream, my mate. You are Dakota Cordova now, and White Valley will be your home. You will want for nothing. Dimitri and I will watch over and ensure that all of your needs are met. When the time comes for your first transformation, we will be with you, guiding you all the way."

"Transformation?" she asked, afraid of what he might tell her. Nothing made sense at the moment. If it hadn't been a dream...

"The transfer of body fluids has already begun the change inside you. Our saliva and semen have mixed with your body fluids." She blushed at his blunt words but when he continued her blood ran cold. "We will stay here for the next week so that you will experience the change at least once before entering the Valley."

"Change? Transformation? What are you talking about?" She felt like a parrot repeating every key word or phrase that he spoke to her.

"The wolf is already forming inside you, Dakota. If you listen you will hear its call echoing in your blood. Soon the need to give it freedom will take over and you will be helpless to stop it." He must have seen the fear in her eyes reflected in the mirror. He turned her into his arms and used one hand to lift her chin so that he could look directly into her round blue orbs.

"It is natural to fear your first time, my mate. But Dimitri and I will be with you the entire time. That is why we have this cabin. So that the males can guard and aid their mate when she undergoes her first shift. Unfortunately our women do not gain their wolf until they are mated."

"Why not?" She remembered the sensation earlier of something shifting beneath her skin.

"It has always been that way in the Valley. Our boys change for the first time at the onset of puberty, around twelve or thirteen. There is something in the hormones at that age that brings it on. But our women don't make the same hormone that is needed to release the wolf. Not until they are mated and the exchange of fluids takes place does this occur for them." He tugged her hand and led her back out to the main room and over to the big bed.

"And once the change occurs the first time?" She couldn't believe that she was actually standing here beside a bed, wrapped in nothing but a quilt, speaking with a gorgeous man who she was fairly certain she had already had sex with — amazing sex with — about changing into a wolf. A wolf. As in a werewolf? She pinched herself and unfortunately felt it all too well. Nope, she wasn't still dreaming. So either she was in the company of a delusional madman or this truly was reality. And heaven help her but she wasn't sure which one she would prefer.

She opened her mouth to say something else when Sebastian got a look on his face and headed to another door that she hadn't noticed before. He glanced over at her and smiled. "Dimitri is returning from his run." He pulled the door open and a huge black wolf bounded into the room.

It came straight for her and she yelped with surprise and tried to backpedal away. It pushed its nose against the quilt where it lay across her thighs and she would swear it was sniffing her female parts. With a quick tug the quilt was pulled loose from her trembling fingers to pool around her feet. The wolf stepped closer and its long rough tongue came out to glide along the lips of her sex. She gasped with shock, startled further when it nuzzled against her folds, the tongue brushing lazily around her clit.

She stumbled back, her knees hitting the mattress, causing her to sprawl back on the bed with her legs dangling off the end. The wolf took advantage of her position and moved closer, burying his wet nose into her exposed folds and inhaling deeply.

She went to move and stopped when she heard the distinct rumble of a growl and felt the slight nip of teeth against her inner thigh. Sebastian stepped into her sight, now as naked as she was. His cock jutted up from his nest of black curls thick with his desire. The head was swollen and red and drops of his semen already beaded in the tiny slit.

"She does not seem to enjoy your games in that form, Dimitri," he spoke to the wolf. "Perhaps you should wait until later for that?"

The wolf pulled away and looked up at her. She knew that her face was white, her eyes huge with fear and uncertainty. There was no hiding it. It was a wolf, a big, black wolf. And its head had been buried between her thighs. And Sebastian had called it Dimitri. Holy crap! That must mean that they were werewolves. But those didn't really exist. Did they?

"Dimitri?" she questioned, terrified of what response the animal might make.

She thought that nothing could startle her more but then she had never counted on what happened next. The wolf began to change before her eyes, a little at first and then the fur began to melt away and skin took its place. Padded feet gave way to human hands and feet and the muzzle receded from the wolf's face, slowly taking the familiar shape of one she had seen before. With one last shake of his hair the wolf disappeared and Dimitri stood naked between her thighs. She blinked once, twice, but he still remained. Her vision swam and black dots took shape before her. Her last thought was that she must be having a stroke. That was the only thing that made sense at this point. Werewolves didn't exist.

"Way to go," Sebastian spoke out loud, his disgust for his brother ripe in his voice. "She has passed out. Was there really a need to show her that so soon?"

"You didn't tell her about us already?" Dimitri queried as he let his gaze roam over the lush body of his mate. "I assumed that you would tell her and thus prepare her for my arrival."

"Of course I told her," Sebastian scoffed. "But it is one thing to hear it and another to see it. You should have shown a little tact, my brother, and kept your muzzle out of her pussy."

Dimitri sighed and shook his head. "It is too late to worry about it now. She will wake soon and we will spend the rest of this day talking and mating. She will become use to the idea."

"You sound so sure," Sebastian whispered. He had seen the fear and worry in her eyes. And now he knew worry of his own. What if she couldn't accept them? Couldn't accept the Valley?

"What choice does she have at this point?" Dimitri queried. "The change is already beginning inside her. I could feel the growing presence of her wolf with mine. It is too late to change anything now. She is part of us, a Cordova." He reached down and wrapped the fingers of one hand around the base of his cock, giving it a few strokes up and down. Dakota lay before them on the bed, her legs spread wide enough that they could easily see the pink perfection of her pussy. Dark hunger filled his gaze and when he glanced at his brother he could see the same reflected in Sebastian's eyes. "I need her already. She is like a fire in my blood. I feel for her." His gaze softened as he glanced back down to where Dakota lay. "I feel things that I have felt for no other. A need to protect and comfort. I want to cuddle her close and never let her go. I want to bury my shaft so deep inside her pussy that we are as one." His gaze sought his brother's once more. "Tell me you do not feel it as well?"

"You already know that I do," Sebastian assured him.

"Then what choice do any of us have?" Dimitri spoke again. "There is no going back, no undoing what we have already begun. She is our mate and only death can separate us now."

* * * * *

Dakota came awake slowly. Her body was screaming with sexual desire and she was pretty sure that it must have something to do with the two men busy pleasuring her body with their hands and mouths. What a way to wake up. And she had dreamed the strangest thing anyway. She glanced down at her breast where Dimitri was busy sucking and shook her head at the thought of him transforming from wolf to man in front of her. It had to have been a dream. Right? But then if that were so he wouldn't really be here right now, would he? Lord, nothing made sense at the moment. Well, one thing did. Pleasure. Raw, carnal, sexual pleasure. With two very talented men. She'd just focus on that for a bit.

"I see you finally decided to join us," Dimitri murmured around her nipple. Sebastian was subjecting her feet and toes to some wicked tongue torture. She never knew that her feet could be an erogenous zone but they most definitely were.

"I see you started without me," she replied and moaned when Dimitri sucked harder at her stiff nipple and Sebastian began to slowly work his lips and tongue up the inside of her legs. It was sheer torture and she never wanted it to stop.

"There is no starting without you," Sebastian whispered against her flesh. "You are the most important one here."

"Ummm…" she moaned as he lapped at her woman's dew that coated the plumped folds of her sex. She was eager for more of them, ready to have sex with both of them for the rest of the night. A laugh tumbled from her throat. From virgin to vixen in one fell swoop. Who would have thought it?

"You are happy with us?" Dimitri questioned and she eagerly nodded, choosing not to read more into his query than what was happening at this moment.

"Yes," she hissed and arched her back, pushing her nipple farther inside his mouth as Sebastian latched on to her swollen clit and filled her pulsing channel with two of his fingers. "God, yes," she cried, giving over to the intense pleasure that was exploding throughout her body.

Dimitri moved from her breast and licked his way up her throat to her jaw. He continued to her open lips and possessed her with a kiss that both took and gave at the same time. He was all carnal heat and hunger, eating at her lips and mouth. Yet there was no denying the hint of something more that bewitched her and held her an eager captive beneath them. His tongue stroked along hers, leading her in a play that was as satisfying as the more carnal act she knew was coming soon.

Sebastian thrust his fingers in and out of her while continuing to manipulate her clit with his mouth. He would suck fiercely at it then stop and gently tease along it with his tongue before nipping it with his teeth. It was a vicious cycle that kept her on the verge of orgasm for longer than should be physically possible.

"Please," she begged as Dimitri moved his mouth back down along her neck to the place where they had both bitten her earlier.

"Please, what?" Dimitri spoke softly against her skin, his breath sending fresh tremors through her core.

"Please," was all she could manage. What could she say? Please make me come? Please take me? Fuck me now? She'd never experienced anything even remotely like this and the pleasure alone was enough to leave her nearly incoherent.

"Everything and more, love, everything and more," Dimitri stated and bit deep into her flesh. His teeth broke the newly healed skin open again and she could feel her blood mixing with his saliva. Once again the euphoria broke over her and even as she exploded with her orgasm she could feel her body relaxing further into the bed. Dimitri licked over her skin and then he was gone and Sebastian was there.

He rolled them over on the bed so that she was draped across his chest, her legs outside his hips. Dimitri's hands helped lift her just enough for Sebastian to line his cock up with her dripping pussy and then with one sure thrust she was filled. Sebastian felt so good buried inside her, like he was always meant to be there. They both moaned with pleasure but two sets of strong hands kept her from sliding her body up and down on the thick cock.

Instead she was positioned so that she lay flat against Sebastian once more. His face was buried in her neck and she could feel him licking over the marks she wore. She knew that he would bite her again soon but she didn't care. She actually craved it, needed it like water. Nothing could be better than this.

Dimitri moved closer behind her. His knees slipped between hers and Sebastian's legs, spreading her wider and lowering her pelvis on Sebastian's erection. He was deeper now than he had ever been and with just that stimulation she was close to orgasm once more.

"Breath deeply, love, and relax," Sebastian whispered and she felt his hands glide down her sides to her hips. Then he slipped them around until he was squeezing and separating her bottom cheeks. He kneaded them slowly, making her relax her muscles and that was when Dimitri let her know his intention.

She felt his finger first, coated with her own juices and some type of lubricant that she had neither seen nor heard him get. His finger slipped in to the first knuckle and she automatically started to tense around it.

"Relax, love. Let him prepare you for the final claiming." It was Sebastian who spoke to her and it was his face she glanced up at with a questioning look.

"The final claiming?" she whimpered as Dimitri continued working his finger in until the entire digit was snugly inside her. Slowly he began working it in and out, coating her with whatever cream he had applied to his finger. The muscles there loosened up and relaxed and she wondered just what he had used on her. She felt him add a second finger but Sebastian claimed her attention again when he whispered to her.

"The final claiming occurs when both of your mates enter your body at the same time. It is a completion of the bond that can only occur when both of us take you as one and all of us achieve satisfaction together."

"And when the bond is completed?" she moaned. "What happens then?"

"Once the bond is completed your transformation will be assured. Your wolf will begin to emerge and fight for the right to seek its form. We will help you, guide you through it." It was Dimitri who informed her of this, his fingers stretching the untried tissues of her back portal. Stretching her for a possession that she both feared and craved.

"But what if I don't want to be a wolf? What if I want to leave?"

Both men tensed around her and she shuddered at the fire in Sebastian's eyes as he looked at her. But it was the guttural command in Dimitri's voice that nearly sent her into orgasm. "What has begun between the three of us was destined and can no longer be undone. With the final claiming there is no going back. You are Cordova and your home is now with us in the White Valley."

"But we haven't joined in a final claiming yet." She stated it calmly and knew that she was daring him to take her now, to enter her anus and thrust deep. Honesty compelled her to admit that no matter what, she didn't want to leave these two men who seemed so concerned with her needs and her satisfaction. Sure, it was mostly lust at the moment but she was certain that it would soon lead to so much more between the three of them.

And Dimitri didn't disappoint her with his response. Strong fingers were pulled from her body and he used his hands to grip her hips and hold her where he wanted her. She felt the nudge of his solid shaft against her anus and pushed back without thinking. Dimitri used her body's motion to aid his entry and thrust home with one hard stroke. All three of them groaned with pleasure as they held still, Dakota filled with the thickened cocks of the men who would be her mates.

"We have joined." Dimitri's voice was filled with dark, carnal promise and she moaned as he licked over her neck. "There is no leaving us, Dakota. There is only the promise of every day beginning and ending like this."

They moved inside her, their shafts rubbing along each other where the thin flesh separated one opening from the other. It was glorious torture, and pleasure built in ever-increasing waves throughout her body. One filled her as the other retreated, only to trade places with the next stroke. Her pussy clasped greedily at Sebastian while Dimitri pulled almost free of her snug anus. Then it was Dimitri pushing deep while Sebastian tugged almost completely out of her. Slowly they rode in and out of her body, torturing her with the sheer pleasure they gave.

She cried out and unknowingly clenched her channels around the cocks invading her. Both men cried out as well and the rhythm picked up until there was little delay between the time when one filled her and then the other. Soon they were both spearing in and out in tandem, two cocks surging into her as one. Harsh grunts and breathless moans filled the room as they all surrendered to the ecstasy they were feeling. No beginning and no end. Only three people who were slowly forming a bond as one.

Something burst inside Dakota and her body clenched and released, tightening deliciously around Sebastian and Dimitri. Their cries matched hers and she pulled them into orgasm with her. Hot jets of thick cum filled her pussy and ass as each man found his own release within her. Without thought or plan she stretched her neck out, leaning her head back against Dimitri and let loose with the sounds building in her throat.

No one was more surprised than she when a wolf's howl filled the air. A howl coming from her.

Chapter Three

Dakota lay snugly between Dimitri and Sebastian in the bed. She must have fallen asleep soon after their last round of lovemaking and they had been content to cuddle and doze with her. She would love to awaken every day for the rest of her life just like this.

And so you will.

Dakota was startled into opening her eyes and found herself staring right into Sebastian's bright green eyes. How in the world did he hear her? She hadn't spoken out loud? Had she?

Sebastian's laugh was joined by Dimitri's. Dimitri wiggled closer against her backside and she almost groaned at the feel of his burgeoning erection. Surely he couldn't be excited again? That wasn't possible, was it?

You will learn that much is possible when you are mated to a wolf. It was definitely Dimitri's assured confidence in her head.

Then Sebastian added, *Two wolves.*

How are you talking to me in my head?

It is the way of our kind, love, Sebastian informed her while nuzzling along her neck and shoulders with his lips and tongue. *With the continued exchange of blood and saliva the bond will grow stronger. Eventually you will learn to read both mine and Dimitri's thoughts as well.*

Perish the thought. It entered her mind without her realizing it and her reward was a sharp nip from two sets of wicked teeth.

"Hey," she yelled out loud and reached out to swat Sebastian with her hand. He caught it instead and pulled it to his lips.

There is nothing that we shall hold from you. Nothing that we will ever think that would be against you. You are our mate now, the woman of our hearts. Nothing will break the bond that we have forged. You are a part of us now. And we are a part of you. Three parts of a whole. Only complete when we are all together.

That sounds like more than lust. Her insecurity leaked into her thoughts and she knew from the growls that both men were now privy to what she had witnessed her ex-fiancé doing with another woman.

He was a fool and undeserving of you. It was Sebastian who assured her of that while Dimitri was much more harsh in his condemnation of her ex.

He is lucky that he never touched your body or I would have hunted him down and killed him with my bare hands.

Dakota laughed and it felt wonderful. Who would have thought that her sudden desire to have some one-on-one time with nature would lead her down this path? Here she was now the mate of two men, werewolves at that. And if what they said was true then soon she would be able to take the shape of a wolf as well.

We do not lie, Dimitri told her and nipped at her neck.

She moaned with pleasure, leaning back into the bite, eager for his teeth to grip and claim her. Would they mate as wolves as well?

Oh, yes. Sebastian growled softly against her breast before tugging her nipple between his teeth. The sensation traveled from her nipple to her womb and a ripple of pleasure traveled through her vagina. *We will fuck often in our animal fur. It will be like nothing you have ever known.*

Everything with you two is like nothing I have ever known. She moaned in pleasure as their lips explored her body, hands plucking and caressing her flesh.

Two masculine grunts filled the air and she giggled at the pure male satisfaction that they conveyed. She had never been so happy that she had not lost her virginity with what's-his-name.

What's-his-name? Sebastian queried.

Who? was all she could manage to think as they continued to play her body with their lips and hands.

Good answer, my love, Dimitri assured her and bit gently at the mark he had made. His teeth sank in and the very eroticism of the act had her shuddering in orgasm, her body writhing between his and Sebastian's.

Sebastian pulled away and went to the bathroom. She heard the running of water and then he was back with a soapy cloth in his hand, which he held out to his brother. His cock glistened with the drops of water from his washing and she couldn't fight the urge to roll onto her hands and knees and make her way to him. When she stopped his cock bobbed in front of her face, a temptation too seductive to resist.

She nuzzled against the wiry hair that surrounded his groin, wallowing in the rich musk that was his alone. She could feel his staff twitching and swelling bigger against her cheek and finally gave in to the need to lick her way from the base to the flared head. She greedily slurped him between her lips, felt them stretching wide to accommodate his width. They both groaned with intense pleasure.

Sebastian took control of her exploration, wrapping his fingers in her tousled curls and pumping his shaft deeper and deeper into her mouth. He eased his cock into the back of her throat and held it there for only a moment before sliding out. She choked a little but as he continued she heeded his voice in her head that encouraged her to breathe through her nose. Soon she could take all of him, swallowing the portion that forged into her throat. It was empowering even though by looks it seemed that he was controlling her. She knew beyond a shadow of a doubt that one word or sign of discomfort from her and he would stop.

Dimitri moved behind her and she knew what he was going to do before he did it. His entry was a slow glide of his hardened shaft into her empty channel. It was perfect and conveyed just how much she had come to mean to him as well. She enjoyed experiencing her mates in this way. There was something powerful about pleasuring with her mouth even as Dimitri pleasured her. She sucked eagerly on Sebastian's cock while thrusting her hips back in a gentle rhythm with Dimitri's strokes. This was what she had been searching for. These two men were the ones she had been destined to love. This was love in its most primal form, a mating of more than their bodies. It was the beginning of a future that appeared brighter than ever before. It was the beginning of life as Dakota Cordova, mate to Sebastian and Dimitri Cordova, newest member of the weres of White Valley.

Also by Elayne S. Venton

ഇ

Indiscretions

About the Author

ഇ

There used to be a time when Elayne would start reading a book in the afternoon and stay up until the wee hours to finish it. Now those hours are spent researching, writing, re-writing, and occasionally making dinner. Multi-published, Elayne enjoys writing in several genres where the characters' passions hurl them together and love binds them throughout time.

Currently, she lives in the rural south with her wonderful, industrious husband, two teenagers, and a lovable golden retriever. In her spare time, she volunteers at the local historical society.

Elayne welcomes comments from readers. You can find her website and email address on her author bio page at www.ellorascave.com.

Tell Us What You Think

We appreciate hearing reader opinions about our books. You can email us at Comments@EllorasCave.com.

Also by Jory Strong

☙

Carnival Tarot 1: Sarael's Reading
Carnival Tarot 2: Kiziah's Reading
Carnival Tarot 3: Dakotah's Reading
Crime Tells 1: Lyric's Cop
Crime Tells 2: Cady's Cowboy
Crime Tells 3: Calista's Men
Crime Tells 4: Cole's Gamble
Death's Courtship
Ellora's Cavemen: Dreams of the Oasis I (*anthology*)
Ellora's Cavemen: Seasons of Seduction I (*anthology*)
Ellora's Cavemen: Seasons of Seduction IV (*anthology*)
Elven Surrender
Fallon Mates 1: Binding Krista
Fallon Mates 2: Zeraac's Miracle
Fallon Mates 3: Roping Savannah
Familiar Pleasures
Spirit Flight
Spirits Shared
Supernatural Bonds 1: Trace's Psychic
Supernatural Bonds 2: Storm's Faeries
Supernatural Bonds 3: Sophie's Dragon
Supernatural Bonds 4: Drui Claiming
The Angelini 1: Skye's Trail
The Angelini 2: Syndelle's Possession
The Angelini 3: Mystic's Run
Two Spirits

About the Author

Jory has been writing since childhood and has never outgrown being a daydreamer. When she's not hunched over her computer, lost in the muse and conjuring up new heroes and heroines, she can usually be found reading, riding her horses, or hiking with her dogs.

Jory welcomes comments from readers. You can find her website and email address on her author bio page at www.ellorascave.com.

Tell Us What You Think

We appreciate hearing reader opinions about our books. You can email us at Comments@EllorasCave.com.

Also by Solange Ayre

ಜ

Emerald Eyes
One Thousand Brides
Wizard's Woman

About the Author

෨

Solange Ayre, galaxy-hopping investigative journalist, also serves as a policy advisor to the United Conglomeration of Planetary Jurisdictions. She makes her home on Ayriana, her private island-republic in the West Caribbean region of Earth.

After a whirlwind childhood living in the capitals of Europe, Solange married St. Georges Ayre, one of the wealthiest men in the world. The crystal palace he bought her on Ayriana is the primary tourist attraction in the area—at least, for those who can find it. St. George's mysterious assassination is still mourned by his grieving widow.

Directly descended from King Louis XVI and Marie Antoinette, Solange graciously supports the democratic government of France and relinquishes her claim to the throne. Under no circumstances will she answer to the title "Your Highness."

In her spare time, Solange enjoys breeding and showing her prize-winning miniature dragons as well as researching and writing erotic romance.

Solange welcomes comments from readers. You can find her website and email address on her author bio page at www.ellorascave.com.

Tell Us What You Think

We appreciate hearing reader opinions about our books. You can email us at Comments@EllorasCave.com.

Also by Rowan West

Roll Play

About the Author

Rowan West believes in finding pleasure in the everyday and pursuing passion whenever she can. Pleasure comes in the form of her children, uninterrupted naps or hot baths, long calls with friends, decadent food (especially desserts), learning new things, and curling up with a good book. Her passions include her husband, writing, and helping women to trust, believe and accept their sexual power (hence her choice of writing genre).

At her home in New England, Rowan's days consist of an unending quest to balance all her roles (wife, mother, writer, daughter, etc.) while maintaining her sanity and/or sense of humor. She is looking forward to hearing what her children say about their mom's work on career day.

Rowan welcomes comments from readers. You can find her website and email address on her author bio page at www.ellorascave.com.

Tell Us What You Think

We appreciate hearing reader opinions about our books. You can email us at Comments@EllorasCave.com.

Also by Cindy Spencer Pape

Between a Rock and a Hard-On
Djinni and the Geek
One Good Man *with Lacey Thorn*
Stone and Earth
Stone and Sea
Teach Me

About the Author

ಬು

Cindy Spencer Pape has been, among other things, a banker, a teacher, and an elected politician, though she swears she got better. Her degrees are in zoology, and she currently works in environmental education, when she can fit it in around writing. She lives in southern Michigan with her husband, two teenage sons, a dog, a lizard, and various other small creatures, all of which are easier to clean up after than the three male humans.

Cindy welcomes comments from readers. You can find her website and email address on her author bio page at www.ellorascave.com.

Tell Us What You Think
We appreciate hearing reader opinions about our books. You can email us at Comments@EllorasCave.com.

Also by Lacey Thorn

☙

Bare Love 1: His Bare Obsession
Bare Love 2: Bare Confessions
Bare Love 3: Bare Seduction
Bare Love 4: Bare Devotion
Island Guardians 1: Earth Moves
Island Guardians 2: Fanning Her Flames
Island Guardians 3: Washed Away
Island Guardians 4: Breathing Her Air
Merciful Angel
One Good Man *with Cindy Spencer Pape*

About the Author

೫

Lacey Thorn spends her days in small-town Indiana, the proud mother of three. When she is not busy with one of them she can be found typing away on her computer keyboard or burying her nose in a good book. Like every woman, she knows just how chaotic life can be and how appealing that great escape can look. So toss aside the stress and tension of the never ending "to do" list. For now sit back, relax, and enjoy the ride with Lacey as she helps you to unlace and unleash the woman inside.

Lacey welcomes comments from readers. You can find her website and email address on her author bio page at www.ellorascave.com.

Tell Us What You Think
We appreciate hearing reader opinions about our books. You can email us at Comments@EllorasCave.com.

Why an electronic book?

We live in the Information Age—an exciting time in the history of human civilization, in which technology rules supreme and continues to progress in leaps and bounds every minute of every day. For a multitude of reasons, more and more avid literary fans are opting to purchase e-books instead of paper books. The question from those not yet initiated into the world of electronic reading is simply: *Why?*

1. ***Price.*** An electronic title at Ellora's Cave Publishing and Cerridwen Press runs anywhere from 40% to 75% less than the cover price of the exact same title in paperback format. Why? Basic mathematics and cost. It is less expensive to publish an e-book (no paper and printing, no warehousing and shipping) than it is to publish a paperback, so the savings are passed along to the consumer.

2. ***Space.*** Running out of room in your house for your books? That is one worry you will never have with electronic books. For a low one-time cost, you can purchase a handheld device specifically designed for e-reading. Many e-readers have large, convenient screens for viewing. Better yet, hundreds of titles can be stored within your new library—on a single microchip. There are a variety of e-readers from different manufacturers. You can also read e-books on your PC or laptop computer. (Please note that Ellora's Cave does not endorse any specific brands.

You can check our websites at www.ellorascave.com or www.cerridwenpress.com for information we make available to new consumers.)

3. ***Mobility.*** Because your new e-library consists of only a microchip within a small, easily transportable e-reader, your entire cache of books can be taken with you wherever you go.

4. ***Personal Viewing Preferences.*** Are the words you are currently reading too small? Too large? Too… ANNOYING? Paperback books cannot be modified according to personal preferences, but e-books can.

5. ***Instant Gratification.*** Is it the middle of the night and all the bookstores near you are closed? Are you tired of waiting days, sometimes weeks, for bookstores to ship the novels you bought? Ellora's Cave Publishing sells instantaneous downloads twenty-four hours a day, seven days a week, every day of the year. Our webstore is never closed. Our e-book delivery system is 100% automated, meaning your order is filled as soon as you pay for it.

Those are a few of the top reasons why electronic books are replacing paperbacks for many avid readers.

As always, Ellora's Cave and Cerridwen Press welcome your questions and comments. We invite you to email us at Comments@ellorascave.com or write to us directly at Ellora's Cave Publishing Inc., 1056 Home Avenue, Akron, OH 44310-3502.

COMING TO A BOOKSTORE NEAR YOU!

ELLORA'S CAVE

Bestselling Authors Tour

UPDATES AVAILABLE AT
WWW.ELLORASCAVE.COM

Cerridwen, the Celtic Goddess of wisdom, was the muse who brought inspiration to storytellers and those in the creative arts. Cerridwen Press encompasses the best and most innovative stories in all genres of today's fiction. Visit our site and discover the newest titles by talented authors who still get inspired - much like the ancient storytellers did, once upon a time.

Cerridwen Press
www.cerridwenpress.com

Discover for yourself why readers can't get enough of the multiple award-winning publisher

Ellora's Cave.

Whether you prefer e-books or paperbacks, be sure to visit EC on the web at www.ellorascave.com for an erotic reading experience that will leave you breathless.